Our Little Secret

Darren O'Sullivan

ONE PLACE. MANY STORIES

HQ
An imprint of HarperCollins*Publishers* Ltd
1 London Bridge Street
London SE1 9GF

This paperback edition 2018

1
First published in Great Britain by
HQ, an imprint of HarperCollins*Publishers* Ltd 2017

ISBN: 9780008285166

For Ben, who shows me that anything is possible.

Chapter 1

5 May 2016
The first final day

10.39 p.m. – March train station, Cambridgeshire

Eight minutes.

Chris looked up at the dial of the train station clock, its ticking unperturbed by what was about to happen. It read ten thirty-nine. He stood and watched the seconds pass by slowly. Eight minutes, that was all he had to wait. Looking around the station he noted how dilapidated it was. The benches that were once sky blue were now covered with an assortment of profanities – as were the walls behind them. Pictures of male genitals and insults to people's mothers were lit by a dull orange light in the roof of the old station and the flickering of a half-empty vending machine.

The old Chris might have had an opinion about it. Not now. Not any more. Instead, reading the walls and the bench just made him feel more tired, more ready.

The station was the kind of place that still had damp autumnal leaves even in the middle of summer. The kind of place the wind always fiercely travelled. He listened as it howled and moaned its way through the entrance and past him, stirring bottles of beer and empty crisp packets that had overflowed from the bins.

Letting out a sigh, he could see his breath hitting the air like cigarette smoke. Although it was May, the weather was unseasonably cold, barely six degrees. He hadn't noticed how cold until now. He hadn't noticed much lately, besides time. It was his only constant.

Chris observed, in the same way a person might observe through a window, that his shirt was wet. It was raining and, now more aware of his surroundings, he realized the wind was giving him a chill.

He had been painfully passing the time walking through the quiet streets of March, a small fenland town north of Cambridge, for an hour before arriving here. A town that was tired and had been left behind, full of charity shops and bargain outlets that displayed items for a pound or less. The shop signs that hung above paint-stripped doors were crude and cheap, almost shouting their names at him as he passed by. He'd noticed those inconsequential things but not the fact it was cold and he was wet. He briefly wondered why before shaking off the thought. He had to keep his focus now more than ever.

He looked again at the clock, it still read ten thirty-nine, and he still had eight minutes. Just eight small minutes.

Then he would be dead.

Chris had chosen the location perfectly. At this time of night there were no passenger trains. The next one not for thirty minutes after the one that he longed for. He had done his homework. In the months before there had never been another person on the platform at this time on a Thursday night. Research that began after his grief and shock had turned into numbness. As soon as he had made the decision to end his life, he knew it could only be in one place. The one place that changed everything.

It was on this platform Chris had known he was in love.

The first time he stood in this spot since, he had to fight the urge to do it then and there. But it was the middle of the afternoon, and there were several people waiting to travel. Each and every one of them would see him die. Something he couldn't live with. He knew it would have to be at night.

Every Thursday he went back to the platform to find the opportune moment. Then one night, a little later than his usual visits, a distant rumbling came over the track and Chris knew this train was different. As it passed, he counted the carriages. There were forty-two. He counted them each week. Sometimes there were more, sometimes less. But they were always in the dozens and always at the same time: 10.47.

He had found a solution.

Researching the company, London Concrete, Chris knew it would be passing through on the date he needed. It wasn't perfect. But close enough. He knew the train driver would be affected by his death. He hoped that the support would be in place to help him come to terms with it. After all, Chris wasn't the first person to step under a train. To minimize the trauma he would cause to the driver, he had to time it perfectly. Yes, the driver would know a man killed himself, but he had a way to ensure he didn't see it happen.

His memory tried to take him back to the night his beautiful wife Julia passed away. Before it could take hold he grasped at a glimmer of something else. He closed his eyes, fighting to hold on to the image. He wasn't ready for the other one. Not yet.

The memory that he desperately grabbed hold of was the moment when he had first laid eyes on her.

It was five years earlier, and he was with Steve, his best mate, who had dragged him out for a few drinks despite his protests. He remembered how that night had begun. Steve didn't call or text, but turned up unannounced at Chris's front door, leaving him no choice but to go out. A taxi sat waiting, engine running as Chris threw on an old T-shirt and jeans – the only things he could find clean, cursing Steve as he did. For a moment Chris felt like he was back there.

'Come on, mate!'

'I'm coming, hold on.'

'Bloody hell, they'll be calling last orders by the time you get your arse into gear.'

'Well then ring me to say we're going out before you turn up.'

'No chance, you would have said no.'

He was right. He was always right.

It had only taken the five-minute taxi journey into the city centre for Chris to forgive Steve's intrusion. An hour later Chris was glad that his mate had turned up; he hadn't realized how much he needed to unwind. The drinks were flowing and he hated to admit it to Steve, but he was having the best evening he'd had in a long time.

Propping up the bar in their favoured place, unoriginally called The Corner Lounge due to its geographical location, Chris sipped his drink — people-watching as Steve chatted to one of the barmen. Chris couldn't help but notice the similarity of everyone. How people all have their go-to outfits for a night on the town in order to stand out, only to blur together. The men all wore the classic jeans and jacket combo and the women all looked glamorous, perhaps too glamorous for a small bar in a small city. Looking down at his fraying jeans and old T-shirt he couldn't help but smile to himself.

The walls of The Corner Lounge were hung with retro wallpaper and adorned with portraits of unknown people, designed to make the modern space feel old and classy. Soft house music played in an undertone to the menagerie of conversations and laughter. He had to give the place its due: it had atmosphere, the mismatch of wallpaper and portraits were somehow warm and welcoming, even if it was all just an illusion to make you spend more money.

Chris's attempts to keep up with Steve's drinking pace had left him a little blurry-eyed and he could hear Steve's conversation with the barman about how well life was treating him. It left him feeling a little envious. He soon shook it off, ignoring the green-eyed monster. It was probably just the lager.

As Steve continued to talk about him and Kristy, his girlfriend, getting married one day soon, Chris scanned the room once more. It was then he first caught a glimpse of her through the crowd. She was sharing a joke with a friend, throwing her head back as she laughed, giving everyone who might be looking at her a clear view of her perfect smile. That was the first thing he noticed: she laughed without a care in the world. At some point Steve had stopped talking to the barman and was focusing his attention back on Chris.

'She's pretty.'

'Who?'

'Come on, don't pretend you're not staring at the woman in the green dress.'

'I wasn't! I mean, she just caught my eye, that's all.'

'Of course she did. She's lovely. Probably the type of lady who eats a lot of avocado. Well … go on, go say hello.'

Chris laughed at the idea of this. He had never found it easy to talk to women, especially women who were as beautiful as she was. He looked at Steve and smiled. It was a nice idea, but they both knew he wasn't confident enough to ever do it.

Chris hadn't had many love affairs in his adult life; he was a shy, awkward teenager who didn't know how to speak to the opposite sex, and this shyness stayed with him, becoming the foundations on which he built his personality. He didn't mind, being alone suited him just fine. Alone he knew where he stood, there were no surprises, no uncertainties. Chris watched friends around him fall in love then be scorned. Their emotional state like a roller-coaster that he didn't want to ride. Single life suited him well. But, he tried from time to time to be in a relationship regardless, although it had always been the woman who had broken the ice and introduced herself first.

'Come on, mate.'

'Wait, what are you doing?'

'If it were up to you you'd never meet anyone. We're going to go say hi.'

'Steve!'

'Fine, you stay here.'

Steve walked away, bopping along to the music, which made Chris realize no one else was. It was something he really liked about his friend: he had such contagious confidence that wasn't intimidating or something that people mocked. Watching him solo dance towards the beautiful woman, Chris drained his glass, cringing at himself as he did – he was that guy who knocked back a drink to gain some Dutch courage before talking to a girl.

He turned to the bar and waved at the barman to order two more beers, his ears burning and his heart rate elevated at what might or might not be happening behind him. He figured that Steve's advances on his behalf would be shut down and he would turn to see him walking back, shoulders shrugging as if to say 'oh well'. A sheepish smile on his face.

After paying for his drinks, he took a sip followed by a deep breath and turned back to face the room in time to see Steve rather unsubtly pointing in his direction, gesturing for him to come over. The beautiful woman was looking at him, making eye contact, and Chris had no choice now but to walk over and introduce himself.

He made his way through the crowd, trying his best not to interrupt the conversations of strangers he walked into, cursing and thanking his mate in equal measure. He had awkwardly offered his hand as a way of introducing himself. At the same time, she went in for a kiss on the cheek, missing and landing near his ear, causing him to accidentally touch her on her side, not firmly, but enough for them both to know. He hoped she didn't notice his face flush.

He would never forget that moment, yet he never spoke of it with her.

Steve stayed long enough to ensure the conversation was flowing smoothly before he splintered off to talk, rather loudly, to her friend about his future plans. It left Chris aware that it was just him and this beautiful woman getting to know each other. He hoped his nerves wouldn't show, though he could feel his face was still burning.

As they talked he struggled to understand how she could be so beautiful, so smart, so funny and, after discreetly glancing down at her hand, so unmarried. He remembered how her soft green eyes never left the smoky grey of his as they spoke, and that he didn't learn her name until embarrassingly late into their conversation because he was so nervous he hadn't asked.

Her name was Julia.

In that first meeting he learnt that she was a journalist for a local paper and had been for seven years, starting straight out of university. He learnt that she loved her job, and that being a writer was something she had wanted to do ever since she started her first diary as a child. He asked her if she wanted to write other things, a novel or perhaps something for TV. She said she liked where she was. Telling people's stories and finding the hidden truth was enough. She told him that she truly believed she could make a difference. It wasn't her being naive, she was an optimist, her positivity was infectious.

He told her about his work. He remembered she was baffled as to what he did, most people were. Chris worked with pensions. Navigating his way through the labyrinth of schemes, both government and private. He tried to explain how his main role was to consolidate schemes ensuring that people didn't have several small pockets from previous employers but one more substantive monthly pay-out when they hit retirement age. She said that she didn't understand, but asked if he loved it. He did, and she said that was all that mattered.

As the night drew on, the crowds left, leaving the quieter murmurs of couples enjoying each other's company, and as Chris ordered Julia and himself another drink he began to think beyond the moment. He wondered if he would see her again. He wanted to ask her for her number but couldn't find the courage despite her giving all the signs of enjoying his company. Steve once again intervened and rather unsubtly asked how they were going to stay in touch. She immediately asked for Chris's phone and tapped her number straight into it.

'So you don't lose it and forget me,' she said.

He wondered if that was remotely possible.

He remembered how the rain felt warm on the back of his neck as he stole a kiss outside the bar before she got into a taxi. And how he laughed into his pillow like a child might on Christmas Eve that night, because he knew in that moment what he still knew now. She was the one.

He remembered being excited at the idea of seeing her again.

He remembered in that moment, meeting her, he felt more alive.

And then jolting back to the present, he remembered she was gone.

Opening his eyes, he was back on the cold platform. He looked at the clock.

Ten forty.

Seven minutes.

Chris took his wallet from his back pocket and opened it. A picture of his wife looked back. Carefully, he took it out and held it in his hands and for a moment time seemed to matter less. It was from their honeymoon nearly two years ago now. Her skin was sun-kissed. Her smile was as wide and as carefree as the day they met. He remembered the beach they were lying on as he took it. Quiet and peaceful, a secret no one else knew of. And they just lay there, her head nestled in the gap between his shoulder and chest as he stroked her hair.

He pictured how they had spent day after day like it. Sleeping and talking and kissing without anyone to interrupt them. He told her stories of his father and she told him about her dreams and plans for the future.

He remembered how excited he felt as they discussed buying a bigger home and having a little family, both fantasizing about a daughter they would call Sophie, with her eyes and his smile. Their fantasy baby would crinkle her forehead when concentrating, and gently rub the bridge of her nose when falling asleep, just like Julia did.

He remembered how she told him he would make a brilliant daddy and how his heart felt full because of it. He thought about the night they stumbled across a cave bar in the side of the Sierra Nevada mountain range. Its locals rough around the edges with their dirty fingernails, stained T-shirts and thick beards. But they welcomed the non-Spanish-speaking couple with a kiss on each cheek. He thought of how she got drunk and he played guitar. He remembered feeling like those were the best weeks of his life.

It was his favourite picture of her. He could feel the Mediterranean sun every time he looked at it. Its warmth reaching his soul through her smile. But it felt cold in his hands, her smile not as bright. It told him what he already knew. He had let her down. There would be no bigger home, no little family, for he couldn't save her from dying, even though every atom in his being had been desperate to do just that.

He wanted to say something, anything. There were under seven minutes left and he desperately wanted to talk about how he felt. It didn't matter that no one would hear it but the slowly moving rain cloud; he needed to voice them. Chris had always struggled to tell her his thoughts. The kind that are frightening for people to reveal, ones that once said couldn't be unsaid. He wanted to share his deepest feelings about how when she looked at him it felt like the whole world stopped moving. As if all of the energy that had ever been created was holding its breath and that when she kissed him he felt lost within it.

He wanted to say that every mistake he had made, all of the times he had failed, were justified because each one brought her closer to him and had shaped him into the man who she would love. He wanted to say that nothing else mattered besides her. He wanted to tell her he would gladly trade places with her and would be happy to have died knowing she could live. But he couldn't find the words. And she couldn't hear him. He couldn't turn back time.

Six minutes.

Closing her smile into the palm of his hand, he placed his wallet on the bench behind him. He had no need for it now. He thought it might be more use to someone else. He left it open, showing a £20 note inside. Stepping back, he thought of the old expression his father used to say.

'It is only money; can't take it with you,' he'd often said to Chris, even when he was too young to understand what it meant.

Even now, after seeing him fall ill and succumb to disease, he always remembered his father as he was when Chris was a young boy. The way his greying beard felt as he came in to kiss Chris goodnight, an air of tobacco wafting across him whilst he pretended to sleep and the way his father told stories about his mother. How they had met, when they had married.

She too had succumbed, although at no age when a person should, an age that robbed him of his ability to remember her beyond the images his father gave him. Then he remembered a moment he had long forgotten. One where his father took him outside into the garden on a cold, clear night.

'Chris, do you know why we are outside?'

'No.'

'I'm going to show you where Mummy went.'

'Where?'

'Look up.'

'I can't see anything; it's too dark.'

'Give it a moment.'

They lay down on the cool ground together. After a few seconds the stars began to show themselves and, as he looked, the more he could see. There were thousands. He had never seen so many stars.

'Wow.'

'Sometimes, Chris, you have to look into darkness before you can see the beauty behind it.'

Chris didn't know what his father meant by that. But he thought he said it more for himself than for him.

He remembered for many minutes he and his father just lying there, close to each other, looking at the wonder of the sky. It made him feel so small, but so safe.

'Chris, I'm sorry that you don't remember your mummy.'

'Me too.'

'Chris, do you know where people go when they die?'

'Heaven.'

'That's right, and do you know what heaven looks like?'

'Clouds?'

Chris's father laughed quietly. 'Yes, clouds, but also stars.'

'Really?'

'Yes. Up there are billions of stars. More than you or I could ever count. Each star is a person who has died and they go into the night sky to watch over us as we sleep. Like your mummy is doing now. You see, darling, we haven't really lost her at all.'

Chris gasped and looked more intently at the sky, trying to find a trace of his mother. 'Is Mummy watching us now?'

'Yes. Chris, if you ever feel sad or alone always remember your mummy is up there, twinkling just for you and me.'

Shaking off the memory, he questioned, knowing what he did now, how his father had stayed so strong. He hadn't thought of that night in a very long time and looking to the sky he wondered if there was a star next to his mother's, maybe two: his father's and his wife's. All he saw were dark clouds looking back. It was right that they were hidden.

Chris wondered what his father would say to him now. Would he tell him to be braver than he was and allow himself to heal? Would he tell him to do the right thing and reach out to someone who could help and then find a way to be happy once more? Not that it mattered – he didn't believe in ghosts. He didn't believe in anything.

For a moment he wondered if things would have been different if his father was still alive, then he forced himself to focus. Taking the note from his trouser pocket that he had carefully worded about the circumstances of his death, he looked for somewhere to place it. Somewhere he knew it would be found to explain why he had chosen to take his own life.

Settling for under the decaying bench, he used the stone that he had carried on him for nearly a year as a weight to stop it blowing away in the wind. That stone had been on him every day since she had died and as soon as it was removed from his pocket he felt vulnerable. He took one last look at its blackness, polished by the waves over endless time. He placed the stone on top of the folded note as far back under the bench as he could reach and stepped back towards the platform edge. Then, he looked back to the clock.

Five minutes.

Chris took off his shoes, the damp, cold floor strangely soothing on his bare feet. It helped him stay in the moment. He did it to feel closer to her. Julia hated wearing shoes, and when Chris first asked her why, she told him that feet were designed to feel the world beneath them. To be connected.

She was barefoot the night she passed away.

Chapter 2

Twenty-five minutes earlier

10.17 p.m. – The bastard's bedroom, Lynn Street, March

It was dark in his bedroom and it smelt of sex, our sex, but I could see just enough to look at the deep-sleeping shape of the man who had once filled my heart with love. My naked body warm under his covers. His jet-black hair limp across his face. Looking at him I couldn't believe that this man had once made me believe anything was possible. But as he mumbled something in his sleep, it felt like I was looking at somebody else.

I remembered how I used to stare at him, admiring how beautiful he was. There was no beauty in him any more, just the shape of a person who mirrored my anger and shame. This man had stolen years of my life. I felt betrayed.

Foolishly I thought that he'd texted me because the day before was my birthday. Special occasions had a funny impact on people, making them nostalgic and longing. I thought that was what had happened to

John. But it was clear as soon as I arrived that he hadn't remembered. That was okay. He was never good with remembering dates.

I thought that we were going to address his infidelity and I was expecting myself to forgive him and rekindle our love. I'd imagined he would sit me down on the bed, holding my hands. Candlelight throwing shadows across the walls as he told me how he regretted what had happened and that he loved me. I half dreamt he would then get on one knee and say he needed to spend the rest of his life righting his wrongs. And that he understood the pain he had caused. He had been unfaithful to me for over a year – we both knew it; we also knew it would take nothing short of a miracle for us to recover, but I let myself dream we could.

Looking at him asleep, I couldn't see how I'd let myself be so stupid for so long. Sex with him used to be about giving over fully, spirit and soul in perfect embrace, but it was clear I was just being used.

The night had started with us watching an old film. We were curled up on the sofa under a blanket as the opening credits rolled. I felt safe, I felt secure, and I felt it could be like it once was. I allowed myself to think that maybe, just maybe, things had changed. He had changed.

Now I knew he had used the familiarity of a classic black and white movie to get what he wanted. It had just been about sex, about primal need, and that sickened me. Still, at least he remembered I liked the old black and whites – surely that was something?

I wondered where it had gone so wrong and why we couldn't have a life more like those old films? The ones where people fell in love. The ones where there would be some problem facing that love, whether it was someone else trying to block it or a class divide, but love would always win. People didn't lie in the old movies. They didn't cheat, either.

Squeezing myself into my tight jeans, the ones that hugged my figure and made me feel attractive at the beginning of the evening and repulsive at the end, I searched for the shoes I had kicked off as things heated up. Quietly swearing to myself when I realized one was on the floor, painfully close to his sleeping head. Holding my breath, I crouched to pick it up, his deep breathing suggesting it didn't matter if I was there or not.

Taking one final look at his beautiful body, I knew there was no going back. Checking my train timetable app to see the next train home was just before midnight I knew I had a long wait, but I didn't care. I couldn't stay any longer. After putting on my cardigan and wrapping my scarf around my neck, I walked towards the door, wanting to, but not daring to look back.

I tried to keep my head held high, as if it would give me a little more dignity. Wondering how I could feel dignified sneaking out of an ex's house in the middle of the night, I grabbed my bag and left, closing the heavy door behind me. Taking with me my shame and the tattered remains of our relationship in one quiet, unceremonious moment.

Chapter 3

10.43 p.m. – March train station

Four minutes.

I paid the taxi driver and stepped into the frigid wind, which carried a drizzling rain. The kind that soaked you without you knowing it was raining. As I shut the door I could hear him cough a little as he said goodbye but the door was already out of my hand and closing, cutting him off mid-phrase.

Pulling my cardigan over my chin, I steadied myself. The cold air mixing with the red wine I had been drinking making me feel a little tipsy. I heard my phone ping from inside my bag. Stopping in the sheltered entrance of the train station I rifled through it, finding my iPhone. I pulled it out and tapped in my security code, 0311, the month and year I first met the man who'd since made me feel so abandoned. Tapping the screen on the new message icon I saw it was from him.

'I had fun tonight.'

I read and reread the message, hoping to find some hidden meaning in its four words until the screen went blank, turning the dark glass of my iPhone into a mirror, one that showed a tired girl who had just been taken advantage of.

I opened my banking app, punched in my security code and prayed. I knew there wouldn't be much, but I hoped there was enough to pay for my ticket in case a train conductor was on board. The station didn't have a ticket machine or a barrier; it still worked on a trust between passengers and the train company. One I'd abused too many times for someone in their late twenties. My account read £3.41. I scrolled to see what was in my savings. A sorrowful 6p. I'd have to jump the train and keep my fingers crossed.

Dropping my phone back into my bag, I stepped into the tired station and saw a man standing close to the edge, looking out across the track towards the other platform. Oddly, he was barefoot. His shoes were carefully placed beside him like someone might do before they entered a mosque. I looked around to see if someone was there with him, wondering for a moment if he was filming a media student's project. Being near Cambridge there was always something of that nature happening. But he was alone, lost in his own thoughts.

I looked at the floor trying not to establish any kind of eye contact, moving slower as I made my way to the bench. Strangely, I felt like I wasn't allowed to be there. Out of the corner of my eye, I could see him swaying a little, obviously drunk. Sitting down as quietly as I could, I hoped he wouldn't turn around and notice me. The hairs on the back of my neck rose as I became aware that I was alone at a deserted train station with a drunk man close by.

Looking up at the rusting station roof, I thought about my evening and felt a sense of déjà vu. Before John there was Micky and before him, in my college days, there was Paul. Men I'd loved who had lied to me. My first two loves committing betrayal had been hard. I'd cried a lot, then slept with a few men, then hated myself for it and stopped dating until meeting the next one.

But John was different. I was no longer in my teens or early twenties. I was nearly at an age where families and marriage would be a factor. I had pictured that with him. And it was all a lie.

I pulled out a packet of Marlboro Lights from my bag and opened them. It took four attempts to get my cigarette lit. Each strike of my lighter possibly alerting the man that I was there. Luckily for me they didn't. I leant forward and rubbed my temple with my free hand, glancing at the damp floor. The man hadn't moved at all and, feeling more confident I didn't matter to him, I looked at him gently swaying. I looked at his shoes beside him, once smart but now scuffed and stained. A dark brown patch across the side of the right one. The black leather worn off the toes.

My mum told me you could tell a lot about a person from their shoes. His told me that he was once someone who cared, and now didn't. I noticed he was too close to the edge of the platform for a man who was drunk. I should have told him to step back – I thought it. Almost articulated it. But stopped myself. He was an adult, able to look after himself. And besides, I didn't want an act of kindness to be misread. As far as I was concerned he was like all men. But still, I watched. Curious as to whether my shoe assessment was in any way true.

I could only see him from behind but could tell he was in good shape, his white shirt tight and damp across his shoulders and back, showing a strong muscular form. He looked down onto the track, his thoughts obviously back from wherever they had been. Thinking he would turn and look at me, I shifted my body. Closing myself off. Despite my curiosity about him, I didn't want to talk to him. I just wanted to be left alone.

***

Three minutes.

Dying didn't worry Chris; the only thing that did was the timing. Not just the date but the moment too. He wanted to step not in front of the train but under it. The idea of the driver having to see his death bothered him too much. He knew what it was like to watch a person die. It was something he wished on no one.

If he waited for the engine to pass and then stepped under one of the carriages, say, the twenty-fourth one, his outcome would be exactly the same, but no one would see it happen and therefore no one would be scarred.

The 10.47 was a cargo-loaded train; there would be no passengers. With the timing of his suicide and the note he had placed under the bench, Chris was confident it would cause only a small amount of collateral damage. He knew that the driver would have to stop because someone died but he wouldn't see it, he would be at least three hundred feet away in his carriage before Chris would step out. The emergency services were used to jumpers. This was his final redeeming act as a human being. The only thing he still had to offer.

Looking at the picture that was crumpled into his palm, once more Chris focused on his wife's gaze, the amber flecks like lightning bolts in her green eyes that seemed to move with fluidity. He focused on the way her smile was slightly higher on one side, giving her a mischievous glint. He kissed it and carefully put her in his shirt pocket. He wanted her close to his heart when the time came.

***

Out of the corner of my eye I watched him kiss a picture. Seeing him kiss it changed how I felt about him. It made me think of an old film I love.

One where a man's heart belonged in one place. And I realized that maybe he wasn't the enemy. Far from it. John and all men like him were the enemy. John wouldn't even have a picture of me, let alone kiss it. This man, he was different. He was clearly in love and the way he kissed the picture, so tender, so caring, made me feel as if I'd assessed him wrongly.

He was clearly a little drunk but not 'a drunk'. No doubt just going home from a date night with the person in the picture or perhaps even returning home to her after a few drinks with friends. I found myself smiling at the idea of someone loving so deeply that nothing else mattered.

Because of that, I couldn't help but be drawn to him. He wouldn't be the sort to try anything on, not with the way he held that picture, and maybe, if we did talk I would learn about the person. It was exactly what I needed to hear after so many wasted years of pretending to have such a love of my own. It was a nice idea. But I knew I wasn't going to interrupt him; it felt selfish.

He shook his head, looking up to the sky, and I looked away before we could make eye contact. Focusing on the tatty bench I was sitting on, I saw something perched on the corner of it, hidden in the shadows created by the armrest and bad lighting: a dark wallet. It was open and exposing money as well as a HSBC bank card. It had obviously fallen from his pocket. I was ashamed to admit to myself, but, part of me wanted to take the cash. Money was always tight, too tight. There were a few notes, and a few notes would mean I wouldn't have to jump any more trains this month. It would mean that when everyone at work went to the pub for lunch, I could join them, if only a few times. Of course, I couldn't do it.

'Excuse me … '

He didn't respond.

'Excuse me, hello?'

***

Chris slowly turned around to see a woman in an oversized cream cardigan sat on the bench; he could tell she'd been crying. She looked tired and cold. How long had she been there?

'Excuse me …' she said.

Chris just looked back at her blankly.

'Sorry, I just wondered, is this your wallet?'

Chris could see his months of planning, months of meticulous attention to detail over time, location and date unravel in a second. Everything had been premeditated, but he had no contingency for anyone else being there.

'Hello?' she said softly, gently, barely at a loud whisper.

'Yes, it's mine,' was all Chris could say as he stepped towards her and took the wallet, his thumb touching the back of her hand as he did. Her delicate wrist exposed from the cardigan sleeve. Goose bumps raising the fine light hairs on her forearm. Staring at her for a moment, he put the wallet in his pocket before turning back to the track. He had planned everything to ensure no one would be hurt by his suicide. But this.

Two minutes.

Staring ahead, Chris wondered what would happen to her if he did what he intended. Would it ruin her life? He knew it probably would, but the idea of him having to orchestrate it all again was too unbearable to comprehend. It had to be as he'd planned. He didn't feel strong enough to have it any other way. So he had to work out a way to get rid of her. He turned around to look back at this thin, dark-haired woman and she was staring straight at him, as if waiting for a response. Had she asked him a question?

'Hmm?'

'I asked if you were waiting for the London train?' she repeated, taking a puff on her cigarette.

'No.'

'So the Cambridge one, like me?'

He knew, from the months of research, that the Cambridge train wasn't for another hour. His train was imminent, then a slow London train with usually six carriages rattled through, then the Cambridge train. He wanted to shout at her for being so early.

'You do know the Cambridge train isn't for another hour?'

'I know.'

'There's a pub on the corner. You look cold. Why don't you sit in there?'

'Well, they kind of want you to buy something,' she said, followed by an honest and embarrassed: 'Payday next week.'

There was his opportunity; if he could get her to go for a drink he could be alone.

'Let me buy you one?' he said, his voice a little softer than before. 'I mean, let me pay for you to have a drink.'

'Sorry?'

'Let me buy you a drink.'

'What? No, thank you.'

'I don't want to come with you. It's not like that. It's just, I can see that you're cold. I don't mind paying for one, saves you waiting here for so long.'

'Really?'

'Yes.'

'That's a really kind gesture.' She said it slowly, clearly weighing up whether to take him up on the offer. Holding his eye to try to work out what the catch was. Breaking eye contact, he looked at her cigarette burning in her hand.

'They'll kill you,' he said, noting the irony, watching her put it out under her shoe.

'I can't accept your offer, but thank you.'

'It's just a fiver.' He proffered a note.

'N-not many people would be so generous.'

'Please. Take it and go get warm. It's cold tonight.'

'It is. Are you not cold?'

'A little.'

'Why don't you have a coat?'

'Why don't you?'

'Long story.'

She looked at his feet, clearly wanting to ask but not wanting to embarrass him.

'To be connected,' was all he said by way of explanation, regretting the words as they fell from his mouth.

'Sorry?'

'Nothing, it doesn't matter.'

'Are you all right?'

Chris opened his mouth to reply. But caught the words before they left. A pause she noticed. Telling her that he was far from it.

'Wanna talk?'

'No, and you shouldn't want to either. I could be anyone. I could be a mugger or worse.'

'I did think that. But somehow I know you're not.'

'How could you possibly know what kind of man I am?'

'I don't know – instinct.'

She watched as the tension from his shoulders lifted momentarily. Her kind words having the impact she wanted them to have. Chris kept eye contact with her for a second. Trying to process what was happening. There was something in the way she looked at him that was unnerving. It reminded him of the way he used to see the world. Hopeful, kind.

He pinched the bridge of his nose, rubbing his tear ducts. His words slipped out of his mouth again before he could catch them.

'It's been a rough day.'

He glanced past her to the clock.

Ninety seconds.

'I've had a rough day too. My boyfriend, I mean ex ... You know how it is.'

As he turned back to look at the track, the girl's voice faded away. Chris's mind raced, as if he was drowning. This was supposed to be a peaceful time for him. He was supposed to be alone with his thoughts so he could reflect upon his short thirty-four-year existence up till the point where he watched Julia slip away – and the ten long months after.

He wanted to be seeing it all in a series of flashbacks, pausing on the highs and lows of his time. He wanted to be thinking of his first bike ride, and the long summers he enjoyed as a child and the way his father smiled when he spoke of his mother, and the terrible day he died and his funeral on a beautiful summer's morning. His first kiss as an awkward teenager, and then how, years later, he met and fell in love with Julia, the way she snored and how she would tease him about his slowly greying hair before kissing him and telling him she liked a silver fox. Their holidays and adventures, their kindness to one another. Their plans for a future.

He wanted, as painful as it was, to think of that night.

Instead he was panicking and his mind grabbed for something he couldn't quite reach. For the first time since he knew what he must do, he didn't know how things would play out. It had all been clear up to this point: wait for 5 May, their wedding anniversary, a date that mattered to her. Find a discreet place that would cause little damage. Leave this earth quietly. Be with his wife again.

It didn't matter if it hurt; it didn't matter if it was quick or slow. It just had to not cause harm to another person and it had to be now, and therefore the girl had to leave. He turned around to look at her once more and she was looking straight back at him. Had she said something again?

'Sorry?' muttered Chris.

'I was just telling you why I'm here.' She waited for him to respond, but he didn't. 'Anyway, so he's been using me and, if I'm honest, I've known for longer than I let on. I guess that sometimes things are rough. You know?' Again she waited for him to reply, but he said nothing, only lowered his head. 'I saw you kiss that picture.'

'That's none of your business,' he said, his guard back up.

'Sorry, you're right, I shouldn't pry.'

He watched her pull her scarf up over her chin to shelter herself from the cold wind that was sweeping through the station.

Sixty seconds.

Chris had forgotten it was cold, but he did notice that her gestures reminded him a little of the way Julia used to hide her face when she was embarrassed or shy. Another memory began to swirl into focus among the million that were circling his mind, unable to fully settle, like a flock of birds feeding at sea. He seized the one that was closest and, as it fell into place, he could see it was one of his favourite moments.

He was lying in bed with Julia next to him, facing him, lit only by a small lamp that cast shadows over her delicate features. The memory was of their first full night together. The night that had begun at this station. They were both nervous and tipsy after a dinner party her mother had hosted. He still couldn't believe he'd summoned the courage to go, but he guessed that's what she was to him: personified courage.

They were both in his bed in their underwear and between gazing at one another and giggling due to their nerves they kissed passionately, her gentle moans and heavy breathing in his ear making his whole body tingle as if suddenly exposed to intense summer heat. His pulse moving at such a rate that for a second he thought his heart would burst and he would die right then in that moment.

He remembered the way he entered her without looking anywhere but deep into her eyes and how it was over quickly, both climaxing together in such a

32

way that Chris didn't know where his began and hers ended. He thought about how she giggled after and hid her face, embarrassed about how loud she had been, with only her smiling eyes showing above the covers. He remembered thinking that nothing else mattered.

The woman in the cardigan was looking at him still. Had she spoken again? Why was she bothering?

'I just wondered why you would want to get me a drink, that's all.'

'I've said – you look cold.'

'I mean, why would you care?'

'Because I can.'

***

Taking a deep breath, I felt something I didn't understand, something in my stomach, a kind of ache.

'I didn't think there was anyone nice left in the world.'

'There probably isn't.'

'And yet a complete stranger offers to buy me a drink so I can stay warm. I mean, who does that?'

'Don't read into it; it's not a big deal. I've only offered because, if you must know, I want to be alone.'

'Clearly.' I took a breath. I needed to keep him talking. Despite him wanting to be alone, I knew I couldn't go. It was becoming clear that this man was feeling as he was because of a love that wasn't reciprocated. I was feeling the same too, but I had my sister to talk with about my feelings and a shoulder to cry on. I don't know why, but I sensed he didn't have the same. 'Did she leave you?'

'What?'

'The girl in the picture?'

'Just take the money, please.'

I chose to ignore him. I had never met a man who clearly treasured love. Despite him not wanting to talk about it, I knew I needed to stay. I knew if I could get him to talk, it would make him feel better. Selfishly, I knew that would make me feel better too.

'Is there any chance she will come back?'

***

Chris thought about the moment he said goodbye as she lay in the ground.

'You clearly love her.'

'Yes.'

He didn't know why but the stranger's persistence had somehow found a way through his walls. Just a small crack that she managed to squeeze in through.

'I wish I had someone love me like that.'

Chris looked at her. He could see in that moment she was hurting in a way similar to him. But on a smaller scale. He knew he would never love anyone like he did Julia. And in return he wouldn't be loved back. But this girl, the train girl, she still had a future.

'You will.'

She broke eye contact, a small smile on her lips. He felt as though in a different time they might have had a good conversation. But the clock was ticking. He needed her gone. He closed the gap she had broken through. His wall solid once more.

'She was a lucky lady.'

'Sorry, I don't mean to be rude, but I need to be alone. Will you please go for that coffee. I insist.'

He glanced from her to the clock and back again, her expression startled by his sudden forcefulness.

Forty-five seconds.

'Sorry,' he repeated a little softer. 'I want to be on my own and I don't really want to talk to anyone. It's sweet of you to care; it really is. But I need you to leave, okay?'

'Okay,' she replied. 'Sorry.'

'Go for that drink.' Holding out the five-pound note, Chris looked up.

Thirty-five seconds.

In the distance he could hear a gentle rumbling. It was coming.

'Please.'

***

I stood up and walked towards him, standing a little too close as I took the money. My hand unintentionally stroking against his, for the second time, and I felt it again. There was something, although I didn't fully know what it was, that drew me to him, to this stranger. As I looked at him, I could see fear in his eyes and I wanted to know what he was frightened of. What I did know, though, was that if I left, something terrible would happen. It was the combination of him wanting desperately for me to leave him alone and the sound of the train coming. I was possibly being dramatic and comparing this moment to one from a film, but it looked like he was going to do something stupid. He pleaded with me again to leave, this time with a little more force. Scaring me a little. I didn't know what to do. I hesitated, unable to commit to anything. Again he said please, taking a step towards me. I stepped back. I was worried if I stayed any longer he might force me with more than words. But I didn't want to leave him. The train was getting louder and he started to look for it down the track. Not knowing what else to do I started to back away. As I did, he turned to face the on-coming train.

Twenty-five seconds.

I thought of all the times in my life I didn't act. I didn't act when my parents split up. I didn't act the first time John cheated on me. I didn't act when my bank account read so little so often. I still don't know why but I knew that in that moment I would do something. Turning, I looked towards the man in the wet shirt and bare feet. The man who reminded me of the old films. His gaze focused on the rail track three feet below.

'Look, I don't know you and you don't know me,' I said with all of the courage I could summon, shocked that the words were coming out of my mouth. 'But I think we both could do with something new; I know I could. I think we could both do with some help. So why don't you come join me? Why don't you and I get a coffee … together?'

***

Chris wanted to scream at her. He wanted to shake this stupid girl who had misread his intentions. He was not being polite. He was not being kind. He was not showing empathy or chivalry. He just wanted some fucking peace before ending it all, but she wasn't giving up.

'I've never met a man who would offer to buy me a drink like that without expecting or trying anything on. Never. That makes you someone good in a world full of arseholes and I can see you are struggling with something and so am I. I'm asking you to join me because we both need someone nice. We both need a good person to talk to, even just for a short while.' Her breathing was shallow, panicked, rising in pitch as she struggled to get enough air in her lungs to speak her words without spilling her fear. A fear of what she hadn't yet learnt.

'You don't know me,' he replied, looking once again to the clock. 'And I'm not a good person. Can't you please just understand that and go for that coffee?'

'No!'

'What do you mean "no"?'

Ten seconds.

Ten months flashed through his mind. He thought about the pain, the suffering. The routines he developed to cope with his great adversary, time. He thought of Steve's attempted interventions as he spiralled into a downward depression. How his best friend wouldn't give up on him despite Chris backing away completely.

He thought about his father, how much stronger he had been. He thought about how sad his friends would be at his funeral, wearing black, tears in their eyes, unable to contain their grief. Although none of them would be shocked.

Then he heard it, the voice he had been waiting to hear for so long, calling out to him. He had longed to hear it say these words, now he was desperate to not hear them yet. He needed more time but the announcer continued to talk, despite his silent begging.

The next train to arrive does not stop at this station. Please stand back from the platform edge.

The rattle of steel on steel with over three thousand five hundred tonnes of moving machine started to build. The screeching of the friction caused by the immense weight became so loud it penetrated deep into his inner ears. The train girl instinctively turned her body away from the direction of where the noise was coming from, as if she would be protected from the monster approaching.

He didn't move. He didn't even blink as he stared out towards the track, its rumbling almost inviting. It was as if the tracks had hands and they would surely pull him down. He looked to his right and could see the eyes of the train approaching. He wanted to step out, but she was there, she would see, and he would damage her as a result. Reluctantly, he knew it wasn't going to happen as he had planned and hoped. He turned to look at her, the girl who'd stopped him being with his wife.

***

I knew that he was too near the edge, but I didn't have time to say anything before the deafening noise of the train strangled my voice as it passed. Its driver desperate to deliver his payload and return home; his mind on other things.

I turned away further, the whipping wind generated by its passing caused me to grip on to my cardigan as my hair was jostled by the monster's phenomenal force.

***

Chris didn't blink; he just stood there looking at her as the train sped past. She shouted something to him. He couldn't hear. He didn't care. To his right he could see the solid mass speed past broken only by the gaps between the carriages, which moved so fast they seemed to be only millimetres long, but still long enough for him to slip under. He would only need an arm to get caught, or a leg, and the amount of downforce created would suck the rest of him under before he could register the pain of his limb being hit. All he had to do was take one step back. Just one. But he couldn't. She was watching him. And he hated her for it.

Then it was gone. As it passed, he looked to his left and longingly watched the red tail lights of the train disappear into the night.

He had failed to do the one thing that may have brought peace to his fractured soul. Unable to think of how to fix it, Chris looked towards the exit. Still facing the train girl, he crouched down to grab his shoes. He looked up at her; her eyes were fixed on him. For a while neither moved.

'Please, can you stay?' She finally broke the silence.

He was unable to form any words. His ears unable to hear what she had said. But she didn't matter; all that mattered was searching through his thoughts for a solution. It was either find one or fail his wife.

'Please?'

He picked up his shoes and then without putting them on, he walked towards the entrance, up the stairs and away from the station, leaving the girl alone.

***

I watched him leave and for a moment couldn't move. Like a rabbit caught in headlights. I wasn't one hundred per cent sure, but it felt like the man who had just left was there to do something terrible. My instincts told me that's why I couldn't leave the platform when he insisted. It was in the way he kissed that picture, the way he stood too close to the edge. The fact he had taken his shoes off 'to be connected'. On their own, they were oddities; together they told something else.

They told me he was there to take his own life. And I had stopped him. For now. Still looking towards the now lifeless entrance, I heard a breeze sweep along the platform and the sound of traffic rattling over the bridge. The sounds returning after a brief moment of not existing. Sitting down on the bench, my gaze shifting from the entrance to the track, I tried to shake off the feeling I had about him. It made me feel sick.

I took another cigarette from my bag and lit it. The adrenaline in my hands made it difficult to hold the flame steady. Once I had taken a few drags, my mind settled and I tried to piece the truth together. I had been mistaken about him. He was not a drunk, or a nut job, most likely just a sad man whose girlfriend dumped him but one who had no intention of hurting himself. I had it made up as an elaborate distraction tactic from my sad little life. He was the real tragedy. I cursed my pathetic loneliness meaning I had to practically beg a stranger to spend some time with me.

Allowing my head to sink, I watched my cigarette ash blowing away in the wind and let out a laugh that quickly turned into a small cry. I just wanted to be home, in my bed, desperately trying to forget the night's events and get on with my life, as sorrowful as it seemed. I wondered if I would ever feel the elation that came with victory. Just once.

Wiping my eyes, I saw there was a letter directly under where I was sitting. One that was carefully folded and placed under a stone that looked alien on the cold, damp asphalt. It was clear the stone didn't belong at the station. I reached down and picked it up to examine it as well as the note it held down, although I wasn't prepared for what it said.

'To the person who finds this letter … '

Scanning to the bottom made me almost throw up and I stood up as I realized what the letter was. My gut instinct had been right. That feeling I had when he walked out of the station was true. He was there to kill himself; he was going to jump in front of that train and I had accidentally saved his life.

'… There was no one who could have stopped this from happening … '

And yet, he didn't do it.

I thought about my reason for being there, how it was a massive coincidence, how it was probably usually deserted at this time of night. If I came any night other than tonight or had decided to stay at John's, I would have never have seen him and then he would be dead.

I felt an overwhelming need to find him. I had accidentally stopped him but that didn't mean I had saved him. He could find a bridge to jump from, or he could step in front of a lorry. He could go to the river in the town centre, stuff rocks into his pockets and jump and no one would know to stop him. No one at this moment, but me. I had to talk to him, to explain I had seen his note, to tell him that whatever had happened to him, it would get better. There was something good lost in him, buried under pain, and I wished I'd forced him to get a coffee with me so I could have helped him see that. I wished I'd left when he did and followed him so I knew where he was going, so I could help, or get him help, or something, anything.

But I hadn't. I'd made me wanting to have a coffee with him about me needing a distraction from my problems. That's why I had given up so easily. Running towards the exit now, I left the train station and stopped in the middle of the quiet road. Looking to my left and then right I saw nothing, only the dark footpaths lit by orange lights. No one could be seen in the gloomy spring night, everything was deathly quiet as if the night couldn't speak of what had happened and what had not.

Only the wind remained unaffected as it blew through the trees that lined the pavements. The way their limbs swayed looked so peaceful, reminding me of *his* gentle swaying when I first saw him.

'Shit, Sarah, he was right there and you let him just walk away', I said out loud. Looking at the letter once more, I learnt his name, which was neatly printed at the bottom: Chris Hayes. I called out desperately. My voice jagged, on the verge of crying. 'Chris? Chris!'

But only the breeze, rustling the leaves, and my echoing voice, desperate and delicate, replied.

Chapter 4

10.52 p.m. – somewhere on the A605, near March

Chris felt numb as he stumbled into a taxi, giving his address. Probably the same taxi that had dropped off the stupid girl who had unhinged his plan. The journey back was the longest of his life. Unable to fully comprehend what had happened and its impact, he rested his head against the window, looking out. His cheeks vibrated as the cab picked up speed. He watched the rain fall and hit the glass in such a way it sounded like it had a pulse. Almost like the weather mocked him for being alive when he should be dead. The driver spoke, interrupting his thoughts.

'You look like you've had a rough day?'

Chris looked at him in the rear-view mirror, shrugged his shoulders, and returned to the rain. Not knowing what else to say or do. He saw the driver's toothy smile change to worry. Chris wondered why he would care about a stranger.

'I see, well we all have them.'

Chris just nodded his head. Looking out of the window again.

'When I'm feeling down I try to see the world through someone else's perspective. For instance, we've not got it as bad as those poor folk in Aleppo. You hear about it on the radio. No water, no electricity. Bombs falling every day. That's someone who's got it rough. And here's you and me, in a warm taxi, driving on a quiet little road.'

'I guess.'

'See, perspective. I'm Giles, mate.'

'Chris.'

'Name suits you. Not like mine. Giles – sounds a bit posh for someone like me. Although I do have a lord in my family tree going back a few hundred years. Could have left me a few quid mind.'

Chris smiled in spite of himself and then quickly cursed himself for it. He looked back towards the rear-view mirror to get a better look at his driver. Chris noticed he was maybe sixty-five with greying hair, weathered skin and a thick neck. A scar ran across the bridge of his nose and the nose itself was slightly bent to the left – he had clearly been on the wrong side of someone's fist in his youth. Maybe even done a little time.

Giles began to talk about the weather and how it wasn't like when he was growing up, but Chris wasn't paying attention. After a while Giles noticed and quietened down. He turned up his radio and listened to a song by Status Quo, which mumbled over the sound of the taxi's diesel engine as they rattled along the A605, cutting through small villages and towns.

Twenty minutes into the journey Chris could see the lay-by he had visited once before coming up on his left. He saw a tree that stood taller than any other. One he and Julia had both rested against once. He watched the tree as they passed – focusing on the intertwining roots, which could be seen curving out of the earth – until it was consumed by the darkness. Once it could no longer be seen, Chris felt a sense of loss. He wanted to ask the driver to go back so he could sit where he and Julia had sat one night a long time ago, him sweeping the hair off her face, holding her tightly as neither spoke; but he didn't ask. Instead he closed his eyes. Pretending to sleep.

It took him the rest of the journey to calm his heart rate, which pounded in his head. A journey that, including a long wait at a train crossing, took just over fifty-five minutes and cost him £60.

Chris opened the door to the house, a modest three-bed he bought after meeting Julia. He hoped in vain there would be some sound coming from within. It was silent besides the ticking clock on the kitchen wall. As Chris closed the front door, he looked back to see the old chatty taxi driver give a small wave as he pulled away.

He felt a small pang of guilt for being so dismissive. At first he'd been suspicious of the old man but it was clear that the taxi driver was lonely and actually trying to care for a stranger by talking to him. It made him think of his father once more.

'Everyone you will ever meet is fighting a battle you do not know, so be nice. Be nice always.'

Chris felt ashamed of himself. He briefly wondered what his father would think of the way he had just treated another human being, but soon shrugged it off, despite his father being right. After all, he was supposed to be dead right now and therefore the driver wouldn't have had anyone to talk to anyway. Besides, his father's view of other things mattered a lot more.

After putting his shoes under the stairs, Chris saw there were two new messages on his home answerphone. He pressed play and sat on the stairs near his front door. Unsure what else to do. The first message was from Ben, a work friend of his. The automated voice told him he had left it just after midday.

'Hi, Chris, it's Ben. I hope you're okay. I've tried to call you on your mobile but can't leave a message. So I got your number from our records. I thought you wouldn't mind. Mate, we've been chatting in the office and it came up today was, well, you know. Anyway. We'd like to take you out for a drink, just a few of us. Just to catch up. No pressure to come back to work or anything, far from it. We miss your face around here and want to see how you are. So give me a ring back when you can and we can set something up.'

The second was from Steve, sent at eight minutes past ten. The same time Chris had been aimlessly walking through March.

'Hi, mate. Thought I'd just give you a quick call. Haven't heard anything from you in a few weeks and Kristy reminded me today was your anniversary. I'm sorry, I should have remembered. I'm rubbish with dates. I came over earlier today, about seven, but you weren't in. Listen. I've got some time off work soon and I was thinking we could go and have a pint or something? Anyway, give me a call.'

Chris was tempted to call back but thought better of it. He remembered the last time he and Steve went for a pint, three weeks before. It was a goodbye drink that Steve didn't know he was sharing. Like a wake for the living. It was a huge risk meeting up with Steve. Chris usually told his best mate everything, but he couldn't tell him the thing that really mattered.

When they had last met at their usual haunt – the same bar where Steve had instigated Chris meeting Julia – it was a quiet Friday due to the pouring rain that hadn't lifted all day. Chris had spent the day in his house, waiting for nothing in particular, before leaving an hour and a half earlier than their agreed meeting. His nerves were frayed at seeing his mate for the last time, so by the time Steve arrived Chris was washing down his third pint and, as he approached, Chris hugged him for longer than normal. Steve glanced at the empties.

'Had a few already I see, mate?'

'I came straight from work. Figured, why not?'

'I can't remember the last time you had more than a couple.'

'Me neither, but tonight we are celebrating.'

Chris then walked to the bar, ordered two more pints, and returned to sit beside Steve who was clearly confused.

'What are we celebrating?'

'Life.'

Raising his pint glass, Chris clinked his friend's and drained half of his before Steve had taken a sip. As he lowered his glass he could see Steve watching him.

'Are you all right, Chris?'

'I'm fine.'

'Are you sure?'

'Of course.'

'Okay. So what specifically about life are we toasting?'

'Just life, like I said.'

'I see. Well I'm glad we are, mate. It feels like forever since we had a pint.'

'It's been a long time.'

Steve watched as Chris took another long drink of his pint, leaving only about a third of it swilling in the glass.

'Chris?'

Chris burped loudly. Drawing the attention of people at nearby tables. 'Yep.'

'Are you sure you're okay?'

'I'm fine, Steve; stop mothering.'

'Chris. What's on your mind?'

'Fucking hell, let's just have a drink. Can't we just get drunk together?'

'I'm not sure that's a good idea – maybe you shouldn't have any more?'

'Don't tell me what to do.' Chris slammed his glass on the table with such force two of the three empties jumped off the table and smashed on the floor.

'Bloody hell, Chris!'

Chris took a deep breath, centring himself. As he spoke, it was quieter but no calmer. 'I'm getting another one. You want another one?'

'No,' Steve replied, shifting in his seat as eyes began turning towards the commotion at their table.

'Please yourself.'

Chris remembered the look on Steve's face. One that recoiled at the aggressiveness of his remark and was deeply worried. He couldn't remember any other time in their friendship where he had been confrontational and he knew Steve knew it.

Chris had forced himself to calm down and they'd spent the rest of the night talking awkwardly about nothing of consequence. Chris didn't ask about Steve's wife; he didn't ask about his work. In fact, Steve had to do all of the talking by asking forced questions Chris didn't answer. Especially when he tried to speak about Julia and how it was okay to admit he was struggling without her.

By the end of that night, Steve had warmed up, Chris had cooled down, and as last orders were called, both stepped into the cold night air.

'Nice seeing you, buddy.'

'You too, Steve.'

'Wanna do this again next week?'

'I'd love to. The next few weeks are chaos at work, definitely after though.'

Chris could see his friend looking at him in a way that showed he didn't quite believe what he had just heard – only for a moment though, and then it was replaced with Steve's infectious smile.

'Sure, buddy, just give me a call.'

They hugged again before going their separate ways.

Chris remembered it being harder than he thought it would be to say goodbye to Steve and hearing his voice again reminded him of how drunk and aggressive he'd been the last time they spoke. He didn't want to try to explain his actions that night. He shouldn't need to. He should have been dead by now.

As the voicemail message ended and the line went quiet, Chris stood up, walked down his hallway and into the kitchen. He picked up a folded letter with a key resting on it that had been placed on the kitchen table. Putting the key in his pocket, he took the letter to the sink. Its contents gave the location of the box for which the key fitted, as well as the detailed reason for why he had taken his own life. This letter Chris had poured his broken heart into and that was why he couldn't leave it at the station. His words were too raw and he worried it would have a lasting effect on the person who found it. That's why he had two notes. The one at the station was cold, detached.

It was devoid of feeling and emotion, it was just a list of facts. He intended it to be found. That's why he had left his full name rather just initials like he originally wanted to do. It wouldn't take long for the investigators to find his address where they would learn his reasons why. He figured they would be more desensitized to death than Joe Public. Foolishly, Chris read it, his sadness amplified and his grief embedded further, though he had no idea how that was possible.

He took a lighter from the cutlery drawer and lit the corner of the paper, watching the orange flame take hold and burn upwards. He couldn't read it again. He didn't have the strength and, although he felt the same as when he wrote it, everything was different. The note became not a clue for investigators, but a reminder he had failed his wife. The flames climbed up the paper until nothing but charred carbon was left in its wake. He held it for as long as he could, the hairs on the back of his hands being licked by the flames, before he dropped it into the empty sink and it burnt into nothing. His innermost secrets gone.

Then, reaching into the cupboard, he took a glass and poured himself some water. His hands shook as he did. He wondered how long he had been shaking, and if the old driver had noticed. As he took a sip, his entire body felt flooded with the cool, crisp liquid. He realized that it was the first drink he had had since waking from a fitful dream that morning.

He felt guilty for enjoying the sensation as he drunk the whole glass, followed by another.

Once the glass was empty, the relief of quenching his thirst turned to disgust that he had found small joy in doing so. Chris slammed the glass down with such force it exploded. Shards scattered over the kitchen surfaces and floor. One large shard sliced against his hand, causing it to bleed. He didn't notice at first. Instead, he grabbed the edge of the sink and, gripping hard, he shook it, screaming in his own head, trying to loosen it from the side, trying to destroy something else. It didn't budge.

Out of breath, he saw blood running down the side of his hand and onto his bare feet. Watching it, he felt no pain or worry, only a mild curiosity as to how much would come. After a few minutes it became obvious that it wouldn't be enough. It wasn't deep enough and was already coagulating. He pulled on it with the fingers of his other hand, causing his skin to stretch and fresh blood to form but soon even that didn't work and it began to heal.

If only all things healed that well.

A memory snapped into his mind like an electric shock. Like the single pulse of a strobe light. So fast he barely registered it, but so destructive. It was Julia as he never wished to remember her. It caused his heart to beat wildly and he felt the need to run. But he shut that out, closing his eyes against the invading memory. He thought back to the events on the platform instead.

It had taken months of meticulous planning to ensure that it would go right and instead it had gone terribly wrong. Because of one person. Because of one stupid fucking person. Could she not see he was desperate to be alone?

Looking up, as if God himself would be on his ceiling, Chris was lost as to what he could do next. He silently waited for an answer, from God, from Julia, from his father. But he only heard the clock continuing to tick and pass time. As if nothing had happened. Before finalizing his 10.47 plan, he'd contemplated taking an overdose or swinging himself from a noose. But he wasn't happy with the idea of his body being found. He knew how scarring it was to see a dead human body. It haunted his dreams; it invaded his waking day. It had fundamentally changed him into a person more in shadow than daylight.

He made a rule in the months after Julia passed that when he went, he would not leave a complete body, so that no one else had to lose their light as he had lost his. The train was perfect. He would be just a red smear that dragged on for a mile and therefore no personification could occur by whoever had to clear him up. They might find a hand or an eye but without it being attached to a full body, one that had a soul, it would just be a surreal piece of flesh that might look like it could be a prop in a cheap horror movie or something found hanging in a butcher's window. He wouldn't look like anything that was once human and therefore he wouldn't look like anything that could ruin someone's life.

He realized that now the rules had changed. He realized that leaving a human form didn't matter. He had done everything he could to protect other people. He had lied and hidden. He had grieved alone because it kept others safe. So focused on that, he'd almost failed to see the only thing that truly mattered. Julia. It would be a stranger who would find him, the police probably. Fuck them, they were not his responsibility. It had to be this date.

Realizing he didn't need to care so much for everyone else made Chris feel anticipation build and course through his body. Like an athlete might feel on a starting block, waiting for the gun to go. His plan hadn't been executed the way he wanted but he was still going to join his wife. Chris opened his cutlery drawer and took out a small fruit knife, its blade about three inches and sharp. Perfect.

Looking around, he wondered where it would be best to do it. Only one place sprang to mind. The bedroom. The room where they'd shared their deepest fears and wildest dreams. The place where they could forget about the world, wrapping themselves up in their own little bubble, where they could laugh and love and lust for one another.

He went to his bedroom, sat on the edge of his bed and opened his side drawer. There were only two items in it: a book, one of its pages folded a third of the way through, which he'd not picked up in a long time, and under it Julia's favourite light blue cardigan. He needed to be close to her as he took his last few breaths, to smell her smell, to have her with him. Although he didn't deserve it.

The rest of her possessions were all boxed up in the small room that used to be an office. He wanted to hold her cardigan as he died. Clutching it, Chris pressed the knife into his wrist. It wasn't ideal. Far from it. He knew that it would take between ten and fifteen minutes to bleed out and in that time most of his blood would cover the room that he and Julia slept in.

It was completely opposite to what he had tried and failed to achieve with the train. It would be messy; it would be disturbing for the poor person who found his cold lifeless body in an ocean of dark brown drying blood. But he would be by her side once more and in that ten to fifteen minutes as his life faded, he could think of her. Taking a deep breath, he glanced at the small digital clock as the flicking of one minute to the next caught his eye. The time it read stopped him before he spilt a single drop of blood.

Chapter 5

11.54 p.m. – Kings Road, Cambridge

I spent the journey watching the scenery rush past, unable to focus on what my vision took in. A heat burnt through my body. My blood pumped through my veins like lava, making my eyes sting. My breathing was shallow and tight. I was obviously in shock. The train went into a tunnel, making me jump and as my ears popped I caught myself in the glass that acted like a mirror against the vast black nothingness. The girl who looked back was blotchy and pale. Her mascara, which was designed to be waterproof, had failed after twenty minutes of crying.

I couldn't keep looking at myself as a fresh tear rolled out of the corner of my left eye. Instead, I focused on my hands, the polish on my fingernails chipped through picking. My hands shook slightly. I pressed them onto my thighs to try to calm them. It seemed to work. I tensed my arms, pressing down onto my legs and took a deep breath in. As I released my tension, I let my breath out and, for a moment, I felt in control of my thoughts again.

Somehow, I felt like I had failed when in fact I had done the exact opposite. I should have felt empowered. I had just saved a life – and yet, I felt like a child, lost, needy. I tried to look at myself again, but as I did the tunnel ended and the flat, dark world came into focus again, broken only by lights from farmhouses and faraway villages until the city lights of Cambridge came closer.

I saw couples sat in front of the television in the houses that lined the tracks as the train slowed into the station. It bothered me less than I thought to see people happy together. I guess stopping a man from killing himself can change someone's perspective.

Once I left the near-deserted station I wrapped my cardigan as tightly as I could around me and, crossing my arms, focused on keeping my breath under control. I began to walk home. Night was clinging fast to everything around me as I wandered down Station Road, making me involuntarily shiver. Shadows from street lamps transformed the Georgian student-filled town houses that were, by daylight, beautiful to look at into something more sinister. Usually if I was out this late I wanted to get home as quickly and as safely as I could, but not tonight. Tonight I dragged my feet.

Although Cambridge on the whole is a safe city, it has its fair share of problems and streets you have to avoid after dark, like all cities do, and usually

I would feel my senses heightened. Waiting for a noise or light that would make me break into a run. Somehow though, I feared the night less. Almost like my self-preservation had been detached. The gravity of walking out on the man I loved and hated simultaneously only to accidentally walk into the life of another man who was trying to end it all was a little too much for me to fully absorb. It seemed too bizarre for my small and ordinary life. It felt like I was watching a black-and-white movie instead of actually experiencing it first-hand.

As I reached the botanical gardens I thought it was safe to relax a little, but as soon as I did an image flashed into my mind, like a lightning bolt illuminating a night sky. It was him, on the platform, jumping under the train as I helplessly stood by. So sudden and violent was the image, conjured up from my broken imagination, it forced the air from my lungs and stopped me in my tracks.

I had to sit down or I was going to black out. I tried to refocus on my breathing but it was too late. Flashing through my mind was Chris and his wet shirt and his note and his sad, fearful eyes that made my heart ache. They were spinning inside my head, shouting at me. Taking my last cigarette out of the packet I tried to light it, my unsteady hands making it impossible to do so. Each strike of the flint failing to spark the gas somehow pressed on my chest, crushing my lungs, until I had to stop and lower my head between my legs. The lack of oxygen made me feel as if I was drowning, as if I wasn't a part of the world.

When I closed my eyes I saw his bare feet on the platform floor and heard his voice saying it connected him. Without thinking I unzipped my knee-high boots and struggled to get them off my feet before taking my socks off as well. My fumbling fingers felt like they didn't belong to me any more and I knew if I didn't get control I was going to be sick. Hot bile began to rise from my stomach and my eyes were struggling to focus as I finally wrestled my socks off.

As soon as I managed to put my feet on the cold, wet, hard, uneven floor I could feel the world begin to slow down and for a moment I focused on the uneven chips and cracks under my cooling soles. It allowed me to get my breathing under control.

After a few minutes, I could feel the blood returning to my hands, enough for me to light my cigarette, inhale a deep lungful, and lift my head back up to hear the sound of the wind in the trees and rain hitting the leaves above me. I knew I should get back up and get home to safety. But I couldn't. I needed to stay put and finish my cigarette barefoot.

Only eighteen hours earlier, I had woken up to just another Thursday with its mediocrity of responding to emails and taking telephone calls. Only the nervous sensation at the thought of seeing John later and what that would bring let me know I wasn't entirely numb. Fast-forward that short time and everything had changed, all because of a man called Chris Hayes.

I saw him kiss that picture again. But in my mind I was standing behind myself watching the whole evening play out in front of me. Like you would in a dream, and my heart ached once more. The poor, poor man. Why didn't he just do it? Was it something he had to do alone or something more? I imagined his sad eyes on mine as he fell backwards in front of the train, the sound of it hitting him and the way his body would explode on impact, it all happening so fast it would be like he wasn't even there. It would have been something that would have stayed with me forever – and I knew then why he didn't do it.

With my boots and socks in my hand, my feet beginning to numb from the cold, I started to walk home again. The sinister shadows of older houses were replaced with newbuilds where the street lamps were more frequent and brighter. Usually here, I would have my senses fully engaged for any movement from the alleys between the houses, or a sound of footsteps behind me, but tonight they weren't. It felt like I was in my own sense-free bubble.

If he really did protect me from seeing him die, even though he wanted to die, then that made him a better person than anyone else I had ever known. It was the most selfless thing someone had ever done, and I knew that I needed to repay his obscure kindness. It was clear that whatever happened he felt like the only option was to end it all. I knew

I shouldn't, but I took his note out and read it once more.

To the person who finds this letter.

On the fifth of May, I ended my life. There was no foul play involved as I made this decision of my own free mind. They say time can heal all pain, but, in truth, some pains are too great.

There was no one who could have stopped this from happening.

Chris Hayes.

I had never read a suicide note before, I was expecting something more profound. More detail. But, only one line offered any emotion. His talk of pain. I could empathize with that. Sometimes pain can feel so great that ending it seems the best solution. I had seen it once before, in my school friend Becky. She was struggling with home life and nobody knew. She hid it so well from all of us in our friendship group right up to the point she tried to hurt herself. She did it in the girls' toilets between second and third lesson. I wasn't there when she was found by a teacher, Ms Tuttle, who was doing the routine checks to catch smokers, but from what had filtered through the school, Becky was lucky. She was even more so because after that day all of us in our friendship group surrounded her to help in any way we could. Even when others called her names. The school spoke with her family and together they helped set up some counselling to guide her in her recovery.

I've not seen Becky in a long time, but, from what I could gather on Facebook, she is happily married and has a little girl who looks just like she did as a kid. I often wondered, what if that break time Ms Tuttle didn't walk into that toilet? What if no one found her? What if no one took the time to care? I was wondering those same questions again, but this time for him. I knew that if someone could reach him, he could find another way. My gut told me he was alone. Which meant I would need to be the one to find him and start the process of getting him help. I just wished he'd said or done something that might tell me where to start.

Finally reaching the welcoming shape of my own front door, I suddenly realized how tired I felt. It was as if the comfort of home allowed me to finally concede to the night. Opening it, I could hear the television quietly playing from the lounge, knowing what that meant – my sister Natalie and her partner George were downstairs. Probably both asleep on the sofa as that was what usually happened. I didn't mind though. I desperately needed the familiarity right now.

I had never had that feeling of closeness Natalie shared with George with anyone, and it made me feel happy and jealous at the same time. After leaving my boots at the bottom of the stairs, I stepped into my small, cluttered front room with its walls covered in photographs. Lots of me and Natalie, some of John, most of Natalie and George.

The bright HD light coming from the TV was cast over the sofa opposite, confirming my suspicions.

There they were, both curled up, her head on his chest, both asleep, barely visible above the sofa's throw, which they used as a blanket. Their breathing in perfect unison. It was nice to see. I loved that Nat and I were so close and could live together in relative peace. But sometimes I wished for my own space, just so I didn't have to feel like a third wheel in my own home.

Natalie was so similar to me in so many ways. Her looks, the way she talked, and yet Natalie managed to make everything seem effortless. She had excelled in school and was more popular despite being three years younger, and she'd managed to meet a wonderful man, who adored her and who she adored in return. Again something I didn't believe would ever happen to me, and Natalie made it seem easy to maintain that mutual adoration.

Normally, I would gently tap my sister and she would stir. She would then wake George and they would sleepily give me a kiss and go to bed, freeing the couch for me to sit on and perhaps wait for a text from John, or channel-surf for an hour to try to help me switch off. But instead I left them there. It seemed cruel to disturb their peace, and after a day like mine I needed the idea of peace to exist. Seeing their tranquillity offered me a brief and fragile hope.

I walked up my narrow, steep stairs and stepped into the bathroom. I turned on the light, which temporarily blinded me with white and chrome. After turning the dial on the shower, I undressed, foolishly looking into the mirror once naked. I noticed how red my eyes were, how tired I looked, and how I was beginning to show the early signs of age – the small and delicate lines around my eyes, the skin on my forehead not quite as tight as it once was, the slight thinning of my lips, and boobs that weren't quite as pert as they once were – until the steam from the hot water blurred me from myself. Thank God.

I got into the shower and turned it up as hot as I could bear, so hot my skin reddened, and then I stood motionless, letting the water cascade over my head and face, trying to wash the day away. After I felt less dirty, I wrapped myself in a towel and fell onto my bed, knowing I needed to get to sleep quickly. In six hours I would have to get up and get ready for work. But playing in my mind on a loop was my moment with Chris.

As the hours ticked by, all I could think of was him and whether I should have done more before he walked out of the station and my broken little life.

Chapter 6

12.07 a.m. – London Road, Peterborough

Dropping the knife, its cold steel sounding louder than it should on the wooden floor, Chris couldn't believe how careless he had been. Time had been his only companion, his only constant since Julia died and somehow he had neglected it. With Julia's cardigan still in his hand, he ran downstairs to look at his wall clock, which continued on its forward journey, completely oblivious to the commotion he was causing.

'Please be fast, please be fast.'

Seeing it, his heart sank further. It said seven minutes past.

He was too late. It was now the sixth.

He had missed his date.

Not knowing what to do, he looked around his room for an answer. He wished he could turn back time, just eight minutes would be all he needed. But if he could turn back eight minutes, why not turn back ten months and bring his wife back to him?

Rage bubbled to the surface and he buried his face into her cardigan to muffle his wounded scream. He screamed until there was no more air in his lungs. He screamed until veins in his forehead bulged, until he was desperate for more oxygen. He screamed until his hands tingled and his vision closed in on him.

Then he was on the floor, lying on his side, his face pressed into the cold kitchen tiles, her cardigan half covering his face. The clock told him he had lost four more precious minutes. He must have passed out. He lay still for a moment. His hand was beginning to hurt where he had cut it. Chris inhaled and Julia's scent lifted from the cardigan, which remained potent after so long.

The dark, lifeless world began to fade into the background as the light of a beautiful moment from their past took over. One that he had forgotten they shared. She was in bed, lying on her side and looking at him. Her skin glowing in the way it did after they were intimate. He stroked her face, running his finger over her eyebrow, across her cheekbone. He remembered telling her that she was beautiful and she hid her face more with the duvet. He laughed, unable to say what he really wanted to. He'd been scared by the intensity of the feelings he already had for her.

She asked him who he admired. Chris said that one was easy, and he told her about his father and of his kindness and strength. About how he always managed to find light, even in dark times. He also talked about his father's father, a man who passed away when Chris was just eight or nine. He died not through illness or accident but because he wanted to.

Chris remembered telling Julia how his grandfather and grandmother met when they were young, and they fell in love instantly. His grandfather a bugle boy in his army outfit, playing on the steps of York Cathedral to thousands of people. When he hit his solo he saw her in the crowd, looking at him. As soon as he finished, he went to her side and then never left. Just like the old movies.

As they got old she developed cancer and, at seventy-one, she died. He, a healthy man of seventy-four, with no illnesses, died less than three months later. His grandfather told Chris's father with his last breaths that the world was beautiful for different people for different reasons. And that his reason for it being so beautiful was waiting somewhere else. Chris remembered telling Julia he wanted to be like that; he wanted to love so much that he couldn't live without it.

He remembered Julia saying it was the most beautiful story she had ever heard.

He remembered how she kissed him then and he tingled at the touch.

Then he remembered the last time he kissed her. Her lips cold and blue.

Taking shuddering breaths, Chris cried. In the rare moments when he allowed himself to cry, he did so quietly, gracefully, and completely unnoticed. This time was different. A loud wounded noise, almost like an animal dying, fell from his mouth. There was no restraint, no modesty in his grief. Its origin unknown, but from some deep and dark part of his body. A part that he had learnt to keep behind a door, one that had been forced open only once before in his life. He clutched his stomach, thinking he may burst wide open, hoping he would, and he sobbed long and hard. 'What do you do now? Jesus, Chris, what do you do now?'

Only the ticking clock could be heard in reply.

Chris staggered towards his back door, unlocked it, and stepped into the cold night air. He walked towards the back of his garden where his shed was, barely visible through the overgrown weeds that had strangled Julia's buddleia. He looked behind him to make sure he couldn't be seen. Satisfied, he unlocked the door and stepped inside.

Chris stepped over his lawnmower and, reaching to the furthest corner from the door, lifted up a large metal toolbox and put it on the counter he had built years before in an effort to be more organized. Using the key he had left with the letter, he opened the box. He needed to make sure its contents were still inside. He counted them off in his head. All seven items were there. Untouched, smelling of damp earth, iron and rust.

He moved the mobile phone that was switched off and picked up a large hardbound book. Inside

70

were the words of his wife. A diary that wasn't his to read. He took it, flicked through the pages. Her smell coming from them. He stopped at a page from August – the summer after they married.

'He took me to a gig last night, an up-and-coming band that neither of us had heard of. The crowd was young and rowdy and when we got there he led me to the bar, holding my hand tight, not letting me go. People pushed, as people do in busy bars, but somehow no one walked into me. He stepped in front or to the side to make sure they bumped into him instead. I don't remember anyone being so protective …'

Chris didn't remember that night. It didn't seem to him it was noteworthy, but that moment clearly meant a lot to her, and he'd had no idea. He flicked forwards in the book, to the following November. At first she spoke of her mum, and her failing health, and how he and Julia visited a few times a week, bringing her flowers, taking her something to eat. If she was feeling up to it.

This day she wasn't. She was tired but in good spirits. They just stayed with her watching *Bedknobs and Broomsticks*. Her talking about when Julia was little and how the cartoon lion had frightened her. Julia pretended to be a little girl to make her mum laugh. He did remember that moment and couldn't help but smile as he read it.

Flicking again, another year passed. As Chris saw the first line of an entry he stopped himself. He knew what it said. He also knew he wasn't strong

71

enough to read it. Instead, he flicked backwards and read one of the first she had put in, just after they met. But rereading her words made him feel a warmth he didn't deserve, so he closed it and held the diary close to his chest.

It allowed him to think more clearly. Work for a solution. She lived in those pages. Speaking of her love. Telling him the things she couldn't say out loud. Remembering the dozens of things they had done that he had forgotten.

After a few minutes, he put it back carefully with the other items and locked the box before hiding it once more in the dark recesses of the damp shed. Chris knew he couldn't wait another year, another anniversary – it was too hard. But the date he did kill himself on *had* to matter. A bittersweet gift.

He took his phone from his pocket and went to the calendar to find something suitable. Her birthday: too far away. His birthday: too difficult to vanish without people being aware. It had to be a date that only mattered to him and her. A date that no one would find suspicious if he was missing. And then he knew when he would do it. After scrolling forward, he stopped and counted backwards.

Twenty-eight days.

Perfect.

Twenty-eight days was all he had to wait. He didn't know why he hadn't considered this date previously. It was a better date to honour his late wife. It would be exactly a year after the day she died.

Going back into his house he felt different somehow. Like a small part of him had passed away on the platform when he had failed to kill the rest. A small part that was good. A small part that was what his father had given him. It had been fading since Julia died and he knew it was nearly gone.

His fathers voice seemed quieter among the others that shouted in his head. Tired. Now he would have to wait quietly, patiently, for another month without his words and lessons, without the good. The fine line between right and wrong slowly evaporating.

Chris made a note of the things he was going to do. He knew he didn't need to, but the first thing on that list was to resign from his job. If only to cement his new plan in his mind. It was something easy to tick off, help him regain control. He would ring first thing – around 6 a.m. before the office opened – and leave a message.

He knew they would accept his resignation when they picked it up without the need to call him. He'd been signed off for depression for so long he doubted anyone would be shocked or even care. He would also follow it up with an email and once done he would have some power back. And a new plan would be set in motion. Knowing it was the first step made him feel like he had a sense of direction. It would also be one less reason to be outside in public. Making his grief easier to contain, his secrets easier to keep.

One of which wasn't so secret any more because of the train girl who had no doubt found his note and his stone. He hated her for her stubbornness in not seeing that he wanted to be left alone, and her naivety in assuming she could help him. For a moment he pictured himself hitting her, wondering why he hadn't just done that. If he'd slapped her hard right across her delicate face she would have run away and called the police, and by the time they'd arrived, he would have been a smear on the track below.

It seemed so simple a solution and yet he didn't think of it when it mattered. That was the part that had died. The part that could do no harm. It made him hate her even more.

Chapter 7

Julia's diary – June 2011

I used to keep a diary as a little girl. All of the girls in my primary school did. It was like you had to in order to be cool. I had a bright pink one, one of the 'My Little Ponies' on the front. The ribbon that was stitched into the seam and tied around, holding all of my six-year-old secrets, was rainbow-coloured.

I found it again a few years ago. My first entry was about a boy I liked in class. My first 'love'. I carried that diary everywhere I went and would always been seen writing in it. I guess, if I really think about it, it was from there the seed was planted to be a writer. Capturing stories, revealing truths. I remember I would often talk to myself in the diary – I guess like I am doing right now. Saying things like, 'Julia, you have to remember Kyle (my crush in primary school) is an idiot.' Or 'Julia, don't forget it's Mother's Day next week.' But then I grew up and other things became more important.

Studying took over, then boys, then a little of both in my college years. My first twelve years of life were well documented by my family pictures and my childish diaries, and nothing much after. It's kind of sad when I think about it. All those years, uncaptured, being lost as I got older. Recently, I've had time to think about life a little more and it seems I've not saved the big adventures I've had in any way.

My secondary school and college days that I loved are only seen through Facebook pictures added by old friends, long forgotten. We all had bad hair and the sense of style that came with the late Nineties and early Noughties. All of us looking like we wanted to be in the Spice Girls.

My university years are just fondly remembered hangover-fuelled dreams of late nights out – going to gigs of bands who were going to be the 'next big thing' only to disappear as quickly as they arrived. And my father: a complicated man who left my mum for Australia when I was in my teens. He's just a speck of an idea. His bad jokes and silly stories seem to have been lost in the dark spaces of my memory. We speak a few times a year – birthdays, Christmas. But the conversations are always short and forced.

I struggled with him leaving and, as an adult, I've forgotten all of the good qualities he had. Ones that Mum couldn't forget. She often tells me he was the kind of man that you rarely see. Funny, charming but fiercely protective of his family. That is, right up until he left us.

In those moments when Mum talks of him before he packed his bags, I can see myself as a child again, lying on his broad chest, his breathing raising me up and down as we both dozed in the garden on a spring morning. I see the bedtime stories, his St Christopher necklace gently hitting me as he gives me a kiss goodnight. His breath smelling like rolling tobacco.

Yes, loads of years have been lost to the archive in my head but, as you can clearly see, I'm going to change that. So hello, diary. Welcome back to my life. You might be wondering why I've decided to come back. It's a good question. One that's embarrassing but as it's just you and me I'll say it as it is.

Yet again, there is a boy. Meeting him has ignited that part of me that needs to write it all down. It's made me not want to lose anything that I might think fondly on later in life. (Or not.) 'The new man', as my friends like to call him, though really he should be called the first man. In my adult life so far I've not met anyone who has interested me in the way he does. There is something about him. Something you can't quite put a finger on. A depth to him I have never seen before. It's exciting.

I've got a good feeling about this and I thought it would be nice to put it down in words to find again when I'm old and grey. Who knows who might be by my side? Perhaps, maybe, him? Just writing that makes me feel funny.

We met a few nights ago in a bar called The Corner something. It was sweet really, his annoying but well-mannered friend had to introduce us as he was shy. Normally guys are forward and confident. Assuming women like that. But not me; shy works for me.

I even had to instigate our first kiss before I left. It wasn't great. It was raining and my hair was beginning to fall down. Plus, we were both quite drunk. But I didn't mind.

77

It felt like a first kiss as an awkward teenager, with all of its wonder and expectation. Today we've been chatting throughout the day via text messages and last night he called to talk. Saying he wanted to hear my voice. It's all happening very quickly but it feels okay too. Nice. Safe.

I don't know a lot about him yet, but I do know he's funny in a geeky, dry way. He's interested in my day and asks questions (which shows he listens) and I like the sound of his voice. I've been dying for him to ask me out, on a real date, and each time we've talked via message I've been hoping he would ask.

Last night I started to think we were only destined to be friends (I even wondered for a while if he was gay) but then he messaged me this morning, about half six asking if I wanted to do something. So, this weekend we are having a day together. I said I wanted something small, and neutral, and close to home so he suggested we meet in Cambridge, on the river, for a picnic.

When I think about it I'm nervous, which is kind of refreshing. Let's hope it's something I'll always remember. Something that would warrant me continuing to write in this diary.

So that's where we are. I'm going to try my very best to write as often as I can. To keep the future me updated. Fingers crossed, I'll have something good to say very soon …

Chapter 8

12 days later
16 days left

10.47 p.m. – London Road, Peterborough

Sitting in his kitchen, Chris watched the second hand of the wall clock tick and listened to the heavy rain beating against the bay window. It made him nervous. The rain took away his ability to listen to his house, hear its noises and alert him if something wasn't right. Chris tried to push out the sound of the relentless hammering of the storm and listen, just in case someone tried breaking in via an upstairs window.

Each time there was no sign of anyone trying to do such a thing. But he checked anyway. If he was going to break in to someone's house, this night would be the kind of night he would do it. The heavy downpour both swallowing noise, like that of broken glass, and washing away any sign of intrusion. Chris knew it was going to be a long night. When you've lost someone you love so suddenly, so violently, it's hard to ever feel safe again, even in your own home.

The past thirteen nights had been the hardest of his life: the waiting, the silence, the hiding. The days felt longer. The only time he had left the house was to get bread, milk, cheap alcohol and anything else he needed to stay alive. Each time he did he was sure that someone was watching. He could feel the hairs on the back of his neck stand up and he couldn't help but continually look over his shoulder. His muscles ready if his fight-or-flight mechanism was triggered.

Once it was an older man who was in the shop at the same time as Chris. Another time it was a young couple. At first, he thought he was just being paranoid but each time he left the house he saw people looking at him differently. It was like they either knew that he had failed or they knew what he was planning.

As each day passed, Chris was left watching and waiting, his nerves fraying. It had been nearly eleven months since Julia's death but every day he was convinced her killer would return.

The only power Chris had was in taking his own life and even with that he had failed. As the clock continued to tick away, Chris took strength from his commitment to his wife, to be by her side on a date that mattered to them. And once all of the secrets were out, how fitting that they would have the same date on their tombstones, as it should have been.

Besides the constant feeling he was being watched, Chris hadn't spoken to many people. Steve had called a few times, left a few messages, and he had bumped into Mrs Mullins, his elderly neighbour, who stopped him once in the street. Her memory was failing and they always exchanged exactly the same pleasantries, but Chris didn't mind and humoured her. She talked about the warm morning weather before asking if he was okay. She said he looked pale. She asked after Julia and he replied saying she was fine. It seemed kinder not to answer with the truth.

He walked over to the cupboard above the fridge. The door was slightly ajar and he removed a bottle of bourbon. After grabbing a used glass off the table, he poured himself a large measure. He raised a bitter toast and knocked back the double in one mouthful, its heat burning down his throat and into his stomach. Chris didn't much like the taste, but it numbed him so he'd grown to love it over the past two weeks. After pouring himself another one, he sat at his small table and, switching on his mobile, he saw he had one new message.

'Hey Chris, I've tried your home phone but can't get hold of you. Listen, Kristy and I are a little worried. I popped round but you weren't home, again. So when you get this drop me a text or something, okay? Speak soon. We love you, mate.'

As he listened to Steve's voice he could hear his worry. He was trying so hard to stay involved in his life but Chris had slowly opened up a quiet distance, like a piece of driftwood floating out to sea. It was necessary though. He had to keep his friend safe.

When Steve came over and Chris was in, he would hide upstairs, waiting for him to give up.

It worried Chris. He feared that without managing Steve there might be future problems. Steve was persistent at times. Bordering on obsessive. If he suspected anything at all, it would make things very difficult for Chris. With just over two weeks to go, Chris didn't need things to become harder than they already were.

Amid his feeling of fear, he felt a twang of guilt on hearing Steve's words. He didn't deserve to be loved like that. Listening to the message again, Chris could almost hear Steve's thoughts. They had known each other for most of their lives and he could sense what Steve was thinking. Chris knew he needed to make a little effort now. Sixteen days was a long time – enough for Steve to become suspicious of his intentions. He needed to, at some point, play the part of a hurt but healing friend. Although he wanted nothing more than to be left alone with his grief.

He took a cigarette out of a packet and lit one. Inhaling deeply, he felt the same guilt he always did since taking up smoking again. He'd promised Julia a long time ago to never have another cigarette, but he also promised to always support her, to love her, to understand her. He promised to have no secrets from her. He promised to never let her be harmed. He figured breaking his promise about quitting wasn't as bad as the other promises he'd broken.

Sitting back into his chair, he sunk another drink and dragged on his cigarette as he poured the third, this time in order to sip. At this point, every day, he would let himself remember something about his past. It hurt him doing so and that was why he did it. Ten forty-eight became his new midnight, the start of a new day, and one less twenty-four-hour period to wait to be by her side again.

As he lost himself to drowsiness and sleep beckoned, a heaviness took hold in his arms and legs. The bourbon glass in his hand turned into one of milk and the old chair was replaced with a leather one from the conservatory. A room he didn't sit in any more. The needles of cold rain beating against his window stopped, replaced with snow drifting calmly and serenely, gently wrapping itself over the trees in the back garden. Chris remembered where his mind was trying to take him: half a dream, half a memory of when he'd stubbed out the last cigarette.

A week before he'd married Julia.

It was the day after a few of his friends, led by his best man Steve, had taken him out for a final drink as a bachelor. Not a stag do but what he hoped would be a quieter celebration before he became a married man. They teased him, saying they would never see him again and he was throwing his life away. He remembered laughing at them, as they all knew that Chris was anything but throwing his life away. They all knew he and Julia were the real thing, that they were perfect together.

His friends had done a great job of giving Chris an amazing night and leaving him with a killer hangover that had lasted a few days. He was thankful for the snow; it meant that he had an excuse to stay in his pyjamas, despite Julia telling him it made him look like an old man.

Rubbing his tired eyes, he'd let his body feel the ache as he watched the snow fall gently in front of a dark purple sky. The white ghostly flecks had looked otherworldly as they floated past the security light outside. Despite the sore head, he'd felt the best he had ever felt in his life. Sitting in the conservatory listening to his bride-to-be humming as she cooked, Chris had stubbed out his cigarette. He'd watched the blue-grey smoke curl upwards before disappearing. As if she knew what he'd been doing, Julia stepped into the conservatory just as the last embers were dying out.

'That's it, my last one.'

'Are you really going to quit for me?'

'I said I would.'

'Thank you, Chris.'

Her lips tasted like cherries as she leant in and kissed him.

'I can't believe I'm going to be Julia Hayes.'

'Me neither.'

'I like the sound of it: Mrs Hayes.' She'd smiled at him then.

'Me too. Do you want any help with dinner?'

'No, darling, I've got this tonight. You just enjoy your hangover.'

'I feel too old to drink like I did last night.'

'That's because you are.'

'Oi!'

'I'm teasing.'

'Partly. You know. I don't mind not drinking much any more. Can't deal with the hangovers.'

'I like that you don't drink often.'

'Really?'

'Of course. Means we won't ever fight about who's designated driver. And I'm not old enough to have to deal with hangovers yet.'

'You'll never be old.'

'Smooth talker.' She laughed as she walked back into the kitchen. He watched her move away, a happy skip in her stride, and he had to kiss her again. He had the burning need for her taste on his lips.

He stood, hearing something crunch under his feet. Looking down he saw he was stood on broken glass. He looked to Julia. She was on the floor, next to the cooker, her eyes looking towards him but glazed over. Her arm was twisted at an unnatural angle. Standing at her feet, soaking wet and breathing hard, was the man who'd killed her. He spoke his final words to Chris before disappearing.

'This is our little secret.'

Then it was gone.

Chris stood, rubbing both hands across his eyebrows.

'Fuck.'

That hadn't happened before. His dreams were a mess but his memories were always clean. He had worked hard to ensure that remain the case, but now, he was beginning to lose the grip he had on his mind. The image of Julia lying dead and twisted was his dream-like imagination working in overdrive and it had forced its way into the happy memories he treasured. The one safe place, one happy place he had left was gone. Chris now had no refuge. The pressure of these extra days was beginning to get to him. The drinking, the waiting. It was tough to manage. This time was stretching out longer than any other in his life. But he had to wait. Julia needed to know his death meant something. His penance for not dying that night in her place. He knew waiting meant he might lose his mind, or worse, he might be discovered.

That night on the platform proved nothing was certain any more. Everything he had planned was to secure his existence until 5 May. Now that had been and gone, every day was another day where anything could happen. The delay meant he couldn't ward off people like Steve, trying to stage an intervention and complicate his plans. Or that stupid girl deciding to do something heroic. Although when rationally thinking about it, if she did go to the police, what would they do? She once saw a stranger not kill himself. He was sure they had bigger problems.

Now more than ever, Chris needed to keep a low profile and wait.

He grabbed his back door keys and stepped into the pouring rain, his skin tingling through the cold. He walked to the shed to make sure the contents of his toolbox were still there. Just being able to touch her things, smell her scent and hear her voice through her diary gave him a small amount of comfort.

Chapter 9

10.49 p.m. – March train station, England

Sitting on the same bench I had revisited every night for God knows how many long nights (too many if I was honest), I listened to the old tin roof above me squeak, as if the bolts that held it on would snap under duress and the station would come down like a house of cards. I felt a little apprehensive being there alone; I jumped as a leaf blew up and hit me on the shin. I pinched it between my forefinger and thumb before I threw it away from me and then wiped my fingers on my cardigan.

I laughed at myself for being so jumpy. What a way to spend an evening in your twenties.

Since that night, the night when I met Chris, my life had returned to as close to normal as I could achieve. From the outside looking in, nothing seemed to be different, like I hadn't accidentally stopped someone killing himself. But, every time I saw a man in a white shirt, whether that was at work or in a supermarket, I thought of Chris and how his wet shirt had stuck to his back.

Every time I watched a person on their own step closer to a kerb before crossing a road, I thought of Chris and how he stood so close to that platform edge. Every time I saw someone looking lovingly at a picture, the man in the Costa queue glancing at a picture of his baby that was in his wallet, the teenager flicking through pics on her iPhone, I thought of Chris and how he'd kissed that picture.

I'd even tried to watch one of my favourite movies last Sunday morning, curled up on the sofa with Natalie, something that usually made me feel safe and warm and loved. But I had to leave, telling my confused sister I had work to do. The man in the film – who usually allowed me to switch off – challenged me instead, because, again, I thought of Chris.

I thought about what his house would look like and what he did for a living. What had happened to make him so sad? I wondered if anyone else besides me knew his wishes and it made me sad to think that they probably didn't, otherwise surely someone would be looking out for him in the same way I wanted to. Feeling in my gut that he was alone with this struggle made me unable to think of anything other than him. I had switched to autopilot in my day-to-day life.

And I knew I wouldn't be able to think of anything but him until I did something about it.

Feeling a shiver run down my spine, I wrapped my cardigan round me and looked at the clock. His train was late.

Being alone at night, I couldn't stop myself thinking of the many different ways he could have taken his life.

He could have overdosed, or jumped from a building smashing into a car below like in the movies. He could have sat in a car and died of carbon monoxide poisoning, listening to Adele. Alone. Unloved. I know it was all a little dramatic, but sitting on a deserted platform allows your imagination to run wild.

The loudest voice in my head told me he was already dead, but another voice kept whispering at me telling me he wasn't. I couldn't ignore that. I knew he never would come back to this place. However, I couldn't let him go. I could, for once in my life, do something good, be a part of something good. Saving both a sad man and a sad me. I could save a man who didn't want to be saved. Surely that meant something?

I had learnt since that night that about one million people per year die through suicide. Numbers I couldn't imagine. I had also learnt the dos and don'ts if we ever talked again. Do: be yourself, listen, offer hope, take him seriously. Don't: argue with him, act shocked, promise you won't try to get him the help he needs.

Also, I knew his risk level was severe. He had planned, and failed to do it. Doing the research and knowing the facts told me he wasn't going to turn a corner and suddenly be well. It told me he would try again, if he hadn't already.

With all of my energy focused on finding Chris, my thoughts about John had diminished. I no longer waited for text messages that never came. I no longer felt I needed him to provide me with a sense of happiness. I didn't know why, but after that night my life had become easier, except that I couldn't stop thinking about Chris.

At work, my boss had noticed my drive increase to the point where he had no choice but to tell me if I kept going I would end up promoted. It was the first time he'd had me in his office to talk to me about doing well rather than the usual weekly meeting about how my heart wasn't in it and how I wasn't even close to targets. Let's hope that lasts. And, weirdly, he then offered me one of the company cars to help with my travel time to and from work. He said he was investing in my new approach.

He was right to as well. Since that night I had exceeded all targets – selling people insurances they didn't need, and often didn't want. Like I said, my mind was on autopilot. Pick up the phone, dial the number, read the script, challenge the questions, sign the deals. No external thoughts, no personality, just mechanics. And my reward: a small but quirky Toyota Aygo. The company's logo magnetically attached to the bonnet and door.

At first I hated the idea of being a walking advert, but having a car that I didn't have to pay for had its perks. I could be at the station at night without needing to wait an extra fifty-five minutes for the Cambridge train. I could be here in case he came back, and I didn't have to risk being caught without a ticket.

At work they all thought I had become a career-driven woman who wanted to excel in the world of insurance but I was only trying to get through my day as fast as I could so the search could continue. Throwing myself into the days helped them seem shorter.

Natalie and George were also happy because I seemed so much more settled, and with a promotion on the cards I was able to talk about getting a place of my own. It meant that finally they could call our shared house their home. Although, on a few occasions, they told me being at work every night until nearly midnight wasn't good for me and if I continued to burn the candle at both ends I would end up unwell.

I hadn't told them about Chris or the note or that I'd accidentally stopped his suicide. I didn't know how to start the conversation, and I quite liked the thought of it being our little secret.

Above me, the squeaking transformed to a groan as the wind picked up and I thought the roof was going to come crashing down on my head. Wouldn't that be ironic? I'm here, waiting to stop a man from killing himself and I'm the one who dies. The wind dropped, the groan went back to a repetitive squeak, and the station was still upright.

The station itself, although functioning, carried a sadness that was impossible not to notice now. It almost seemed that because of his chaos I had found peace, and knowing this only reinforced my drive to find him and help him find something similar. That was, if he was still alive.

I heard footsteps coming towards the entrance. Sitting upright, ready to stand, I held my breath. I waited to see if it was him. If he did walk out onto the platform I wondered what I would do. Part of me thought I would just throw myself at him, knocking him to the ground as the train sped past. Another thought was connected to the way he'd looked so peaceful two weeks ago before I had interrupted. I ignored that one.

After a few seconds no one came. It wasn't him; it wasn't anyone. I was alone.

Since that night I'd started scouring the obituaries in the back of the local papers and reading stories of people who had died. Widening my net to not just look at the March area but Cambridge and Peterborough too. I'd spent my nights before sleep scanning the local paper's online content, just for an hour or so each evening, sometimes longer. It messed with my dreams and often I'd wake up because of them.

Death was everywhere and so many people had passed away since I started my search. Too many.

It was bloody scary. Most were older, but there were some young people as well, and some too young, far too young. Each time I saw a child had died I couldn't help but choke back a small tear. Babies dying before they had a chance to live.

During my search I had found a few men called Chris but no one called Chris Hayes. I knew that didn't mean he was actually alive. But it did offer hope. Then I heard it, the voice that had become so familiar to me.

'The next train to arrive at this station does not stop. Please stand back from the platform edge.'

The rattle of steel on steel began to build, overtaking the sound of the rain hitting the corrugated iron and the squeak of the wind rushing through the old station. His train was coming. It would sail past at speed and I would catch a glimpse of the driver. So familiar was this ritual now I had even begun to recognize a few of the men who drove the route at this time – and I gave them names.

There was blond boy driver. Old hat driver and diva driver – he was the one who was always singing. It almost became a game guessing which one it would be. After the train left, I would watch its red tail lights head off into the distance and then when I was satisfied they were out of sight I would leave, drive home, and come back the next evening to repeat the process all over again.

I stood up and walked towards the platform edge, not daring to go over the white line. Looking to my right down the track, I could see the train rumbling forward towards me, its headlights temporarily masking who was driving inside. When my eyes adjusted, the train was a lot closer. Looking into the carriage I saw blond boy. His light hair gave him a sense of youth although he was older than a first glance would suggest. He always looked tired as he passed. It made me wonder how safe trains actually are with drivers looking so distracted.

As he passed by, the driver gave a small knowing nod to me. Shockingly, he had recognized me. I tried to nod back but didn't have the time; he had already rushed past. I didn't like being so predictable, but even more troubling was the way he looked at me. His nod wasn't one just of recognition, but one filled with worry. Following the train that sped past, my eyes darting from left to right as I tried to absorb all of the imagery created by the rush, I thought about what blond boy's look had told me.

It said I was someone to be concerned about, someone whose welfare might be in jeopardy. It said I was someone like Chris.

Had it really gotten so bad that a stranger who drives a train looked at me with such concern? Seeing me standing on the platform every time he passed, often looking cold and waiting for no one? For the first time I saw my situation through someone else's eyes. I thought about what I would say if it was a friend who was displaying this dangerously obsessive behaviour. I would tell them to move on, to not waste any more time on a stranger who would have completely forgotten her. I would say that yes, she had accidentally saved this man but he was not her responsibility. I would tell her that she shouldn't try to forget him, as that would be impossible, but to stop obsessing.

Finally, I would tell her, as a way to show a silver lining, that if fate wanted them to be together it would find a way. It was funny that although I had learnt to listen to my inner voice and pause to reflect, I couldn't see any of it until a train driver flashed me a look at high speed. The train carriages kept rushing past and as I watched them I tried to imagine what would happen if I stepped under as Chris had wanted to. I raised my hand, wondering how much it would hurt if I tried to touch it, but I stopped myself.

The last carriage passed and the sound of rain hitting metal returned along with the squeak caused by the wind. I knew it was time for me to leave this place, and I knew I wouldn't be back. I knew that I had to close this chapter and move on. I watched an old Starbucks cup, caught by the wind, rolling towards me before veering off and falling onto the track. It told me all I needed to hear. Saying a silent goodbye, I made my way towards the exit.

Stepping away from the station and back to my car, I took my phone out and rang Natalie. I asked her to put the kettle on and wait for me to get home. I had to tell her what I had been doing for the past two weeks. Just to make sure I didn't come back to the station again.

Chapter 10

Steve was a man who usually slept contently and soundly, much to the annoyance of his wife. However, these past few weeks his mind raced in the dark hours. He spent more time than he had in years staring at his ceiling when he should have been sleeping. He was worried because Chris, for all intents and purposes, had completely cut him out. The last time they had spent any time together Chris was uncharacteristically drunk and not at all engaged. Chris had told him nothing about how he was, what was new and why they were celebrating like he'd stated at the start of the night.

It wasn't like him. It wasn't like him at all. They had been friends for most of their lives. Meeting in Year 7 when they both started at the same secondary school.

Steve had been the popular one because even as a twelve-year-old he was big and good at sports. All of the girls liked him. Something that had transferred into his adult life until he met Kristy. Chris was the opposite: he was the awkward one who was reflective and quiet. A boy who'd tried to keep a low profile.

They'd met when Steve saw other kids picking on him and jumped to his rescue, picking a bloodied Chris up from the floor. Beaten and bruised, he'd dusted himself off and thanked Steve, shocking him that despite how intense the beating was, he didn't cry; in fact, he didn't even look like he was hurt. He'd thanked Steve and walked away like he was a man going on a Sunday stroll rather than a boy who had just been beaten up. Steve knew then that Chris wasn't what he looked. He was far tougher than anyone could imagine.

Their friendship spanned over two decades and it wasn't the first time Steve had seen him in this way. He remembered how Chris was after his first proper girlfriend left him when he was in his early twenties. How cut off he became. How distant he was. Chris struggled with that break-up and put himself at risk too often.

Then one night he got really drunk and ended up in the cells. Steve didn't know exactly what happened but Chris had been hurt in a fight. Apparently down to being in the wrong place at the wrong time. He got mixed up with some people who were known to the police and Chris was mugged. He managed to defend himself, hurting one of the attackers in the process.

Apparently the man ended up blind in one eye. But no charges were pressed against Chris. Instead, a warning was issued, telling him to not let himself get mixed up with those people again and that the man he fought off was known to be dangerous. Chris was told he had been lucky to come away with only a few cuts and bruises. It was a rough time for Chris but it did act as a wake-up call. Steve picked him up from the police station the next morning and helped him start the process of moving on.

Steve hoped he wouldn't end up feeling the same way now. Especially as it was coming up to a year of Chris being on his own. Life without Julia couldn't be easy. After Kristy reminded him it was Chris and Julia's anniversary, Steve was sure he would get a text or a call, asking if he wanted to go for a drink.

Chris's silence troubled him.

Unable to work out what he should do, Steve let out an involuntary sigh. Kristy turned to face him.

'Are you okay?'

'Sorry, love, yes, go back to sleep.'

Kristy sat up and switched on the bedside light. Steve propped himself up on his pillow to join her.

'It's okay, I was awake anyway. What's up?'

'Nothing.'

'You never were a good liar.'

Steve smiled at his wife before his expression changed to a frown. 'It's Chris.'

'I thought so.'

'What do I do?'

'Give him time.'

'He's had time.'

'Give him a little more. He's not like you; he doesn't wear his heart on his sleeve. He's not able to say what he feels and move on. He keeps things in.'

'I know. I'm just worried he'll get himself mixed up in something, like he did before.'

'I'm sure he won't.'

'How can you be sure?'

'How old were you two when that happened?'

'I don't know, twenty-one, maybe twenty-two.'

'Exactly. It was a long time ago. Chris isn't stupid.'

'I just feel like I'm letting him down.'

'You're not; you're being a great friend. Giving him the space he wants, but also reminding him that you're there if he needs you.'

'Kristy, I'm worried. What he's doing isn't healthy. He needs someone to talk to.'

'So what are you going to do?'

That was the question that had kept Steve awake. He loved his friend. Trusted him and respected the decisions he made. Even if he didn't agree with them all. It went against his principles to try to force his way into his life. But sometimes people needed tough love.

'What would you do?'

'If I was as worried as you are, I'd do something about it.'

She leant over and kissed him on the head before switching off the light and lying back down, her back to him.

'Thanks, love.'

In the darkness Steve thought about sending a text right then, but decided against it. He would sleep, think about what he would say, and then somehow work his way back into his best friend's life.

Chapter 11

11.31 p.m. – Kings Road, Cambridge

It felt like such a relief when I finally shared the secret that I had been holding on to for weeks. Telling Natalie had been far easier than my imagination had ever made it. I had been dying to talk with her. To have another person's perspective and thoughts on the situation. To share my burden and give me a moment of rest from the constant onslaught of unanswered questions that played in my mind.

However, more than that, more than the constant wondering what if, bad dreams, and anxiety, I struggled because I was hiding something from the one person I'd always told everything to. Nat was my best friend. We had no secrets.

As I stepped into the kitchen, Natalie was sitting at the table, book in hand and two cups of tea steaming beside her. Seeing her there for me filled me with happiness and relief. Sometimes I wondered who in fact was the big sister in our relationship.

I was by age but, by level of emotional intelligence, I always felt like a child around her. As I sat down, I picked up the mug and wrapped both hands around it, using it to warm me. She didn't press or ask questions but patiently waited for me to drink some and work out how I would begin talking.

Struggling to catch my breath and with my voice shaking, I told her everything. Once I began I couldn't stop until everything was out. Everything I had been thinking and feeling since that night at the station. Finally, once I was done, it felt like a huge weight off my shoulders.

I was expecting her to tell me off for taking as many risks as I had over the past two weeks and not letting her know where I was. But instead she reached over and took me by the hand.

'Sounds like you've had a rough time.'

'It's been something.'

'You should have talked to me earlier.'

'I know.'

I could feel myself begin to well up and Natalie stood and walked to my side. Then, dropping to her knees, she gave me the hug I didn't know I needed so badly.

'You're too caring for your own good, you know that?'

'I just wanted to help him.'

'I know you did. I know.'

Natalie then told me what I needed to hear. 'But you have to let it go, Sarah. He isn't your responsibility.'

'I know.'

'Things are going really well for you at the moment; you should be focused on that. Not trying to find a suicidal man. He could be dangerous.'

'He isn't dangerous.'

'How do you know that? Because he was sad?'

'Yes, and other things.'

'What things, Sarah?'

'I don't know, just things.'

'He was there to kill himself, Sarah.'

'I know, Nat. I just want to … '

'Do what? Help him? Save him?'

'Yes.'

'He's not yours to save.'

'I know that, but he's a good man.'

'How could you possibly know that, Sarah?'

'I just do.'

'No offence, sis, but you don't exactly have a good track record with identifying goodness in men.'

'What?'

'Micky was as emotionally intelligent as a three-year-old. Paul liked a drink and John—'

I shot her a look that stopped her mid-sentence. We both knew what John was. She looked down briefly as a way of saying sorry before continuing, her tone softer.

'He is not your responsibility. He didn't even want your help. You've done enough.'

I couldn't look at my sister any more. Instead, I focused on the kitchen floor near the cooker where a piece of uncooked pasta poked out from under it.

'Nat, you don't know that.'

'It was a complete coincidence you were there. He expected to be alone.'

Hearing her say it out loud hurt. She was right. It was a fluke I was there and stopped him. I felt a tear escape from my eye.

'Sarah. Look at me. It's so sweet and kind that you're this upset about a stranger. But obsessing about him won't help anyone.'

I couldn't stop myself crying as I spoke. A hole that had been opening over the last two weeks was finally big enough for my feelings to fall out.

'But he doesn't have anyone else, Nat.'

'You don't know that.'

'I do.'

'You don't. You're assuming.'

'I can't get him out of my head.'

'That's because you're not letting yourself. This is going to sound harsh. But some people don't want to be saved.'

'What if Becky didn't want to be saved?'

'Becky, from school? So that's what this is about? Sarah, that was a long time ago. We were just kids. Of course she wanted to be helped. That's why she did what she did at school. She wanted to be found.'

'All I know, Nat, is that Becky got the support she needed, and she is fine now. I just want to help him, like I helped her.'

'He is an adult. If he wanted help, he would know how to ask for it.'

'But ... '

'Sarah. People will do what they want to do regardless of how you feel about it. Paul wanted to drink, despite you trying to help him stop and John ... '

'Don't say it.'

'John wanted to cheat.'

I dropped my head further. Hearing her say it out loud hurt more than I was ready for.

'You cannot fix everyone's problems, you just can't, and from what you have told me, he doesn't want you to help him.'

'I guess.'

'You wouldn't have wanted to talk to me if you didn't already know all of this. I'm telling you. Let it go.'

I told her that I wouldn't go back to the station. I had to let all of it go, not just the physical searching but the quieter emotional searching too.

I nodded at my sister's sound advice, trying desperately to ignore the thought that had recently grown in my mind, its branches beginning to stretch down past my eyes and towards my chest. The thought that I knew was ridiculous, for I knew nothing about him besides his wish to die. It wasn't a thought I could put into a sentence yet, but knew that it wouldn't be long before I could.

It was in the way he looked at me. It was something in his gaze, and although I had tried to justify it by the intensity of the situation, and his desire to die, there was more to it. His glances penetrated deeply into my very being, cutting through all of the hurt, touching my soul.

The few words he said to me were so real and raw it felt like I had known him forever. It was ridiculous I know, but even though it was stupid, I couldn't help thinking it could be like an old movie. If only I could work out where he was. I would find him and our lives would change again, but this time for the better. However, life wasn't an old movie. I knew that. It was hard, at times sad, and good people didn't always win; good people sometimes died.

Looking at my younger sister who was trying to read my thoughts, I could see myself in her eyes and I could see that the girl looking back was not someone I wanted to be. Natalie was right. It was time to leave the past where it belonged.

I said I needed some time and Natalie agreed, saying she would see me tomorrow. Then she kissed me on the cheek and went to bed. Leaving me alone to make a mental list of things I needed to box away in the morning. The newspaper clippings, the notes I had made. The letter of his I had found. It all had to be filed away in a place where I couldn't accidentally find it. I knew I should bin it all and yet, I knew that wouldn't happen.

As long as it was packed away and collecting dust, that was enough. I finished my cold tea and went upstairs to bed. I undressed and emptied my jeans pockets, laying out a packet of chewing gum, £3.18

in change and his black polished stone. I kept it with me in case I ever saw him again, so I could give it back. Maybe that was all I could do for him. Return a lost item. The more I thought of it the more it made sense. It would show him I cared. It would extend a hand, telling him he was understood.

I had just promised Natalie I would stop looking, and I would ... after this one thing. I knew she wouldn't approve but I needed to make sure he had it back before I tried to forget about him. With the stone still in my possession I knew I wouldn't be able to shake him. I would tell her that she needed to do one thing for me to help me get on with my life like she wanted.

I remembered seeing his bank card poking out of his wallet: HSBC. She worked for the same bank he had an account with. She could find out his address for me. I just had to convince her it was a good idea.

Chapter 12

August 2011 – Julia's diary

Mum always tells me to trust my instincts. She says that they are the one part of us that cannot lie, even if we want them to, but, if I'm honest, for a long time I have dismissed it as an old wives' tale. Just Mum tending to lean towards superstitions in her own whacky, wonderful Mum-like way.

Although, since meeting Chris my instincts have told me things. Deep things, things I shouldn't know after only a month of knowing him. Things I still can't let myself say, not yet, but what I will say is that I am hoping he feels something similar. I think he does. I think I can see it in the way he looks at me – a sort of tenderness that happens in his eyes – making me feel a little lost.

I first saw it a few days ago. When he took me on a surprise day out, like something out of one of the romance books my mum reads that make me secretly wish something like that would happen in my life. Just me writing that down makes me sound like I'm writing a Mills & Boon novel.

He picked me up at eleven, perfectly on time. As I got into his car and gave him a kiss, he told me we were going to the seaside for the day. He had packed a picnic hamper and a throw for us to sit on. He even had a cool-bag with strawberries and fizzy wine. Serious brownie points were scored.

The drive took about an hour and although we chatted I could tell he was still a little nervous, even after a month of us spending time together. Most of the time guys I've been with aren't nervous at all. They usually overcompensate with manliness that's designed to be attractive. Some women like it, but it has never really done anything for me. His almost meekness is different and I find it unusual and intriguing.

As we drove with the windows down, I watched him, his strong jaw, muscles flexing, his wide hands gripping the steering wheel leading up his toned arms to muscular (but not too muscular) shoulders. He was wearing a white shirt and sky blue shorts that allowed me to see his legs for the first time. I was hoping he wasn't a gym buff who forgot to train his lower body. But as I looked I saw they had the shape of a cyclist's legs. More brownie points scored. I didn't want to, but I couldn't help but think about us having sex. For a moment wondering when it would be.

I was expecting us to go to Hunstanton, the usual destination when driving to that part of the coast, but we passed it and continued for another ten minutes to a lesser-known beach called Brancaster. I hadn't been there before and was amazed at how long the stretch of sand was, and how quiet it looked. We walked along the coastline for about fifteen minutes and as we walked he asked to hold my hand.

Once we were far enough away from the kite flyers, dog walkers and occasional family building sandcastles behind windbreakers, we stopped and he laid out the throw for us to sit on. We talked about everything. Our pasts and plans for the future, although we were a little guarded about the latter. I mean, who knows right? We might end up as a proper couple; we might not. Sometimes you just can't tell and a month in it's too soon to think of us doing anything other than dating, isn't it?

We ate and then walked to the sea and splashed in it. Laughing as we did. I like his laugh. It's bright and unreserved. During one of our quiet moments as we were walking in the surf, the cold water lapping at our toes and the sun warm on our backs, I let myself see something in the future with him. A happiness that I'd not had before. It felt good to think about it, but also terrifying.

At Brancaster there is a shipwreck which, when the tide is in, looks far out to sea. But, as the tide goes out, it ends up beached. He asked if I wanted to go exploring so we walked to it, strolling over the uneven wet sand for what seemed like miles. Its hull was half buried, creating small pools of water that clung to the side of the life-supporting rusted metal.

He pointed out a seagull that swooped down and picked up a crab before carrying it away to be eaten. After it was gone I watched him looking into the sky, a smile on his face. I wanted to ask why he was smiling but stopped myself. Instead, I turned to start walking back towards our stuff, only to see the tide had come in and swept around us, meaning we had to wade in water to get back to the shore.

By the time we were back, my hair was soaked by the spray on the breeze and my T-shirt clung to me. He took his off and gave it to me to wear. Maybe his sense of being a gentleman outweighed his shy demeanour? That would be nice if that's the case. After he gave me his shirt I leant in and kissed him. My lips pressing firmly on his. The sea seeming to stop around us. As he pulled away, he stroked my cheek and looked at me, with that expression that told me more than either of us could say. It was only for a moment before he looked down shyly, but it was there. And I know he saw the same look in me.

We walked back in silence, hand in hand, my fingers fitting perfectly in his strong grip, and drove home. Him putting on an old jumper from his boot that smelt strongly of him. The journey back felt very different to the one there; it felt calm, peaceful. For long parts of it we didn't talk, but it wasn't at all awkward. I just watched the sun begin to change colour as it started setting. I ran my hand through the wind. I've not done that since I was a kid.

He kissed me again after he walked me to my door and I wanted to invite him in, but before I could he stopped me. Saying that he really liked me and he didn't want to rush.

I've never had a man do that before and I know it's way too soon to be thinking into the future. But still ...

Chapter 13

15 days left

9.31 a.m. – St Andrew's Street, Cambridge

Natalie knew I was up to something when she came into the kitchen, and saw me up and making breakfast for both of us. George had left for work an hour before, tiptoeing out of the house so as not to disturb us on the rare mid-week day when both Nat and I had a day off. He was good like that. Kind, considerate, not realizing I was already awake, not knowing I'd struggled to sleep and had been lying there, waiting for him to leave before I got up.

'Sarah, are you okay?'

'Yep, I'm fine,' I lied. I was nervous, and I knew she could see it. What I was about to ask her would go one of two ways, but despite this I knew it was something I had to do.

'What do you want?'

'What makes you think I want anything?'

'Because I know you, Sarah, so just ask.'

'I need a favour.'

'Okay?'

'You're not going to like it, but I need you to listen.'

'Sarah, just say it already.'

'That night I saw that he banked where you work.'

'Sarah, I thought we agreed you were going to leave it behind.'

'I am, I really am. But first, I need you to find his address for me.'

'You want me to do what exactly?'

'I have something of his and I want to give it back.'

'Let me get this right: you want me to go to work and risk my job to find his address.'

'I know it's wrong … '

'It's illegal, Sarah.'

'I know, but … '

'I waited up for you last night and gave you advice, which you agreed with, and now you ask me to do this so you can find him?'

'Nat, please just listen … '

'No, Sarah. You're unbelievable.'

I looked at my sister, who, head in hands, was sitting at the kitchen table, clearly upset with me. I knew I was wrong to ask and I was putting her in such a difficult position, but I had no choice. As I spoke, I did so at barely a whisper.

'I'm sorry I've asked, but I need your help. I need to get it back to him.'

'Why?'

'I think it's important. Besides, I want to forget him. I really do.'

'Do you?'

'Yes, or I'd not have talked to you. But I can't forget him when I have this.'

'Throw it away then.'

'Natalie. Please.'

She lifted her head and looked at me, *really* looked at me, and I held her gaze. I think she took pity on her big sister. She could see in my eyes I was desperate. And I was. This was more than just returning the stone. This was me finding out if he was still alive.

She told me that if she found his address I had to post the stone to him and leave it at that. I pleaded with her. What if it was lost in the post? You can't trust Royal Mail. I needed to hand-deliver it. That wasn't true. I wanted to see his front door, where he came and went. I wanted to stand where he stood. And, if I was lucky enough, to see him. Although I would have no idea what to do if I did.

So we left for the city centre. The weather finally picked up and within a few minutes both of us had to take off our jumpers as we walked. When we got to her work she told me to wait outside. Doing as I was told, knowing it was safer, I crossed the road and leant against the wall of an Italian restaurant. Its owner, the sole inhabitant, watched me momentarily before shaking his head and returning to his work.

Smoking my cigarette, I watched the automatic door of the bank. Every time it moved I expected Natalie to step out, and although the only thing my sister was doing was getting an address, my heart beat like she was robbing the bank and I was her getaway driver.

While I waited, every person who walked by looked at me suspiciously. Two young-looking university students breezed past me on their way to Starbucks to get a coffee, flashing me a glance, and I thought they knew. An old man with his poodle and a garishly bright blue scarf caught my eye, and I looked away, thinking he recognized me. As he passed, he wished me good morning. Was he saying good morning or was he saying it's going to be a good morning? Like he knew what I was wishing for. I tried to shake it off; it was me being paranoid. I needed to calm down.

Natalie was only gone for about ten minutes, although it felt like I was standing watching the world scrutinize me for hours. When she came out she wore an expression that told me three things. She felt terrible for abusing the system. She knew what I wanted to know, and she was still annoyed I had asked her to do it. I didn't blame her. As she crossed the road, I stood upright and flicked my cigarette.

'Don't ever ask me to do something like that again.'

'I won't, I promise. I know it's too much.'

'It is too much.' And her look proved it. Her eyes were steely and her face set in a way that screamed disappointment. 'I mean it; don't ever ask me to do something like this again.'

'I won't.'

'Are you listening?'

'Yes, I promise. I won't.'

'I love you, but I'll not risk my livelihood for you again. This was your one and only time.'

'I know. I'm sorry.'

I expected Nat to thrust the piece of paper in my hand, give me one of her looks that mirrored the ones Mum used to give and leave me alone to read his address. Instead, she gestured for me to follow her. We walked away from the bank and crossed onto Downing Street. We passed the Museum of Earth Sciences, a formidable-looking building with hard stone steps that swept up to it. They were guarded by some sort of animal, its details faded over time.

'Did you find it?'

'It's so like you. Do I not even get a thank you?'

'Thank you, but please, did you find it?'

'Sarah!'

She stopped in her tracks and looked at me angrily. Her look softened, turning into sadness. Directed at me. 'This is really important to you, isn't it?'

'Yes.'

'Why?'

'I don't know. I think it will help him.'

'By giving him a stone?'

'Yes.'

She took a long deep breath and looked up at the clouds that hung above us, threatening to rain down. Weighing up her options.

'There are a few people called Chris Hayes. But the closest lives in Peterborough.'

'Peterborough?'

'Yes, and if you're going now, I'm coming with you.'

Chapter 14

Sitting on a gurney in a curtained-off box room containing only the bed he was perched on, a waste bin, and a wall-mounted hand sanitizer, Chris could hear the sounds of a drunk man somewhere in the accident and emergency department. He was shouting obscenities about how he was a victim of assault and no one seemed to give a shit. For a moment he thought it was him, the man who stole everything he held dear and quietly he opened his curtain to check, coming eye to eye with a drunk who was twenty or thirty years older than him, his right eye swollen and bloodied.

'What the fuck are you looking at?'

Closing the curtain, Chris took three deep breaths to calm himself. It wasn't who he thought it might have been; it was just a drunk and clearly not a victim. He had to remain calm; he had to keep his appearance as such, knowing if he didn't more people would be hurt.

The drunk continued to shout at Chris but he didn't care. His foul language was eventually hushed by nurses who were still on shift from the busy Friday night before. Their voices were tired. Chris heard the man apologize, but then mumble to himself, the only audible words being 'fucking bastards', which Chris heard a few times before the man was told that if he didn't stop swearing the police would be contacted. It seemed to work.

Now it was quieter he could hear the crying of a small child who sounded scared by their unusual surroundings, as well as the moaning of someone from the opposite end of life's spectrum who felt exactly the same.

It made him think about the cycle of it all, how people are born and then grow and then fight for independence, but in fact never achieve it. Despite how it may appear. For when it mattered, everyone was exactly the same: they fought and cried and eventually became terrified of what was after that thing they call life. It was all so fragile and no one was exempt from that. No one. He knew this first-hand.

With his heart rate back to where it should be, Chris thought about what had brought him here.

How he had been startled awake by the sound of what he could only describe as a table leg snapping. After a few seconds, he realized that nothing was broken. The noise wasn't something he'd heard but something remembered from a dream, something more organic than a piece of furniture.

He had sat upright and taken a deep breath. His dreams felt more and more real each day and each one was leading him closer to the nightmare that was his wife's last moments. As his eyes adjusted to the early morning glow he once loved, a glow that was fighting to seep through the thin curtains, he felt sick with the realization. The day he dreaded coming was upon him. A day he would have avoided if he hadn't failed in his May plans. It had been just over eleven months since she died and he fought desperately with himself to delay this moment, but he couldn't.

Chris tried to picture his wife in his mind, and he failed.

Not wholly. He could still see the image he had once been shown of her glazed-over eyes as clearly as he could his own hand. He could see her leg twitching as nerves fired for the final time. The fear on her face, permanently embedded. But he couldn't see anything other than those fragments. He couldn't see the way she looked at him lovingly on their wedding day. He couldn't picture her intimate gaze or the universe that existed in her irises. He couldn't see her depth; he couldn't see her soul.

After rolling out of bed, Chris had stumbled to his bathroom and ran the cold tap. Leaning over the sink, he drank the cold water. He washed his hands and splashed his face, the icy water forcing his mind to focus on the moment. He was awake. He was still alive despite not wanting to be.

He didn't want to look at himself any more. He didn't want to see the man he now was. But he had to; he needed to punish himself for being so careless with her memory. Facing the mirror, he examined the wounded thing that looked back, bloodshot and broken, dark, hostile, dirty, and hated by every atom of his being. It spoke to him.

'Fuck you, Chris.'

Chris felt a hot numbness begin to sweep over his body, the way it felt when being lulled to sleep with anaesthetic. It began deep down in his stomach and spread like a virus through his lower organs and limbs until his hands tingled.

Leaning against the sink, he closed his eyes. He needed to be able to see his wife clearly or everything would be lost, but despite searching he couldn't fully bring her into his mind. She remained teasingly on the edge of what he could grab, her image like a pavement chalk drawing after a heavy rainstorm.

Opening his eyes again to see the animal looking back, Chris felt the numbness travel through his chest up to his throat, choking him until it burnt with rage behind his cheeks. He couldn't look at himself any more and he hit the mirror, smashing the glass and distorting the image of the broken man that continued to look back.

Then, he grabbed a glass that held his toothbrush and threw it. He liked the way it spun in the air as it left his hand. It felt right – the release of it –

as though he was doing something. The glass representing something that he could control. He liked the way it splintered into a thousand independent pieces on impact with the wall. The shattered glass sat like fallen stars on his bathroom floor, glittering and beautiful and harmful. He liked the way he saw the beauty in its demise. It felt strange but exhilarating at the same time. He felt powerful, even if it was just for a moment.

He let himself imagine that he was back in that night when Julia died and the things in his bathroom were in fact the monster who had killed her. He pictured hitting him, again and again until he was broken on the floor like the glass under his feet.

Chris didn't stop until everything he saw that could be shattered had been shattered. Looking around at the destruction caused, he saw the toilet seat ripped off. The bathroom cabinet hanging at an angle, everything that was inside smashed on the floor or covering the walls.

He felt like he needed more. He picked up a piece of smashed mirror. Four inches long, shaped like a dagger. Resting his left hand on the sink, he pressed the point of the mirror into the back of his hand. Dimpling his skin. As he pulled back, a small circle of blood formed. But it didn't hurt. He pressed again, harder, the tip penetrating a few millimetres, enough for him to be able to let go of the glass and look at it stuck in his hand.

He knew he needed to stop himself, calm himself and clean up the bathroom. But, somehow, causing himself damage made him feel good. Closing his eyes, he hit the top of the glass with his right hand, forcing it deeper. A scream forced its way into his mouth but he held it. Instead, focusing on the pain. Something he needed to feel. As he pulled it out, blood poured from the wound to his feet. And the rage passed. And he could see his wife's face once more.

As he came back to his senses, Chris could see that his hand was bleeding badly, much worse than he had intended, and he thought about getting a needle and thread and stitching it back together himself, like he had done before, but he knew it needed to be done by a professional.

As he drove to hospital, he knew that despite it feeling good to hurt himself, he couldn't do it again. He couldn't afford another trip to A and E. Someone would surely begin to question his 'accidents'. He had to remain vigilant and ensure he made it to his new date without anyone else getting hurt, anyone except him.

***

The moaning outside his hospital cubicle intensified, snapping him away from his thoughts. Getting up, he pulled the curtain that separated him from the rest of the ward and looked outside. He saw the source of it. Lying on a bed, only a matter of ten feet away from him, was an elderly woman of an age Chris dared not to guess. The side of her head was covered in dried blood from a gash to her temple that had been crudely patched up as she waited for a doctor to stitch her tissue-paper-thin skin back together.

She had a needle inserted in the back of her veiny arthritic hand and she looked truly terrified. Chris couldn't work out why he was in a curtained-off section whilst she was left on public display. He wondered if it was to appease other patients who could look at her broken old body and see their situation wasn't as bad. Her suffering almost like an advert for how lucky they really were.

She looked so alone although the ward was busy with the constant movement of doctors, nurses and porters. She looked vulnerable. Despite not wanting to, he felt ashamed. She was all alone in the world and he couldn't even guess how long that had been the case, but one thing was clear: she was terrified of dying. He could see it in the desperate way she raised her head every time an official person walked past. She still had that desire to live in her broken body with all of its pain, in a world that had forgotten her.

And there he was. Wanting to be dead. Having to begrudgingly wait. He thought of his father, and how he was exactly the same. Fighting for life until it left him, and quietly he wondered, for a second, what if?

Shaking the thought, he saw her eyes resting on his, cataracts clouding them over, making her gaze smoky grey. His mind began to shift. A memory began to bleed into the forefront of his brain and although he still saw the eyes of the old lady her face had changed. She was no longer in the corridor of a busy hospital ward but a quiet room, the smell of fresh flowers filling the air. And beside this new older woman was Julia.

It was the memory of when they had both visited her mother whilst she was in hospital. They didn't know it then, but it would be the last time they would see her alive.

He remembered the doctors had previously talked with both him and Julia to tell them she was slipping away but her pain was being managed and that she would soon fall asleep and probably not wake up. He remembered how Julia lifted her head a little higher after hearing that, how she stuck her beautiful chin out a little, emphasizing her elegant jawline, the way she did when she didn't want anyone to know she was upset.

Chris knew; he had spent every available waking moment watching the woman he loved.

He remembered how he spoke to Julia's mother when Julia had finished applying her make-up. 'You look beautiful, Mum,' she said. Again Julia's jawline came into focus.

Her mother called for him, unable to see him at the end of her bed, partly through disease, partly through medication. He leant close, close enough to smell her skin, which had now lost its floral scent, replaced with the smell of clean, antibacterial soap.

She told him he was a good man, and that he needed to look after her daughter. He said he intended to forever.

He remembered her pulling him closer. Her voice barely a whisper. 'I'm scared of what is to come.'

He told her what was next was the biggest adventure of them all. That she looked beautiful and her spirit would thrive. That she had nothing to fear for she would always have that grace everyone admired. She smiled before closing her eyes and falling asleep.

He remembered Julia letting herself cry at that, and how her tears broke his heart. He then held her in his arms, stroked her hair, and whispered that everything would be okay until Julia fell asleep also.

That night as Chris held his wife in his arms, he watched Julia's mother pass away.

As he rubbed his eyebrows with the balls of his hands, the moans from the hospital ward flooded back, like they were being turned up by a television remote. He was once again eye to eye with the lonely old lady. She looked as if she had said or asked for something. Desperation on her pale face.

Chris closed the curtain, unable to say anything back.

Sitting back down, he tried to think about something else, anything other than her. He couldn't deny that he had just created a barrier between him, a seemingly healthy man and an older lady who looked desperate for someone to tell her everything was going to be okay despite her probably knowing that the end was close.

Chris couldn't see the life leave another person, not again. But closing himself off to someone in need was more proof that the good his father had instilled in him was dead. The old Chris would have held her hand, or stopped a doctor, or taken more action and wheeled the woman into his bay so she could maintain her dignity. He instinctively reached out to feel the stone that was usually in his pocket, forgetting it was gone.

And, as much as he tried to, he didn't care that he'd shut her out.

Looking at his hand, all raw and bloody, he moved his fingers. One of them didn't quite bend properly, possibly due to him cutting into a tendon, not that he cared one way or another. Soon it wouldn't matter. It became something curious rather than uncomfortable. Someone pulled back the curtain that separated him from the rest of the ward, startling Chris. A young man, possibly only in his twenties, stepped in.

'Mr Hayes?'

'Yes.'

'I'm Dr Bhari. Now, it says you have cut your hand?'

'Yes.'

'May I have a look?'

After stepping in and closing the curtain, Dr Bhari put on a pair of blue surgical gloves from his top pocket. He then took Chris gently by the hands, as if holding a quail's egg, and looked into the wound.

'It's quite deep. What happened?'

'I cut it.'

'I see. May I ask how?'

'It was an accident.'

Chris could see that the doctor didn't believe him. He could see it in his dark brown eyes, eyes that reminded him of the train girl. Part of him wondered how she was, and immediately he hated it. It was her fucking fault he had to wait.

'I see. Well, you've managed to cause a bit of damage in here, but, luckily, you've missed the major blood line into your hand. Although there may be a damaged tendon.'

The doctor paused, looking at Chris, clearly knowing he had done this injury to himself.

'Is there anything else you want to discuss before we patch you up?'

He wanted to tell the doctor it came easy to him to cause damage. That he was broken following Julia's death and he couldn't recover. He wanted to spill everything, unbottle the secrets he'd been keeping for months, torturing himself with. He wanted to tell the doctor about his wife being killed and how he had failed as a husband to save her.

He wanted to tell him that he had started having thoughts of not only hurting himself but others as well, because he couldn't find the man who stole his wife and make him pay. He wanted to say that he hadn't been allowed to grieve properly, and because of that he didn't have closure.

But he didn't.

Chapter 15

As Nat drove along the long, sweeping dual carriageway that lined Peterborough, I suggested we get a coffee before trying to find out where his house was on London Road. Google Maps told us it was only a fifteen-minute walk away from the city centre so we thought we could park at the multi-storey and walk.

Natalie said we should just drive to his house, drop the stone and leave, but I said I wasn't ready; I needed some time. It was happening too fast. I needed to calm down and prepare myself. I dug my nails into my sweaty palms to try to keep my nerves under control. I didn't want Natalie seeing how terrified I was feeling. She was still pissed off at me for asking her to perform her clandestine visit to work, but begrudgingly agreed, so we parked and walked through the shopping centre to the first coffee shop we could find. Needless to say I paid for the drinks.

Since leaving Cambridge, I had the growing feeling that I was going to throw up. A latte would hopefully calm my nerves a little, nothing like a cigarette would, but I decided not to smoke. I didn't want him to smell it on me if I saw him. I knew it was stupid. It wasn't like there was actually any guarantee we would find him and even if we did there was no guarantee he would speak to me. But still, I wanted to make a better impression than I had that night.

After queuing for an impossibly long time in Costa, I ordered our drinks and we found a small table to sit at. We sat in silence, watching people toing and froing, carrying shopping bags. I knew that my sister was wishing she could do something to make me feel happy. My sister always meant well, even if sometimes she was a little pushy. I could see Natalie was about to say something but before she could I saw someone over her shoulder, walking towards us, and I felt the colour wash from my face as shock set in.

It was like I had seen a ghost. For a second I thought it couldn't be real. But then he walked straight past where we were sitting, without seeing me. Without seeing anyone. His eyes only focusing on the patch of ground a pace away from his shoes. He looked tired, more so than he did two weeks before. He looked thinner. He looked older somehow, but still very much alive.

The fact that Chris walked past without seeing me upset me more than I thought it would/should.

He was the man who had been on my mind every day since that night. I'd hoped for something similar, that he wouldn't be able to forget me. Rationally, though, I knew that would never be the case.

He passed so close I could have reached out and touched him, drawing his attention. But I couldn't. I was paralysed by my own fear of what would happen as a result. I wondered, would he be pleased to see me or would he hate me for stopping him that night? Or would he look blankly at me with no idea who I was? Without daring to look behind, I knew he was gone, among the crowds of people.

'Sarah, who did you see?'

I couldn't respond. A tear began to form in my eye.

'Sarah, was it him? Did you just see him?'

All I could do was nod yes, my ability to form words imprisoned beneath my diaphragm, trapped alongside my despair and shock.

'Did he see you?' she asked, looking beyond me to see if she could make him out among the crowd of bobbing heads. I shook my head, allowing the tear to escape, quickly brushing it away. Looking at my sister, I could see her weighing up the options.

'Well, come on,' she said reluctantly, finishing her now-cold coffee and grabbing her bags. 'Let's go talk to him.'

I was shocked by Natalie's readiness to confront him after being so reserved about us being in Peterborough, but I suppose she wanted to get the whole thing over with, so we could return home and be done with it. She looked at me, waiting to get up. But I couldn't. I was too frightened to move.

'I can't talk to him.'

'Fine, let's follow him then.'

'What?'

'Sarah, you think I don't know that you'll regret it if you don't? We cannot have another day of you thinking only about him. Finish your coffee. We're doing this.'

Natalie began to leave. I just looked at her, astonished.

'Sarah, come on, we don't want to lose him.'

As he moved cautiously, we followed far enough behind to not be seen but close enough to not lose him. It was difficult work. Every now and then he would stop and look back where he had walked, almost like he knew he was being followed. As we left the shopping centre and stepped onto the main square, the Guildhall looking impressive in the sunlight, fountains built into the footpath shooting water high into the air with children jumping in them, he looked around him constantly, searching for someone.

He walked into people without apologizing. Keeping his head low, he moved faster so Nat and I had to jog to keep up. It wasn't until the city centre was behind him that he slowed down. When he did, he looked behind him, straight at Nat and I, but he didn't see us. Whoever it was he was looking for wasn't me. He looked fearful, like someone was after him. Once he'd turned away from us, we both looked behind to see if we could see anyone who might be after him. There were lots of people, none of whom looked suspicious.

The busy city centre streets were replaced with the quieter, cleaner ones and he didn't stop walking until he got to the river where he watched it moving gently as it relaxed in the summer sun. We had to stop when he did, next to the city's old police station. Obscured partly behind a wall, I watched him look out over the water.

I wished I could know what he was thinking. I tried to see him properly from where I stood but could only see his left side, his dirty white shirt and contrasting clean bandage on his hand. It was a fresh dressing. He had hurt himself recently. I pictured him cutting his wrists to bleed to death, or hurting himself as penance for his failure, the failure I had caused. But of course it couldn't be that; I couldn't let myself think that. If he had succeeded, he wouldn't be standing so close, looking so alive.

Thinking it made me want to run out and shout his name. But I stopped myself and continued to watch. I could only see the side of his face. His jaw muscles flexed and I wondered if he was enjoying the serenity. Or was he thinking that the water might just be deep enough for him to be dragged to the bottom and drown? But then, something caught his eye. Something that physically lifted him.

I looked down to the river to see a family on the bank. A mother, father and a boy of about two throwing bread to a gaggle of geese. The boy giggling as one pecked some from his hands. Looking back at

Chris I could see him smiling. Just for a split second before he took a deep breath and rebuilt his walls. Becoming hard and iron-like. It was the same thing he did on the platform after I got through to him. There was a good man fighting to be freed under that hardness; I just knew it.

I was about to ask if Nat had seen what I had but he was on the move again. His thoughts collected, composed. Ensuring that we kept our distance, we continued to follow. After another few minutes of gentle walking, he abruptly stopped and we hastily had to hide behind a tree.

He was standing next to a postbox. At first I thought he was posting a letter. Foolishly, I thought for a moment that it might be a letter for me, but I knew that was impossible. He knew nothing about me. Instead, he fought to take his keys out of his left pocket, the bandage on his hand making it difficult, before he stepped off the main footpath and towards a front door.

He didn't look for anyone inside. He didn't call out a hello. Just looked down the street, towards us and the other way, before shutting the door.

A new fear pulled at me, smothering my thoughts and making it impossible to process what I could about the new information I had just learnt. I turned to Natalie. She looked back in a way that made me feel safe and understood.

'Do you want to go knock?'

'No.'

'Are you worried he won't remember you?'

'Yes.'

'What do you want to do?'

'I don't know. You're good at this sort of stuff. What would you do?'

'If it was me, I'd go and knock.'

'But what if he really doesn't remember me?'

'Then he doesn't, and you pretend you have the wrong door, say sorry, and leave. When he shuts the door, post the stone. Then you get on with your life and he stays out of it.'

'I can't just forget I've seen him again.'

'Listen, Sarah, I watched you with John and I saw you change and lose all of your confidence. I watched everything about you wither. I watched the adventurous sister I grew up with disappear, and it was all because you didn't speak when you should have. You stayed quiet and hoped things would be better or different all by themselves, and you wasted years of your life doing it.'

'Why didn't you say something?'

'Because I didn't want to seem like an interfering little sister; besides, would you have listened to me?'

'Probably not.'

'So I'm saying now, you should knock. If he remembers you then you have a conversation. If he doesn't then you leave him behind.'

It was only for a second but a real sadness overcame me at the thought of actually leaving him behind. Natalie saw it.

'Sarah, what exactly are your feelings towards him? It is just about you wanting to help, isn't it?'

I couldn't respond. I just looked down at my feet, hoping my inability to speak didn't tell her too much. I didn't know what I was thinking. Yes, I wanted to help. I was desperate to help. But the way he saw me that night on the platform, the way he offered to buy me a coffee, didn't want me to see what was about to happen to him – I couldn't ignore that.

'Do you want me to do it?'

'No, it's okay.'

Taking a deep breath, I walked the few steps, leaving Natalie behind. From the tree to the postbox and then to his front door.

***

In his kitchen Chris took off his bandage and looked at the stitches: five in all. They pulled his skin together, allowing it to begin to heal. He pulled at one of them, curious as to whether it would hurt. It didn't. He pulled a little harder until fresh droplets of blood formed and dripped onto the floor. He stopped himself from doing any more damage. He couldn't afford another trip to the hospital.

Using a cloth, he cleaned up. Dropping it in the sink, he looked into the back garden. Whilst the inside of his home looked dead and sterile, his garden looked the opposite. It was wild, dangerous and unkempt.

The grass was knee-high and weeds had attacked what once was a beautiful buddleia.

He couldn't help but think that both parts of his home reflected who he was now: part silent, lifeless and ashen; and part angry, chaotic and unrecognizable. Neither part a shadow of how it used to be when life made sense.

It saddened him to see the garden like this. It had been hers. The bushes were regularly pruned, the weeds dealt with. The flowers cut and brought into the house to add fragrance and life. All he did was mow the lawn. The rest of their garden Julia did with as she pleased. Seeing it unloved highlighted how unfair life was. He remembered her in it on an early October day. Warm enough to be outside with just a jumper on.

***

She was on her hands and knees tirelessly working, a content expression on her face, deep in concentration as she planted daffodil bulbs for the following spring. It allowed him to walk right up behind her without being noticed and tickle her, making her jump. She swore at him and mock hit him for scaring her and he said sorry, then asked if he could give her a kiss to make it better.

She refused at first but then as he pretended to be upset she kissed him before telling him to go away. She turned to carry on planting and he placed his hands on her shoulders, massaging them. She sighed in pleasure. Leaning down to kiss her ear, he whispered that he would give her a proper massage later. She told him she would love that.

***

Sitting down, his back resting against the cupboard, Chris took three deep breaths. His memory felt so real he could smell the cut grass from that autumn three years ago. He could taste her kiss. He could feel her warmth. Closing his eyes, Chris forced the memory out. He was too tired to see it.

His thoughts shifted to the toolbox in the shed. He wanted to check the items inside it, read some of her diary. He needed to hear her and talk back to her. He needed to tell her he missed her and hated that she was alone, but he had no choice. Looking out towards the shed, knowing he needed to wait for the blanket of darkness, he noticed the long grass was downtrodden where he made his frequent walks to it. He knew he needed to cut it, make it seem normal. He was just about to put it on his list of things to do when he heard three taps on his front door.

At first he thought it was his imagination playing tricks on him, as it often did. But he heard it again and his body tensed, alert, not knowing what to do. There were three more taps. Whoever it was, they were persistent. He wondered if Steve had come to see him. Maybe Ben from work? Or perhaps someone from Julia's life? Although he didn't know who. She had become solitary in recent years.

He could see someone standing there. Whoever it was cupped their hands and pressed them against the glass. He hid behind his doorframe. After a few moments it went quiet. Knowing he was being paranoid as it was probably just some door-to-door salesperson, he stood. As he did he noticed his hands were shaking.

He opened his fridge and stuck his hand into the small top freezer section to pull out its one inhabitant: a bottle of cheap vodka, half of which was gone from the night before. With hands still shaking, he swigged half of the contents to steady himself. As the liquid burnt his throat and stomach, he heard a woman's voice coming through his letter box, freezing him to the spot where he stood, a sickness rising in his stomach as he placed it. There was no mistake. He knew who it was and he wondered how she had found him. It wasn't the man who had killed his wife at his door but the woman who had saved his.

'Chris? Are you there?'

Not daring to breathe, Chris stared towards his front door and letter box, hoping it was all a trick his mind was playing on him.

'It's Sarah. I was there that night. You know, at the station?'

He didn't know what to do, so he continued to listen, feeling adrenaline course through his veins.

'I know you were going to … I didn't say it, but I knew.'

Fear gripped him, so much so he couldn't blink. He couldn't move and, despite every muscle in his body burning, telling him to run and hide, he didn't flinch. Like something unseen was holding him in place. A fear similar to an animal in headlights. He didn't want to hear her voice ever again, but he couldn't focus on anything else.

'And, I want to thank you for not going through with it. I'm not sure I would have ever been okay. Chris? Are you there? I know I shouldn't be here, but I just wanted to make sure you were alright.'

If he stayed quiet she would think he wasn't there and she'd leave, but perhaps she would come back and try to talk to him again, and that would no doubt put her life at risk. Weighing up the options, he took a deep breath.

'Fuck off!' he said in a stern, unwavering tone, a tone that suggested the prospect of conversation was terminated.

***

Kneeling outside with my face pressed to his letter box, I was taken aback at the sound of his voice. I'd hoped he was there and yet knowing he was made me feel sick. I had a hundred things I'd planned to say to him, nice things, supportive things that I hoped would make a difference to him and help him find peace. Yet, standing there and hearing him dismiss me caused the anger I had been holding on to for all this time, anger I didn't even realize I had been suppressing, to rise to the surface. It temporarily robbed me of my words.

He offered up a sorry, afterwards, said in a softer tone. But that was it. I could tell he wasn't by the door any more, that he had left the conversation, if you could even call it that.

Those two words felt more like a break-up than when I left John. I'd been waiting for this moment for weeks, and this was all I got? I looked back to see Natalie, but she was just out of sight, giving me the space I needed. As I walked away I wondered what I'd been expecting to happen. In the back of my mind I'd hoped he would be glad to see me, but that was me being stupid.

In fact, him saying fuck off was what I should have expected. *Fuck off*. Those two words hurt me more than I thought they could. Joining up with Natalie we both walked towards the city, neither of us saying a word for a while. When I was sure I wasn't going to cry, I told Nat I needed some time on my own and that she should go home without me. I could see she wanted to protest, but thought better of it. I told her I would be okay and that I was going to walk for a while and then get a train home later.

***

With his ear pressed to the door he heard her quiet footsteps walking away. He was still in shock that she was there in the first place. Questioning how she had managed to find him. With a sickening feeling, Chris wondered how much she knew. It was clear she had found his note ... and therefore knew his name.

Somehow she had managed to find his address. But what else? Did she know about Julia? He racked his brain to try to remember every word he had written on his note, the one he'd left with the stone. Was there any mention of her name? He was confident there wasn't, but still, he needed to be sure. He was so close to being at his end the last thing he wanted was to be found out.

Chris couldn't have anyone else stopping him from joining Julia. But, knowing nothing about the girl at his door, he knew he wouldn't be able to find her and assess what she did and didn't know. All he could do was hope she didn't know enough to have the police come knocking, not now, not so close. He walked back into the kitchen and looked at his wall calendar.

Two weeks, one day.

After getting the keys to his shed, he moved towards the back door and stepped into his garden. He knew it was risky in the daylight, but he didn't care. He unlocked the old rotting door to his shed and stepped inside. He pulled out his toolbox and opened it. Everything was still in its place. He skimmed her diary. It calmed his mind.

'Nothing's changed, Chris; stick to your plan,' he repeated to himself over and over until he almost believed it.

He left the shed and locked it behind him, then went back into his house. The train girl coming into his world made things unpredictable. She might never come back, but she might also speak to the police about his intentions that night. And he needed to prepare for the worst eventuality. Which meant he needed to be in public, being that man whose wife was on the other side of the world, in case there were questions.

Getting himself another drink, Chris knew that despite not wanting to, he had to be where people might know him, just to ensure things looked normal from the outside.

Chapter 16

14 days left

1.32 a.m. – London Road, Peterborough

Stepping into his house and locking the door behind him, Chris exhaled loudly and let his head sink. The night had been far more exhausting and difficult than he thought it would. But it had worked. The risks had paid off. Absolutely no part of Chris wanted to be out at night, especially after the train girl had found where he lived. He wanted to lock his doors and stay in the shadows. Keeping his secrets contained.

But her arrival changed things and he knew that it was about appearances. If she did something stupid and talked to the police, he needed to look like a man who was not suicidal. If they thought otherwise they would ask questions and not only would his plans be jeopardized, but the man who killed his wife could be watching, and assume Chris had talked. He had been warned if he did it would place others in danger. He needed to go out, just to keep the people he loved safe. Some might say he was paranoid, but if it was a game, it was one he intended finishing on his terms.

So, after Sarah left, he prepared himself to be seen by people who might know him. An alibi for his intentions. He went into the city centre just before ten, already drunk, and went to The Corner Lounge. It was quiet for a Thursday night, but as he stepped in he could see some of the usual faces that drank there. That was good; it wouldn't take long for someone he knew to come and talk to him.

After ordering a lager, he found a small table, one where he could put his back to the wall. He sat and waited for someone who knew him to approach and talk. As he quietly drank, he noticed how people glanced his way when they walked past. It made him glad he was back against a wall; that way if the man came for him, he could see him coming. It didn't take long before a lanky, long-haired acquaintance called Matt approached. His long limbs awkwardly swinging as he walked towards him. Getting up, Chris gave him a hug.

'Chris, buddy. I've not seen you in here in ages. How's things, man? Shit, what have you done to your hand?'

'DIY accident.'

'Mate.'

'It looks worse than what it is – a couple of stitches is all. Let me buy you a drink.'

'Sure, man.'

Matt sat as Chris went to the bar to get him a beer. As he ordered, he thought about that night when he was standing in a similar place to where he was now. His back to the room as Steve talked to Julia. Moments before he had walked across the dance floor and introduced himself softly.

He shook it off.

He sat down and handed Matt his drink. Matt thanked him and for a while they both chatted about work and football before the beer began to take over and the conversation moved on to more serious themes. They discussed Syria and the fact they were both getting older. Chris could feel himself becoming impatient. But after three more beers Matt asked the question Chris was waiting for.

'So, how's Julia?'

It was show time. He took a deep breath, getting himself into character. The sad shrug of the shoulders. The moments when he didn't keep eye contact. The deep, introspective, longing sighs. He had rehearsed it so that if he was confronted before he could die he could still keep his secret. He loved and hated doing it in equal measure. Loved because this version of events meant Julia was still alive, hated because he desperately wanted the truth out, so she could be grieved for properly.

'She's visiting her dad in Australia.'

'That's nice, man. Not tempted to go with her?'

'She said she needed to go alone. Her mum died last year and she needed to get away.'

'She went alone?'

'Yeah, I didn't even get to say goodbye to her. I came home one day and she was gone. She just upped and left. Took a suitcase and left a note. She said she couldn't cope with a goodbye and just needed to go.'

'Chris, that's rough. How long has she been down there?'

'A long time.'

'Mate, that must be really hard.'

'I miss her a lot.'

'When is she coming back?'

'I don't know.'

'Shit.'

'Has she been in touch at all?'

'Not really, she just tells me she needs time to heal.'

'When was the last time you spoke?'

'A little while ago now.'

'Days? Weeks?'

'About five months.'

Chris could see his lanky mate was drunk. This was good. Drunk people argued and challenged. If there was an obvious flaw in either his story or how he appeared, Matt would raise it. The beauty in it was Matt would do this without knowing exactly what he was challenging.

'And you've heard nothing else from her? I mean, she hasn't said when she will be back or said sorry or anything?'

'Nothing.'

'She will come back, won't she?'

'I thought so for a while, but no; Julia is gone.'

'What a bitch. Fuck her, Chris; you deserve better than that.'

'Matt!'

'How can she do that to you? It's fucking cruel, man. I hope she bloody hates it over there!'

'Stop it. She's still my wife.'

'Divorce the bitch.'

'Matt. Enough. She *is* still my wife. And I hope one day she comes back to be my wife again. I won't give up on her. She's grieving.'

'Sorry, Chris, sorry. I know you still love her. But waiting for her isn't healthy, man. How long ago did she leave?'

'Eleven months.'

'Eleven months? Dude, time to move on, get over the bitch. Have a summer fling. Loads of single young hotties about, mate, all desperate for an older chap. It would be good for you. Get out, live the single life again.'

'I don't want to live the single life again.'

'Mate, it will be good for your ego to get on it. I would if I looked like you do.'

Chris thought about it for a second. About someone else in his bed. Someone else lying in the space between his shoulder and chest. *Her* space. It wouldn't feel right. Before they knew it, last orders were called and they left, having a hug before going their separate ways. Chris promising to be there the following week for another drink.

***

Walking home, Chris had tried to replay as much of the drunk conversation he'd had with Matt as his foggy brain would let him. He was amazed that Matt not only believed his story about Julia leaving, but hated her for it too. Chris felt confident his fake truths were airtight and when he did meet with Steve no new questions would be asked, especially now he'd honed his lines.

For the last eleven months he had longed to tell Steve the truth. But he couldn't tell him about Julia being killed; as far as he and everyone else was concerned, Julia was with her dad in Australia following her mother's death, taking a sabbatical from work to do so. Because if Steve knew what really happened, he would be in danger. Chris was sure her killer was still close, and watching. One little slip would mean Steve would be next. He knew because the night the man killed his wife, the night Chris helplessly watched, unable to do anything to save his beloved Julia, he promised he would kill again unless Chris kept quiet.

As he walked down Bridge Street, he was startled by the presence of a man sitting in a dark shop entrance. As Chris looked down at him, the man, a tramp, didn't avert his gaze.

'Have you got any spare change?'

There was something in the way he was looking at Chris. He knew, and was watching to make sure Chris didn't fuck up and tell the secret he was warned to keep. For a moment Chris thought that the tramp was the man he had longed to be face to face with. But that wasn't likely. No, that man was hiding, as he always was. Somewhere close. The tramp was working for him.

'Tell him I've not told a soul.'

'What?'

Lowering himself to be eye to eye with the homeless man, their noses inches apart, Chris spat as he spoke.

'Tell him I've not told a fucking soul. No one.'

'I don't know who you mean, please, leave me alone.'

'Leave you alone? You're a fucking joke. I know why you're here.'

'Please.'

'You can watch me all you want; it won't change a fucking thing.'

'Please, just leave me alone. I only asked for some spare change.'

'You don't scare me. He doesn't scare me.'

'I don't know what you're talking about. Please, man. Just leave me alone.'

Chris stood and looked around, seeing only a group of young lads and an older couple arm in arm. No sign of him anywhere. He looked back at the homeless man.

'Leave me alone; leave me alone? That's fucking rich,' Chris spat, as he turned on his heel and hastily left the cowering man behind.

Despite that moment, the night had been a success.

Later, as he got himself a drink from the fridge, Chris looked towards the shed. He wanted to read some of her diary and as he pulled it out he could feel a wave of pain hit him. Being drunk and sad wasn't a good idea. All of his emotions came to the surface with the help of liquor and they were emotions he didn't always want to face. He would end up doing something stupid, more stupid than what he had done to himself only eighteen hours before. So instead he looked at his wall calendar and counted the days.

Fourteen left.

Everything was in place. Everything besides the train girl who had come to his door hours before. She was a potential threat. He hoped she wouldn't appear in his life again.

After staggering to his bedroom, Chris took off his clothes then fell into bed. Talking to someone as if Julia was still alive made him feel more desperate than ever for his old life. He wanted his wife beside him, like she had been for thousands of sleeps.

Chris opened his bedside drawer and took out the book that waited for its reader. He turned to the first page and read the opening lines out loud. Like he had done with Julia resting in the space between his chest and shoulder that now bore an angry scar. He tried to focus on one of the many moments in which he'd read to his wife as she half dozed, pressed against him, but there were too many. So he thought about the first time.

It started before they were married when her mum's health took a turn for the worse. On those nights Julia cried herself to sleep and one night Chris picked up one of his books and instead of reading quietly from where he left off he started from the beginning and told her the story until she was in a deep and peaceful sleep. Julia's mum lived for another three months and every night Chris read to help with the struggle, then with the passing, then with the healing, until the ritual was so embedded neither could sleep without him doing it.

Turning to the dog-eared page, the place where he'd last read to with his wife nearly a year before, Chris read out loud until he drifted into an alcohol-fuelled sleep.

Chapter 17

13 days left

12.54 p.m. – Lynch Wood business park, Peterborough

Parked in his black Audi, Steve watched the entrance to Chris's work. He was in the area so figured he'd time his lunch for when Chris had his and grab him for a burger from the van that parked in the lay-by half a mile away.

He felt the urge to just make sure his friend was okay. Steve knew that Chris always took his lunch at twelve thirty. He had for years. It had become a joke that he was so predictable. He started doing so because Julia also had her lunch at a similar time and they often rang one another, or with their workplaces only being a mile apart, they would have lunch together.

Part of Steve kept an eye out for her too. Although he didn't know why. He knew she was thousands of miles away, probably sat on a beach enjoying the weather, forgetting her old life and her abandoned husband; but Steve looked anyway. Force of habit, he supposed.

He had been sitting there for twenty-five minutes and Chris still hadn't emerged from work. He was just about to give up and drive away when he spotted a familiar face. It wasn't Chris but one of his colleagues, Ben. They had met a few times on nights out. He was a nice chap and probably the closest person to Chris at work. Steve jumped out of his car and walked towards him. He had to quicken his pace to catch up.

'Ben.'

Turning around, Ben couldn't hide the surprise, and confusion, from his face.

'Ben, sorry, it's Steve. We met a few times on nights out? I'm a friend of Chris's.'

'Yes, of course. I remember. How are you?'

'Good, thanks. Sorry to stop you, Ben. Is he in today?'

'Chris?'

'Yes, is he in the office today?'

'No.'

'Bugger. When is he next in?'

'Steve. Chris hasn't been at work for a long time.'

'What do you mean?'

'He's been on long-term sick leave. I thought you'd know this?'

'What? No. How long has he been off?'

'I'm not sure of the exact date. Ten months, eleven maybe.'

'Do you know when he's back?'

'He's not; he resigned.'

'When?'

'A few weeks ago. Is he okay?'

Steve stood in shock. Chris had not been at work since last summer. All this time without mentioning it.

'Steve? Is he okay?'

'Yes, sorry, yeah, he's fine. Thanks, Ben.'

Getting back into his car, Steve watched Ben walk away, his head low until he disappeared around the corner. Chris hadn't been in work for eleven months and had just resigned. He counted backwards. Last summer. Around the same time Julia left. He knew it wasn't a coincidence. He also knew that he was right to be worried about his best friend. Chris had taken Julia leaving a lot harder than he thought. He hadn't been at work and, worse, he had lied to Steve about it.

Chris was many things, but he had never been untruthful with Steve. It was part of why they had been so close for so long.

As he started up his car to drive away, a thought popped into his head. Chris was in trouble and clearly wasn't coping as well as he led people to believe. Julia's leaving him had broken Chris. They'd spent so much time together and suddenly they lived on different sides of the world. Steve tried to imagine how he would feel if it was him. He knew he wouldn't be doing very well either.

Steve knew he had to do something to help. But if he confronted him about it, Chris would disappear completely. He knew this because, when they were young, in the wake of his last break-up, Steve had tried to force his way into Chris's life and Chris had vanished for a while. When he eventually came back, he told Steve he had been having dark thoughts. As long as Chris was in control, he would feel safe. He wouldn't leave; Steve was sure of it.

As Steve merged onto the A1 to head south towards London, he knew that he would have to keep a closer eye on his friend. Swing past on his way home from work sometimes, find an excuse to be in the area. Insisting on that beer sooner rather than later, but making it look like it was on Chris's terms.

He couldn't help shift the idea that Chris was going to do something stupid.

Chapter 18

Mum has been forgetting a lot of things recently. For a while now I've kidded myself, telling myself it's because she's lonely, that I can fix that by being around more to help with things like shopping and cleaning. So, I've decided to go part-time at work. I've spoken with my boss, James, who wasn't overly keen on the idea as a boss, but as a friend he told me that being there for a loved one was one of the most important things anyone can do, and I should definitely reduce the amount I'm at the office.

So, that's that. As of next Monday I'm part-time for the first time in my adult life – to help Mum more. I know she's old, but she's not that old. She shouldn't be frail yet. For weeks I've seen her forget things and I've rationalized it by thinking, So what if she occasionally gets muddled about what day of the week it is, or who is Prime Minister? She's retired. Why would she need to know?

She's been forgetting silly little things like that and the occasional word for months. Losing keys, forgetting to put the oven on when making dinner so it just sits there for an hour or two defrosting. It wasn't until two weeks ago when I popped round for a cup of tea that she looked at a picture on her mantelpiece of me, her and Dad. Back when I was young. She asked who he was. Dad was her world until he left for Australia. Her one true love she could never get over. Even after all these years, there hasn't been another man in her life.

In the picture we were all smiling. I was in his arms, only two, maybe three. Mum loved that picture. She said it captured a time when everything made sense. Her forgetting who he was turned my worries from something I could dismiss as a lonely mind forgetting and losing things to something that was taking things from her.

So, I've been researching Alzheimer's and I've concluded it was a silly thing to do. Most of what the internet tells me is about how terrible it is and life expectancy after diagnosis. It's only made me worry more. I know I need to talk to her about it, and for us to go to her doctor for tests. But I'm scared. What if it is what I think? What if my mum is on a slippery slope to somewhere terrible? Part of me would rather not know.

That said, I know I'll broach the subject tomorrow when I see her. Although I'm not sure how. Do I come out and just say it? Or do I lead her and allow her to voice the concern herself? Surely she knows in herself something isn't right? But, when you know something for sure there is no undoing it.

I've spoken with Chris a lot about it, about how scared I am. He's offered to be there when I talk to her, to give support where he can, even if it's just making us a cup of tea. I really want to say yes, but I think this should be between Mum and me. Having him there would be more about me and that's not fair. Still, it was lovely of him to offer.

Chris also hinted last weekend, when I was drifting off in his arms, that I needn't worry about going part-time with regard to finances. I told him I didn't want his money and he replied that was a good thing because he wasn't going to offer, making me laugh. He did say, however, that it seemed daft that we were both paying rent. Before kissing me on the head and telling me he loved me.

It was the first time he had said it and he said it in a typical Chris way. Not attracting attention to himself. Not making it a big thing. Just three quietly spoken words that I truly and deeply believed. I wanted to say I loved him back, but couldn't. Chris has never asked for anything from me in all the time we have been together. I wanted him to have his brave and touching moment. So I said goodnight and snuggled in to his shoulder.

Just as I was dozing off, he whispered that he had put in an offer on a place, and if it was successful he wanted me to move in. So I wouldn't have to worry about money, and could spend as much time with my mum as I needed.

I've really missed not being with Chris much this week. I've been staying with Mum. He's been so understanding and patient with it all. I was sure when it all started he was going to get fed up with me being upset and away all of the time. I mean, who wouldn't get fed up with that? But he hasn't (so far). In fact, he's been more attentive, more available. He messages me all the time, seeing how I am, wondering if there is anything he can do. I even told him if he needed a break from the constant misery, I'd understand. But he said he couldn't think of a worse idea.

Sometimes, I don't know what I would do without him. Even if sometimes I don't treat him in a way he deserves. For instance, the other day I was tired and fed up and worried about Mum. Chris could see I was off and asked if I was okay. And I shouted at him, told him to leave me alone. Told him I needed space and he just stood and took it all.

He didn't leave, he didn't raise his voice, and he didn't do anything that would fuel my outburst. He just waited patiently for me to calm and once I had I was devastated I had spoken that way. He forgave me instantly. Telling me it was one of those things and that he understood. Not a hint of anger. I don't know what I've done to deserve such a good man.

In the morning I think I'm going to ring the doctor and get Mum an appointment. I hope to God it's just a tired and bored mind. Although my instincts tell me otherwise ...

Chapter 19

11 days left

8.42 p.m. – London Road, Peterborough

Sitting on his back doorstep, his bare feet basking in the last of the evening sun before it continued westward and over the horizon, Chris watched the sky begin to softly change colour. He thought about what he and Julia would be doing on such a nice day if she were still alive. What had they done the previous year?

He pictured them going for a nice walk along the river – the place where he had asked her to be his wife – before finding a pub to get a drink and perhaps some food. They would then walk home slowly, enjoying the warmth of the evening, perhaps sitting on the bank to talk about work or holiday plans. A warm summer evening, just before the sun started to set, was his and Julia's favourite time of the day. It reminded them of the lazy Spanish ones of their honeymoon, which seemed to be timeless.

On a day like this Chris missed his wife even more.

And if they didn't go out but stayed at home she would be in the garden with him right now, sipping a glass of white wine whilst he nursed a lager and played guitar. She would be sitting at the patio table, looking up at the sky and gently swaying to whatever he played. Neither talking. Neither needing to. They were content with each other's silence.

It would get dark and they would go inside before the mosquitos feasted, heading to bed where Chris would read to her as he always did. Her head on his chest, in her space, as they immersed themselves in chapter after chapter of whatever book had captured their attention.

Chris closed his eyes and let himself see it. Both of them naked and close. Her arm wrapped around him as he held the book in one hand and stroked her hair with the other. Their breathing in unison. The sound of the warm wind gently blowing through the open bedroom window. The world still and calm. He imagined putting the book down and lifting her chin with his hand to kiss her on the lips. Her pulling away and smiling at him before kissing him back. Their bodies intertwining. Her legs wrapping over him. Him rolling on top of her. Her hands held to the bed by his. Her back arching slightly, inviting. Him pulling up, straightening his arms to see his wife.

Her glazed eyes looking back.

Standing up, Chris rubbed his eyes until it hurt. Partly to shake the image, partly to stop himself crying. He hated that he couldn't think of his wife as his wife any more but as a dead person. He hated that her memory was becoming tainted by his inability to manage his thoughts. He hated that she wasn't there with him making new memories. Looking at the sky, its colours starting to come alive as it does with a sunset, he knew that he couldn't sit and enjoy a moment like this again. This would be the last sunset he would let himself watch before he saw one with Julia. If that was what happened next.

He went into his house and locked the back door behind him. Walking into the lounge, he saw his guitar stood beside the sofa, against a wall. Dust covered the top of it. He sat and pulled it out. Placed it on his lap. He cleaned its strings with the bottom of his T-shirt and plucked each one individually. It was out of tune, but not horrifically.

He rested the guitar on his lap and prepared to play a few chords and go to the place he went when playing. A quiet place with no other sounds or time or memory. But the last time he picked up his guitar, she was sitting with him. To play now would be unfaithful.

As he stood to put it back, knowing he would never play again, he paused. The guitar firmly in his hands. He had never been in a band; he only played for pleasure, and then, for her. And she was dead. With one hand still on the neck, he held the base with the other and drove it down onto his knee, snapping it in half, the neck swinging wildly, still attached by the strings. It would never make music again.

After dropping it on the floor, he sat and put his head in his hands. Chris let himself cry. It was right to have snapped the guitar. It was right that he couldn't ever play it again, and neither could anyone else. It was only for Julia. But it still broke his heart because of the memory attached to it. One of the best times in his life.

Wiping tears from his eyes, he picked up the beheaded instrument and rested it back where it had always lived. Disfigured and dead. He needed a drink, to numb this fresh wave of grief. As he stepped into the kitchen, he heard the sound of footsteps in high heels walking towards his front door. The steps sounded official. Panic climbed up from his stomach, clawed its way into his throat, squeezing on his windpipe. Ducking down, he scuttled towards the doorframe that connected the lounge to the hallway and pressed himself against it. He peered out towards the door. He hoped the visitor would post something and walk away, but she didn't. She hesitated, and then he heard three quiet taps.

'Chris?'

The train girl was back.

Hearing her voice startled him.

'Chris? Can we talk?'

He didn't want to talk to anyone. Especially her. But he didn't know what else to do. He still had eleven long days. If he didn't talk now then she would be back again and again and maybe even on the day when he needed to leave his house for the final time.

'Chris, I know you're in. Please, talk to me. I just want to know if you're okay.'

Chris realized part of him wanted to tell her he wasn't. He wanted to say that today had been one of the hardest since Julia died but her death had to remain a secret so no one else would be hurt and he could join her without anyone stopping him. If the train girl knew he wasn't okay she would keep coming. But if he told her he was okay she would know he was lying and still want to help. So he just sat there, peering out towards his door. Not saying anything.

'Listen, I know you're in there. I can see your upstairs light on and I also know you'll ignore me, which is fine – whatever.'

He'd left an upstairs light on? When had he done that? Had it been on all day alerting anyone who would want to know that he was in? He cursed himself for being careless.

'I know it's weird me just turning up but I've been in London today, on a course, and had to come via Peterborough so I thought, whilst I was here, I would come and say hello. I hope you don't mind?'

She waited for him to say something, only to be greeted by silence. 'I should hate you.' Her voice suddenly sounded angry. 'You know I've not been able to forget about you since that night; you know that right? Not a single day goes by without me

167

wondering how you are. You haunt my dreams. You haunt me when I'm awake. I was in London today and it was busy at King's Cross and a man was stood on his own, close to the edge, and I thought he was going to jump. I can't look at anyone standing close to a platform edge without immediately thinking they're going to jump now. That's because of you, Chris. That's on you.'

Holding his breath, Chris crept to his front door, as quietly as he could, knowing he should either retreat to his garden and block out her sound or scream at her to go away.

'You've ended up being everywhere, and I wish I could let you go. Instead, I follow you home after randomly seeing you in the city. Eventually, I pluck up the courage to knock on your door not once but twice despite you clearly not wanting me to.'

Her voice sounded out of breath, like she had been running. She was on the verge of crying and he understood her reasons why. It still didn't make it his problem.

'And it doesn't stop there. John, my ex, he messages me more now than ever, and today would have been our five-year anniversary. I've blocked him now, this evening in fact. I know he's a bastard and I deserve better but I've closed that door because that night you made me see that there's another way, that men can be better. Men can care! Someone reminded me there is some good in the world despite that person now hiding from me.'

Sarah went silent for a moment and Chris shifted his weight to get his ear closer to the door. When she spoke again, it was softer, more vulnerable. 'I loved him, Chris. And I can't any more.'

Chris placed his head in his hands, trying not to let her honest words upset him. He didn't want to know this woman, he didn't want her in his life, and he didn't want to impact hers in such a negative way. And yet, her voice was soothing to him, calming him in a way only one person could before.

She needed to go but he wanted her to stay; he hated himself for it.

'When I first met him I knew straight away I couldn't see anyone else; it was just me and this perfect stranger. He didn't know I existed, of course – and why would he? He was so charming, so beautiful and I was just, well, me. I don't suppose you would understand.'

He understood. It reminded him of when he first saw Julia in that bar all those years before, her carefree laugh and his terror at trying to talk to her. Most of the memories of Julia made him sad. This one in particular he struggled with the most.

'That was five years ago. Five years.'

***

I thought about those five long years of me hoping John would be the right one and couldn't help but think I had wasted all of that time. Getting a

169

cigarette from my bag, I looked to the trees that gently swayed in the evening wind and wondered what five years meant to them. How much had they grown? Would they even notice five years like humans do? Would time matter in the same way?

I wondered what I could have achieved in those years if I hadn't met John. I could have been married with children, or have emigrated as I always dreamt of doing, the north-western shores of New Zealand beckoning me. Or would I be where I was now but in a more senior role? I wondered if I'd not wasted those years with him, would Chris have died as he planned?

On the other side of the door I heard him exhale, quietly but still loud enough for me to realize he was right there. After turning around slowly, I raised myself to my knees and pulled back his letter box to look inside. I could see his dark messy hair. He was only a few inches away from me, listening. Quietly, I closed it again and sat back down.

'Chris, I know you're there.'

I waited, but he said nothing.

'I just want to know if you're okay.'

Silence again.

'Chris?'

A sadness began to build inside me. I was trying to make him talk to me, trying to show that I cared for him, and he couldn't even say hello. It had taken so much of my courage and strength to be here on his doorstep and he couldn't even acknowledge my existence. I was opening up to him and he was more closed off than before. I thought of that time when I saw the train driver's pitying look as he drove past and I wondered what he would think of me now, of how low I had sunk for the sake of someone who didn't care one way or another. Enough was enough.

'You know what, Chris, fuck you. Fuck you for your silence and fuck you for being on my mind as much as you are.'

Then he spoke. His words not being what I was expecting.

'I don't care what you think. Get off my doorstep. Leave me alone.'

Getting up, I flicked my cigarette, his words cutting me deeper than I had ever felt before. I knew he didn't care for me as much as I did for him, but I also knew I had gotten through to him. And he knew that someone wanted to help. For him to say he didn't care was possibly the worst thing he could have said. I had never wanted to be home more than I did then, not even the night I discovered he wanted to die. I knew then that Chris was as bad for me as anyone else I had ever fallen for – possibly worse.

'Fine, Chris, I'm going. But, just so you know, I went back to that station every night waiting for you to come back.'

***

Although he would get what he wanted by letting her hate him, the idea of it wasn't something he

171

enjoyed. Those words spoken aloud were clearly so difficult to say and hearing her tell him she went back to March train station made him feel terrible. This was exactly what he hadn't wanted; he hadn't wanted his actions to affect anyone else.

Pressing his ear to the door, he listened to her walk away until her footsteps were no longer audible. Confident she was gone, Chris rubbed his eyebrows with the balls of his hands and then hit himself, as if he could beat her out of his head. He hated that he wanted her to know he cared. He hated that he wanted to speak with her. He hated that he was being an arsehole to protect her and she would never know.

He walked upstairs, a heavy feeling in his legs, but before he could make it to the top he turned around and headed back to his front door. He pressed his ear against it and tried to hear if she had returned. Then grabbing the handle, he paused for a second before opening it. He half expected, or rather hoped, she would be standing at the end of his path, but she wasn't.

The ground felt cold on his bare feet as he walked to the roadside and looked right. In the distance, her head low, he could see her walking back to the city. It made him feel something, and not knowing why, he wondered how he would have felt if he'd let Julia walk away from him when he first met her. He almost called out to Sarah, but stopped himself before he did. He needed her to hate him. He needed her to never come back.

He went back into his house, closed the door, sat down, and cried long and hard. He hated what he had become. He hated the man he now was, a man his father wouldn't be able to look in the eye any more. He tried to think of his dad, of one of his stories or life lessons he was so good at sharing with Chris when he was young. But his image stayed hidden in the shadows of his memory, ashamed.

Chris walked into his kitchen and grabbed his phone. After scrolling to Steve's messages he began to type. He knew he shouldn't, but the weight of his world was beginning to crush him. He wouldn't tell Steve anything other than he and Julia hadn't spoken recently and he was starting to become frustrated with the lack of communication from his wife; maybe he could even say he was worried about her. He just needed something that would resemble normality after nearly a year of secret grieving. He needed someone to grieve with, but he could never tell.

Instead he typed: *'Hi, mate, sorry it's been so long. I really need a drink. Are you free this evening?'*

Chapter 20

11.38 p.m. – Cherry Orton Road, Peterborough

Sitting at his kitchen table, Steve felt shaken as he pressed a packet of frozen peas to his face. He could feel the swelling coming out across his eye and knew that he was going to have a huge bruise by morning. Some people already thought he looked like a thug; a swollen eye wouldn't help his cause. With three meetings in the next week with potential clients, he would need a good excuse for a battered face. He'd already decided that he did it playing rugby. The swollen eye wasn't what troubled him. Or the fact he had been punched in the face. What troubled him was who had hit him.

Hearing footsteps coming down the stairs, he turned his body slightly so Kristy wouldn't notice the swollen eye as soon she stepped into the room.

'Sorry, darling, did I wake you?'

'No, not at all. I was just worried. Why haven't you come to bed?'

'I just needed some time to think.'

'Is everything all right?'

'I don't know, honey.'

Turning, Steve looked at his wife, wincing as he did so.

'Jesus! Steve, what happened to your face?'

'There was a fight.'

'What do you mean there was a fight?'

'In the pub tonight.'

Kneeling beside Steve, Kristy placed the pea bag back onto his eye, receiving a grimace in return.

'God, Steve!'

'It's not as bad as it looks.'

'What happened?'

'Chris happened.'

Steve relived the evening as he told his wife about the events. How when he got to The Corner Lounge Chris was there and, as before, he was already drunk. Steve told her how he seemed edgy, wired, not himself. He noticed how Chris struggled to make eye contact all evening, his eyes always darting from side to side, watching the room. And when last orders were called, he stood and walked out of the pub without saying goodbye, leaving Steve at the table, confused.

'Do you think he's having a breakdown?' Kristy asked in all seriousness.

'Something terrible is clearly going on inside of him, Kristy, and I don't know what to do.'

'I still don't understand. How did you get hit?'

'After he left the pub I sat a little stunned. I thought he was going to the loo or getting another beer, but he just walked out the door and by the time I reacted he was halfway down Bridge Street shouting at anyone near him. Telling them to fuck off, asking if they wanted a fight.'

'Chris was saying this?'

'I know, I couldn't believe it either. It was like I was watching someone else. There was a young couple, early twenties, and he grabbed the guy, shouting at him that he needed to look after his girl. Treat her right, love her dearly, or he would find him and he would make him pay.'

'Make him pay? Chris really said all this?'

'I ran over and pulled Chris off of the guy, who was fuming. He wanted to call the police but I told him my friend was going through a difficult time and that I was sorry on his behalf. I then turned to Chris and asked him what the hell he was doing, asked if he was out of his mind, if he had taken any drugs, but instead he said the strangest thing to me.'

'What?'

'He said that I wasn't safe; we weren't safe because of him. He said that he needed me to leave him alone and he started running towards the river. I chased him, telling him to slow down, but he wasn't listening. He just ran and ran. I had no choice but to grab him, both of us falling as I did.'

'And Chris hit you?'

'Yeah, I could see he regretted it straight away. He said he needed to be with Julia, before storming off, leaving me on the deck.'

'Oh, Steve, I'm so sorry.' Kristy gave Steve a long hug.

'I just don't know what to do to help him through this. Julia needs to come back. I just don't think she will.'

'Me neither.'

'Kristy, do you mind if I have a few minutes on my own?'

'Of course not. Just come to bed when you're ready.'

'Thanks, love.'

After kissing Steve on the head, Kristy went back to bed. Steve put the peas back in the freezer before looking at his eye in the kitchen mirror. The darkness of broken blood vessels was already flooding to the surface. He couldn't believe how Chris had been towards him. Pouring himself a drink of water, Steve thought again about his friend's behaviour. It was far worse than he had told his wife. It was true, Chris had hit him, but what he hadn't told his wife was that Chris didn't hit him in the street and that he'd followed him home and stopped him before he went inside.

'Look, Chris, I don't know what the fuck is going on with you but you can't have Julia leaving you to turn you into this.'

'She hasn't left me!'

Chris went into his house, and before he could close the door, Steve pushed his way in.

'What are you doing?'

177

'I'm not leaving you, mate, not when you're like this.'

'Steve, get out.'

'No, Chris, we've known each other a long time. Something is going on and I want to know what.'

'It doesn't matter; just get out.'

Chris had tried to push Steve out, but with Steve being both bigger and stronger than Chris he failed.

'Fine, stay; I'm going to bed.'

Steve watched Chris go upstairs slowly, holding on to the banister to keep him upright. He knew that Chris would sleep it off and be very different in the morning. Whatever was going on, Steve was more likely to find out if he put on a little pressure.

Steve followed Chris up the stairs and grabbed his friend's shoulder to turn him around. As he did, Chris lunged at him, hitting Steve in the chest with his shoulder, forcing him backwards against the banister, which creaked angrily at the sudden weight. He couldn't believe how explosive it was. It happened so fast Steve didn't have time to prepare for the hit and the wind was knocked out of him.

Steve stood up to grab Chris and both men staggered into the bedroom and fell onto the bed. It was then Chris had hit him, just once before Steve put up his guard ensuring the other blows glanced off his forearms. With no choice, Steve pushed Chris and he fell off the side of the bed. Chris rose to his feet and tried to attack him once more. His arms flailing and thrashing without landing any clean punches on Steve. The whole time he was telling Chris to calm down. Chris lunged again and Steve had to take action.

As Chris leapt for him, he dropped his shoulder and turned, allowing him to glance past before putting him in a headlock. Chris fought to remove himself and drove himself at a wall. Both men hit it hard before Chris spun again, grabbing a knife from seemingly nowhere. Steve immediately stepped back, panting hard.

'What are you gonna do with that – stab me? Is that it, Chris? You're gonna stab me?'

'Just get out.'

'She was great, and I'm sorry she left you. I really am. But look at you. Are you really going to stab me, Chris?'

'Steve, just get out.'

'You need to get a grip. It's about time you let her go.'

'I can't let her go. I need to be with her, Steve.'

Steve took a small step towards Chris and Chris stepped back, hitting his back against the wall.

'What do you mean?'

'Nothing, just get out, please.'

'Or what?'

'Don't, please. Steve, just go.'

'Fine, all right, I'm going.'

Steve walked backwards, his arms still raised defensively and his eyes flicking from Chris to the knife until he was at the bedroom door. Then he turned and walked down the stairs. Chris followed and watched from the top as Steve opened the front door. He looked back, sighed, and left, closing the door quietly behind him.

As he walked into the city, his whole body shook. The adrenaline began to wear off. He couldn't believe what Chris had just done to him. There was something more going on than a man trying to cope with his marriage failing. But he didn't know what. And he knew he couldn't talk to Kristy about it because she would call the police. Steve had to work it out on his own.

Chapter 21

8 days left

6.52 p.m. – Kings Road, Cambridge

I loved and hated date nights in equal measure. Not my date nights, obviously – they are about as active as the mating habits of the dodo. I mean my sister's date nights. I loved them because when Natalie and George were out I had the entire house to myself, albeit only for a few hours. I hated them because it was a reminder of how easy those two have it with one another. A stark contrast of how shit it was with John and how lonely I felt in the wake of it. But, still, I didn't want to complain.

So I spent the time doing a little extra work from home. A presentation to my boss about how insurance claims are rising on household contents and the preventive measures we had in place to combat it. It was all a bit unethical in my view. Most people only claimed when they needed to. But work's work and needs must.

It also helped me forget the argument with Chris. If you could call it that. I couldn't believe what he had said to me and how much it had touched a nerve. I still felt bruised by it; however, I couldn't help still wanting to save him and to talk to him about his problems.

Nat was right from the very start. His life wasn't mine to protect. His problems weren't mine to manage. She was also right about my choice in men. Why did I always want to save them?

After finishing my presentation, I rubbed my eyes and made a mental note that I needed to get them tested. They felt overworked and strained, making me feel like I was getting old. I looked at the poster George had put on our living-room wall. 'Life isn't about waiting for the storm to pass, but about learning to dance in the rain.' At first I hated it, but now it was a quote I tried to adopt as often as I could. Well, in the last few days anyway. I read it in the mornings as I had my first cup of tea and said it to myself as I headed for work. I know, how 'America' of me.

Saying the quote in my head, I closed my laptop lid, stood up and stretched, uncurling my fingers towards the ceiling. It felt good to have my muscles do something. It was getting late and I'd not had any dinner so I went into the kitchen and began to rifle through the cupboards for inspiration. Lacking any, I settled on a Pot Noodle. I wondered if I shouldn't be so lazy and cook a proper meal. That thought didn't last long.

As the kettle started to boil, I flicked on the radio, Radio 2, hoping for something I could jig to whilst I waited. Surprisingly, one of my favourite songs was playing. A Nineties classic by a band long forgotten. A rare treat for airtime. I sang along, a little out of tune, but that's another good thing about their date nights.

Twirling the noodles on my fork, I blew on them to cool before putting the food into my mouth. And still managed to burn myself. But I hadn't realized how hungry I was and ate them quickly regardless. The song finished and the news was being reported. Its reader unimaginative and emotionless as he announced world events. How people couldn't get on the property ladder and the chaos of the Middle East. I chose to zone out from it. The news always made me feel a little helpless and I knew I couldn't be helpless any more. Helpless was what kept me with John. So I changed the station, finding BBC Cambridgeshire instead. It was the news again. At least it would be relevant to the area and possibly a little less depressing. I sat down and continued to eat quietly as I listened to the local travel update:

'There are delays to train services out of Cambridge this evening due to an incident that happened approximately three hours ago, which means that services between Cambridge, Peterborough and London are cancelled. If you are travelling this evening, please check before beginning your journey as the lines are closed.'

My fork slipped out of my hand and clattered to the floor. It sounded like there had been a suicide.

Going back to my laptop, my hands shaking, I clicked on Google and typed into the search engine 'train line delays today'. It took me three attempts to spell it correctly as I was panicking, wondering. Could it be him? I clicked on the third link, taking me to the BBC news website. As I scrolled down my worst fears were confirmed. I felt as if my heart was going to explode out of my chest as I tried to read, missing words and confusing the narrative as I'd been temporarily robbed of my ability to focus.

It said there had been an incident involving a man on the line, and there was a fatality involved. There was a link to a police inquiry page. They needed witnesses to identify who the man was. I clicked on it. I was beginning to feel light-headed. There was a description of the man. As I read I thought I was going to throw up. CCTV footage confirmed he was between twenty-five and thirty-five. Around six feet tall. I was convinced it was him until I read he had blond hair.

Scrolling down, there was a grainy picture of the man who they thought had died. I didn't want to look but knew I had to, and relief washed over me with such force I needed to sit on the floor.

It wasn't him. A wave of gratitude followed by another of guilt flooded in. It may not have been Chris, but it was another person, someone like him who had friends and a family who would learn of the tragedy. Regardless, I couldn't help myself in feeling more relieved than guilty.

I curled my knees up to my chest to make myself as small as I could and tried to take calm, measured breaths. Each one becoming more difficult until I began to cry. I had really thought it would be him. That he had done it, and that moment was a kind of pain I would wish on nobody. I didn't ever want to experience it again.

I'd convinced myself that that part of my life was behind me, that I was moving forward reluctantly, even though I knew it wasn't. I knew that he was still there in his house, probably planning his end, and that no one else would stop him. I knew now that I would forever live with the guilt if I didn't try. I had to go back. I had to get him to talk to me. I had to show him another way and part of me was so angry with him for making me have to.

I still had the stone; I would use that as an excuse. After grabbing my car keys and shoes, I texted Nat to say I was going for some drinks with work friends so she didn't worry, and then I left.

I got into my car, put it in gear and, still shaking, I drove.

Chapter 22

Since his fight with Steve, Chris had wanted to call or text to say something. He hated that he'd hurt his friend, who had only ever wanted to help him. He hated that for a moment he could have really hurt him with that knife, even though he had done it for Steve's own good. But if Steve was angry and stayed angry, like the train girl was, it would make the next eight days easier to manage and he could die knowing they would be left alone.

He hadn't been outside since coming back from his night out with Steve. He knew he'd have to soon; he was running out of food. But, following his meeting with Steve and the train girl knocking at his door hours before, he felt increasingly paranoid.

Each time he heard a police car go past he thought it was for him. Every time the postman dropped something through his letter box he thought it was a knock, a detective on the other side ready to ask some questions or tell him his friend had been involved in an incident and the man who killed Julia had attacked Steve or his wife as he said he would if he thought anyone knew anything about that night. But no one came. It meant that somehow, despite having a knife pulled on him, Steve hadn't told anyone.

He lay back on his sofa and looked at his ceiling. Its dated, bobbled Artex looked like tiny upside-down mountain ranges. He let himself imagine they were. And his ceiling was a tiny country full of life. He imagined people eating, sleeping, laughing, making love. Going to work, being born. Dying. He tried to picture where Julia would be and what she would be doing. Would she be with him, would she be with another man, or would she be dead somewhere with no gravestone for people to mourn at?

He started to wonder where her killer would be in this Artex kingdom but stopped himself. He imagined instead the power he could have over him. He could create night and day with a simple flick of a light switch. He could create a devastating tsunami with paint and roller. He could stand up and crush him under his thumb.

Rubbing his eyes, Chris laughed at himself. He knew he was beginning to lose his mind. Hearing something, he suddenly stopped laughing and listened. He thought he heard a tapping from somewhere in the house. He made his way into the kitchen, thinking the sound was coming from the back garden. Then he heard it again.

Chris looked at the clock. It was too late for it to be anyone he knew. He heard it again, louder this time, and quietly, quickly, he took the small knife he had returned to the drawer after Steve left. White-knuckled, he walked into his living room to look out of the bay window to try to make out who it was. The figure on the other side of the glass was one he had come to recognize. Unbelievably, she was back. He ducked down into the shadows, not knowing what to do.

***

Looking at the small object in my hand, the weight of it heavier now than ever before, I knew I had to knock on his door one more time. The object should be reconnected with its owner, well, that was my excuse, but really, I needed to see him. To talk to him. I hoped my returning it would open a conversation, that he wouldn't dismiss me for the third time.

I knew why he was doing it. He was hurting, wounded. I hoped my perseverance would pay off. Standing there, I couldn't help but think of *It's a Wonderful Life*. One of my favourite films. I thought of how the central character, George Bailey, wanted to kill himself because of bad luck in life, because of debt. He was saved by being able to see his future. Maybe Chris was the same, and I could be the one to show him something different. A thought I shook off with a sad smile. Life wasn't like that.

I stepped onto his front lawn and sneaked a look through the window into his lounge. I couldn't see much as the only light was the overspill from a lamp in his hallway, casing his living room in a lifeless glow. As there was no sign of him, I pressed my hands against the glass and took my time looking at his world, trying to see any sign of who he was.

I focused on the walls. There were no pictures but light marked where they must once have hung. There were no plants or personal items of any kind. Just a sparsely decorated space, like a show home. I was starting to think he had left but then I saw a pair of shoes. And immediately I knew they were the same shoes that had sat on the platform.

I knocked once more but still there was no answer. Feeling stupid for driving all that way for no result, I quietly opened the letter box, placed the small black stone inside and closed the lid. The stone dropped off the shelf between my world and his, sounding louder than I hoped as it hit the laminate floor on the other side. It was time to leave and I promised to myself I'd not return.

Once again I was that pathetic girl on the platform being silently pitied by a stranger. Only this time I was the stranger looking in, and seeing me as I was felt disgusting. I couldn't allow myself to feel this way. I couldn't go back to being her.

Only when I had passed his front gate and was on the main footpath did I let my composure slip, just for a second. My chin wobbled, giving my feelings away, followed by a long, shaky intake of air as I fought to hold the sadness that was pushing against the insides of my cheeks, wanting to spill tears.

In the silence between inhaling and exhaling I heard him, a few feet behind me, just behind his door, picking up the stone I had tenderly held, and knowing he wouldn't thank me, I began to walk away. A voice telling me not to look back.

But I did.

Standing in the open doorway of number twenty-nine, the stone cradled in his hands like it was as delicate as a butterfly, stood a barefooted Chris. His unblinking eyes were focused on me. An expression of confusion on his face. He looked like he hadn't slept in days.

Chris didn't hold my gaze for long and instead looked back to his hands, his shoulders rolling in as he did. It made him look young, like a child holding some treasure they had discovered. I stood unmoving, not knowing what would happen next. As he lifted his head once more, I saw an openness in him that I'd not seen before. His eyes, although tired, had a brightness in them. I noticed he had a small scar running from the edge of his right one. I wondered how he had got it.

***

As soon as the stone had dropped through his letter box he knew he couldn't ignore her any more. As he opened the door, she turned. The fruit knife pressed against his forearm, hidden from view. Her arms were crossed, protecting her, and he noticed the goose bumps on her skin.

'Why did you keep this?'

He could see the disbelief in her eyes that he had stepped outside his door. He watched as she forced herself to appear calm, despite her voice giving her away. 'I thought it was important.'

'How could you possibly know that?'

'I don't know, instinct.'

She had said the same thing on the platform. The stone meant something to him; they both knew it.

'Chris, I ... '

He should have told her to go home again. He almost closed his front door, but not quite. Chris had tried to be unkind, tried to make her leave him alone. But perhaps this was the wrong tactic; perhaps he would try the opposite, then, hopefully she would see he was okay and that she could get on with her life. Besides, she had returned his stone. He owed her a small act of kindness.

'How are you getting home?'

Her blood started rushing to her face, brightening her cheeks.

'How are you getting home?' he repeated.

'I drove here.'

He told himself not to be too friendly.

'You look cold.'

'I am.'

'Do you drink tea?'

'Yes.'

'Do you want a cup?'

'No, it's okay. I can buy my own.'

'I wasn't going to offer to buy you one.'

'No?'

'No.' Chris looked at her pointedly, his head tilting to one side.

Looking left and right to make sure they were not being watched, he stepped back into his house and walked towards the kitchen, questioning himself as to what he was doing. He should be kind, yes, but he had invited her in. He hated that he was so weak.

***

In complete disbelief I watched Chris walked away from me, going into the darkness of his house, leaving the door wide open. I didn't know what to think as I watched him walk down his hallway and into what looked like a kitchen. I waited for him to come back, but he didn't. Instead, I could hear a kettle boiling.

I assumed he had invited me in, although in a very odd way. I stepped into his world, closed the door behind me and put my bag on a small table. I could see him, both hands on the sink, his head lowered. It looked like he regretted inviting me in and I wondered if I should politely say I could leave. I dismissed the thought. I wanted to be with him. But I wasn't mentally prepared for it. As always, I assumed the worst.

When I had dreamt of talking with him face to face – after he clearly wouldn't open the door to me – I had imagined that it would one day happen somewhere neutral: a coffee shop, a park, or the train station again. Never had my dreams included being inside his house. So, despite his obvious and unguarded sense of regret, I had to stay.

As I walked into his kitchen neither of us spoke. All I could hear was the ticking of the clock hanging on the wall beside the cooker. Its glass casing cracked through the middle. He handed me a tea and I said thank you. I blew on it, giving me something to do in an attempt to alleviate the tension that I felt by being in his home. Once it was cooled enough I took a sip and tried to think of something to say as the ticking of his wall clock soldiered on.

After handing me the cup, Chris kept his back to me. His hands firmly placed on the sink. White-knuckled. I started to think being in his house was a bad idea and, as I put down my tea to make my excuses, he turned and looked at me. It made me feel like something inside was pressing on my lungs, slowly forcing the air out. I told myself to take a deep breath as he looked away. His focus landed on the side where he had put the stone I had given back to him. He then looked away, his head low, tears silently streaming down his face.

'Chris?'

'Sorry.'

'Don't be. Are you okay?'

'No.'

He looked at me, his eyes sad and low. That one word was so truthful and soul-baring I wanted to cry for him. But I stopped myself. This wasn't about me. This was about him.

***

In that moment Chris wanted to tell her everything. He wanted to talk about how on a wet and windy night nearly a year ago he was forced to watch the love of his life die, while he was helpless to do anything about it.

He wanted to tell her he needed to be able to mourn Julia like a normal husband should mourn a wife. He wanted to tell her that since that night he had been waiting for her killer to come back. But he couldn't. So he said nothing and sipped his tea while the tears fell and the silence hung until Sarah quietly broke it.

'Chris, I'm sorry for swearing at you last time I was here.'

'It's all right.'

'It's not. I was angry but it still didn't give me the right. I just wanted to help.'

'I know.'

'To find out what is going on in your head.'

'I know.'

'But you'll still not tell me?'

'How's your tea?' Chris avoided answering her question.

'Perfect, thank you.'

Sarah turned away from Chris and looked out of the kitchen window – despite it being dark – allowing Chris to watch her. As they stood quietly he couldn't help but notice how nothing of the fragile, petite girl he'd met on the platform actually existed. Before him was a quiet, strong woman, one who was attractive. He felt a pang of something before realizing it was because he was lonely. She must have sensed him staring because she turned and looked at him, a small smile flashing across her lips.

Chris had to look away and distract himself. He shouldn't find her beautiful; he shouldn't let himself feel anything for her. Stepping towards the back door, he picked up his cigarettes.

'I thought you didn't smoke?'

'I thought so too. Want one?'

'Sure.'

He unlocked the door and stepped outside. A warm breeze danced in the trees behind his garden, making it sound like they were by the ocean. Chris closed his eyes for a moment as he was transported to that beach with Julia. When he opened them, Sarah was a few feet away, eye to eye.

'The wind in the branches is one of my favourite sounds.'

'Mine too.'

As he gave Sarah a cigarette their hands touched and, stepping closer, he cupped the lighter to protect the flame from the wind. She placed her hands on his to help. Chris couldn't help but feel something pulling on him. It forced him to take a step back. He lit his cigarette and they smoked in silence, listening to the wind. He watched her close her eyes, and lift her head up, a smile on her lips.

'You know, this is the first time in a long time I've stopped and just enjoyed the sound of a breeze. It feels nice to slow down for a second.'

Chris couldn't help what he did next. The yearning to be close was too powerful to ignore, so he stood beside her, facing the rear of his garden and the tall swaying trees. She rested her head on his shoulder. For a moment the wind stopped and Sarah turned to him. He wrapped her in his arms and they stood silently holding each other and looking at the moonlit trees. Connected by a moment, a coincidence that neither of them could ignore.

Chris knew he wasn't supposed to hug her, and yet, the feel of her warmth close to him and the smell that a woman had were intoxicating. Despite the voice in his head telling him to let go, he couldn't. He thought that maybe if he kept his eyes closed he could pretend, just for a moment, that it was Julia he was holding; although he knew it wasn't. Worryingly, it still felt good, but feeling good wasn't part of his plan.

He wanted to pull away from her but she turned in to him and began to quietly cry against his chest.

Instinctively, he held her tighter and began to stroke her hair whilst gently saying he was sorry. Telling her everything was going to be fine. He didn't know if he was speaking to her or Julia or both.

His lips were so close to her ear he touched it occasionally, causing a surge of heat to flow through his body. Pulling her even closer, he ended up holding the back of her head, pressing her face into his neck where she began to calm herself and breathe at a slower, more controlled rate.

Her tears of relief and anger were slowly being replaced with the anticipation of something else. He shouldn't feel this way, not when he was so close to being reunited with Julia, not when he still loved his wife. But as Sarah's warm breath cooled on his neck it caused a wave of arousal. She angled her neck, inviting him to kiss it. An invitation he accepted, and as he placed his lips on her neck she moaned gently.

He closed his eyes, feeling no memory, no dreams, no past or future. Just his lips on her neck and a stillness as his senses took hold. A stillness he had not experienced for so long. Chris knew he needed to take a step back and stop his impulses. Although his head and heart were telling him to step away and tell her it was all a mistake, his body was saying something entirely different. It was reacting to something that was happening between them, a heat like atoms colliding. No matter how he tried to subdue his primeval impulses, he ached to touch her body, feel her heat, to be inside her.

She moved her hand onto his chest, and felt his heart beating wildly, his breathing jagged and shallow. It felt so good to have a woman touch him, so easy to give in even though he was desperate to resist. Kissing up her neck and towards her ear, he wanted to turn his head and press his lips to hers; but knew he shouldn't. She bit his ear gently and pushed her hips into him, his hardness apparent.

He wanted to grab her arse and pull her harder into him, their intimate areas pressed to one another, but he resisted the growing urge and instead moved his hands onto her hips. It kept her body close, but not touching. As he squeezed them he couldn't help but imagine what her hips looked like. He pictured them jutting out of her petite frame, the bones angled, guiding him between her legs. As he could feel himself getting hotter, he wanted to know what it would feel like between her legs. Putting her other hand behind his head, she pulled on his hair and whispered in his ear.

***

I said I wanted him. I said it to harden him further and release that pent-up sexual frustration I could see he had – that we both had. I expected him to pick me up, my legs wrapping round his waist as he walked towards the house and his stairs, where he would climb as we kissed, his hands holding my thighs until he was in front of his bed.

He would throw me down and take off his top, revealing the well-defined body I knew he was hiding under his T-shirt. I expected I would look up at him and take my jeans off, lifting my hips up to slip them down my thighs, never breaking eye contact until his instincts caused him to look at what was now before him, waiting for him to explore. I expected him to kiss the insides of my thighs, eager to take off my underwear. I expected it because this is what had happened before, with John, with other men.

But that didn't happen. Instead, he pushed me away, my sexual image cracking like heated ice.

'You need to leave.'

'What? Why?'

'This is a mistake. I need you to leave.'

'But, Chris ... '

'Please, get out.'

He turned his back to me and stepped into the house, stopping in the doorway between outside and in. It seemed the conversation was over and I was shocked by the sudden change in his behaviour. I wanted to know his secrets and I knew with certain clarity that if I left now, after what had just happened, I would never see him again. Everything had changed when I stepped over the threshold of his front door, when he pressed his lips on my skin.

'No, Chris, I'm not going.'

He hadn't anticipated I would say that and before he could compose himself I noticed his shock in the way he straightened his back where he stood.

The sinewy muscle in his closest forearm flexed and relaxed, only briefly, but noticeably.

'I said get out.'

He tried to sound forceful, and he did, but in a way it was a strained forcefulness, one that was filled with his uncertainty.

'I'm not leaving.'

***

She had to go. For a second she had reminded him of Julia. She couldn't be here in his home; it was too dangerous. It frightened him. Turning around, he looked at her, unsure of what to do next. Should he be more forceful and try to scare her, or maybe physically remove her? He didn't feel he could act on either option.

Last time he'd tried to scare someone it had ended badly. He didn't want to get into an argument. It was his fault she was in his house in the first place. He still hadn't fully established what she did or didn't know, but it was becoming clearer by the second she didn't know enough to interfere with his plans. Unable to throw her out, he walked into the house, leaving the door open again. That was a mistake.

Sitting on his sofa, Chris put his head into his hands to try to stop himself shaking. He took several deep breaths, losing himself in the rhythm, like he had learnt to do when planning for 5 May.

Once calmer, he began to focus on where he was again and listened to his quiet house, trying to pick up the sound of Sarah, still outside.

He sat upright again and there she was, standing in front of him in his living-room doorway. Her fixed gaze unnerved him. It reminded him of his wedding night. His nerves, her passion. He couldn't help but stare back, like a rabbit in headlights whose frozen expression betrays that the animal understands its fate is about to change.

Without saying anything, Sarah took her jumper off and dropped it. Stepping forward, kicking off her shoes, she pushed Chris back and climbed on top of him.

'I … ' began Chris until Sarah placed her lips on his. Their lips barely touching, her top one between his, he felt a rush run through his face. Pulling away, she focused on his mouth.

He was about to protest, but, as he made eye contact with her, the dark brown in them clearer than he imagined, he was almost sure she understood everything about him, about Julia and about what had happened and what would come. And it was all right. The world stopped moving and it held its breath in anticipation, like it had once before.

He should have been thinking of Julia and he forced himself to, but as his mind began to drift from the reality of Sarah on top of him to the memory of Julia he was forced back by the feeling of Sarah kissing him again, harder, with more desire. Kneeling back so she was upright and straddled across Chris, she took her blouse off, one button at a time, revealing her slim torso. Running across the line of her exposed collarbone was a tattoo of three black waves. So small he almost didn't see them. Leaning forward, he kissed each wave before taking off his T-shirt.

***

His body was less defined and thinner than I had anticipated but still in good shape. As I looked at him, I was drawn to a scar on his right shoulder near his chest. It almost looked like a bullet wound, although not quite. For a moment I wondered if he had been stabbed. I leant in to kiss it, but he gently pulled me away.

I looked back up at his face and noticed he was looking at me differently. He wasn't more relaxed than before but more engaged, more present. Whatever the dark secret was that he held on to so tightly it wasn't with him in that moment. We were just a man and a woman who wanted each other. I could see the lust in his eyes. It made me feel warmer between my legs.

Standing, I took him by the hand and led him towards the stairs. Once we reached the bottom he stepped in front and led me up them without talking. At his bedroom door, he stopped and looked at me.

I watched his tension melt away. He kissed me again, this time harder, and, stepping backwards, he guided me into his room. And gently he laid me on his bed. I reached over him towards the lamp and switched off the only source of light in his room, throwing us into darkness.

Chapter 23

10.45 p.m. – London Road, Peterborough

As he snapped awake, for a moment Chris didn't know where he was and he didn't know what time it was. All he knew was he had slept deeply and dreamt of Julia. This time it was one where she was gently stroking his hair as he saw animals floating in the clouds. They were on Brancaster Beach near Hunstanton.

She turned to kiss him, her hair soft, her lips slightly open and inviting, but cold and blue. Like marble. Then the sand beneath them turned to thick wet mud, slowly swallowing her as he watched helplessly, his feet stuck to the ground with long, thin roots wrapping around his ankles and calves. He tried to fight but the more he fought the quicker she vanished. Her open right eye was the last thing he saw. The image stayed with him for a moment after waking.

Rolling onto his side, Chris expected to see Julia's golden hair close to him on the pillow but the hair he saw was dark brown. He wondered for a second if she had dyed it until his mind was awake enough to know that it wasn't hers at all, but another woman's.

Sitting up, he looked over at the train girl who slept with her back to him, feeling surprisingly unmoved despite his dream. She looked peaceful. In the low light Chris could still see the shape of her face. Her full lips closed and relaxed. Her neck, the artery throbbing on the surface as it pumped blood to her brain, fuelling her dreams.

Reaching over, he stroked it, feeling it pulse with life under his touch. If he pressed down now he would cut the supply. She would pass out quickly. If he continued to press she would be starved of oxygen and within a few minutes she would be dead. He shouldn't have thought it, but it was there in his mind as a clear image. Since Julia was taken from him Chris saw life as a fragile line and on either side death. The line itself being narrow, something easily broken, and, in that instance, that thread was as wide as a blood-pumping artery, and it frightened him to think it.

She mumbled in her sleep, a content soft tone that reminded him again of Julia. Something he loved and hated in equal measure. He slipped out of bed, careful not to disturb her from her content slumber. He couldn't look at her any more. Walking as quietly as he could, he went downstairs to the kitchen. He poured himself a glass of water and sat on the floor, not quite believing what he had done.

He knew that after that night on the platform the train girl was going to change everything he had painfully and patiently planned and he knew it was a mistake to let her into his house. He hated himself for being so weak, but it had happened and he couldn't change that. All he could do now was get rid of her somehow, in a way that wouldn't expose her to any truth or put her in any danger. Racking his brain for a solution to how he should deal with the turn of events that he hadn't anticipated, he looked at the wall clock that ticked the way it always had, the way it always would. He saw the time.

10.47 p.m.

Chris began to laugh quietly to himself. A laugh filled with hate for the clock and its relentless displaying of how time was moving so slowly now that he wanted it to move fast and how it had flown when Julia was alive.

He thought of her smile and the way she held his hand and how both could fill an hour of his day but feel like seconds. He thought of the way she giggled at his jokes and the way she fidgeted in her sleep. He thought of the sound of her begging for her murderer to stop, until she screamed no more, pleaded no more, her eyes wide and knowing before the silence fell.

Standing, to shake the horror of the image, he closed his eyes. It wasn't supposed to be this way. He was supposed to be keeping a low profile until he could complete what he needed to. He wasn't supposed to feel any desire other than the desire for it to be his time to die.

Chris grabbed his keys, went into his garden and walked towards his shed. He needed to hear Julia's voice. Before he unlocked the door he looked to the night sky. He looked to where his two stars should be, but they couldn't be seen.

Chapter 24

10.49 p.m. – Almond Road, Peterborough

Steve hadn't intended to come to Chris's house. He was supposed to be doing some late-night food shopping, but as he drove to the supermarket he felt the urge to check in on the man who had once been his best friend, and somewhere under the depression, still was.

First, he drove past the front of his house slowly. Seeing no movement or lights he drove round to Almond Road – the road that backed onto Chris's garden – and parked. It was dark. Assuming Chris was asleep, Steve was about to leave. But then a kitchen light was thrown on and Steve could see movement coming from Chris's kitchen through a gap in the old fence. He got out of his car, ran to the back fence, crouched down and hid in the shadows. Looking through a gap in the wood panels into the garden, Steve saw Chris outside in just his underwear.

He watched as Chris looked up to the sky and then winced as he rubbed his right shoulder. After a few seconds of rubbing and then shaking out his right hand, as if he had pins and needles, Chris walked towards his shed. Steve watched his friend look around, almost as if to make sure he wasn't being watched, before unlocking the shed door and stepping inside, closing it behind him. It confused him. What was he up to? Where had that scar come from and why didn't he tell him about it? Chris usually told Steve everything. His silence felt like another lie.

As Steve made his way to his car he couldn't help wondering what he had just seen and what he knew. Chris had become a drinker, a violent one, and now he was making late-night visits to his shed. There was something not right about this situation.

Chris wasn't moving like a man who was depressed. He was moving like a man who was hiding something.

Chapter 25

7 days left

6.31 a.m. – London Road, Peterborough

It was the second time I had woken up in his bed and for the second time he wasn't beside me.

The first time I woke it was the middle of the night, the noise of a creaky door stirring me from my peaceful dreams. For a moment I assumed it was Natalie leaving for work. It took me a second to remember where I was and that it wasn't Natalie at all. I looked to my left and he wasn't in bed with me, an empty space where he should have been. I assumed that he had gone to the toilet and, stretching, I smiled, feeling satisfied.

Sex with Chris hadn't been what I expected. I thought it would be disconnected, rough even. Like it was with John. But it was anything but that. It was soft, tender, caring. He wanted to please me; he was unselfish. It felt as if our bodies were a perfect fit for each other.

I heard a noise coming from outside and, getting out of his bed, I found my clothes and put them on, wondering how much longer he was going to be in the toilet, if that was even where he had gone. The noise sounded like someone was in his garden. I pulled back the curtain to see outside. In the darkness I could just make out the shape of him near an old shed, almost hidden among the overgrown trees and weeds.

It looked like he was trying to find something. He kept scanning from his left to right and then he looked up towards me. I froze, unsure if he could make me out in the darkness. He stayed looking up at me for a few seconds before turning to open the shed door. Just as he stepped in, he looked back once more. My eyes had now adjusted to the night and I could see him trying to work out if I was there, but I realized he was unable to see me. Once again, I wondered what his secrets were and if some answers were in that shed; maybe there was something I could use to help him.

Twenty or so minutes after he went inside he stepped back out. He looked sad, beaten. He started making his way back to the house. I didn't want him to know I had been watching so as quickly as I could I took my clothes off and put them back where they had been, scattered on his floor like before. I climbed under the covers and pretended to be asleep.

As he climbed back into bed he smelt like soil. I stayed awake, listening to him breathe as he slept. Feeling his chest rise up and down against my hand that rested on it. Wondering what was happening in his dreams. It had taken me two hours to fall back to sleep and now, waking up properly, I realized I was feeling sick from tiredness.

Grabbing my phone, I looked at the time. There were three missed calls from Natalie and a text. I opened it up. She had sent it just before 5 a.m.

'*Sarah, where the bloody hell are you? George and I are worried.*'

I knew she would be beyond worried now. She would be pissed off. I texted her back saying everything was okay and I was on my way home. I needed to get up anyway. It was a long drive back to Cambridge and the A14 was notoriously shit during rush hour.

After putting my clothes on, I looked at myself in the mirror that covered a wardrobe door. I hadn't noticed it the night before. I hoped he couldn't see us in it. My hair looked wild, post-sex wild, and I assumed he wouldn't have hair straighteners anywhere. I hoped I was lucky enough to miss most of the traffic so I could nip home for a shower before work. Otherwise it was the dreaded walk of shame into the office.

Once dressed I called his name. The house was eerily quiet. I called again and headed for the stairs and still nothing. Going into the bathroom, I went to the toilet and washed my face. I noticed that the sealant around the basin was damaged and a narrow gap sat between the sink and wall. The wall itself was damaged also, like something had been hanging and had been pulled off. I assumed it was a cabinet.

Plaster and paint missing, exposing wall plugs where screws would sit. The rest of the bathroom was tidy, but the sink and missing cabinet said something. The damage reminded me of my first boyfriend. He would lose his temper and break whatever was in his way. Then, feeling ashamed and embarrassed, he would clean it up. But the scars of his blinded violence remained. I didn't see Chris having such a temper. There must be another explanation. Quietly, I left the bathroom and walked downstairs into his kitchen. I saw the two cups washed and on the draining board from the night before, but no sign of him. I walked into his lounge. He wasn't there.

There was a picture frame sitting on a small table beside his sofa. I picked it up and in it was him with another man and woman, all three of them arm in arm. Smiling, happy. Putting the picture down, making sure it was in exactly the same place, I walked from the lounge into the hallway, calling his name. My phone pinged in my hand. It was a text from Nat.

'You better have a bloody good reason for not coming home and not telling me!'

I did have a good reason, but I knew what she would do if I told her. She would go ballistic. The idea of lying didn't feel right, but I wasn't sure if I had a choice. I messaged back to say I would tell her everything later.

I called out again: still no response. I was alone in his house. I remembered him in the garden in the middle of the night and walked towards his back door. The keys were in it. Calling out again with no reply I unlocked it and stepped outside.

I'm not exactly green-fingered but even I could see that weeds were taking over what was probably once a beautiful small garden. I could see a bench half hidden behind a bush and walked towards it. It made me think of that night, his sadness, his note. I daren't sit down. I could see the grass had been trodden down to make a path leading towards the shed he was in the night before and I walked towards it.

I tried to open the door but it was locked. Whatever was in there I wasn't going to see it without a key. Walking back towards the house, I jumped when I looked up and saw him standing in the doorway. The bag that I had left by the front door was in his hands. His expression was hard to read.

'What are you doing?'

'I was just getting some fresh air,' I lied. I don't know why I lied, but I felt if I said I had seen him in his shed he might throw me out. He seemed to believe me.

'Coffee?'

'I really have to get going. I've got work.'

'I see, well let me make you one for the road.'

Chris put my bag on the kitchen side and made me a coffee in silence. He told me to take the mug to drink on my drive back, saying I could return it next time we saw one another. I felt my heart beat a little faster. He wanted to see me again. I mattered to him. And then I knew what I should have known all along. My desire, my obsession with him wasn't just about saving his life. Of course, I wanted to help, but it was something deeper. That night on the platform I felt something I couldn't explain, but now I could. It was like electricity. It jolted me into existing in the present. He had restarted a part of me that John had almost killed. The long nights waiting at the train station platform and door rejections were beginning to feel worth it. As I left I wanted to give him a kiss, but lost my nerve. Instead I asked for his phone. He handed it to me and I put my number in.

'So you don't lose it and forget me.'

I thought I had said something wrong for a second because he registered a shocked look but it quickly turned into a smile.

'I don't know how that would be remotely possible.'

I smiled back at him before thanking him for the coffee, grabbing my bag and getting into my car to go to work.

***

As soon as the door was closed and Sarah was gone, Chris went into his kitchen to check the shed key was still in its place. It was. He walked into his back garden, noticing the fresh footprints in the grass she had caused. There was no sign of any damage. She hadn't been inside. But still, she knew something was there. She must have seen him in the night. He was getting sloppy. He didn't want her in his life.

He poured himself some bourbon and, swilling it in the glass, he realized that despite how he hadn't grown to love the taste, he couldn't wait for the effects caused by drinking it to kick in. It was barely 7 a.m. as he washed the first glass down and, as it burnt its way down his throat, he knew that his once only constant that was time now had a friend. Time and alcohol, arm in arm, until he finished what he started weeks before. He looked at his phone and her number. He couldn't believe she had used the same words as his wife had when they first met. He thought of that night again, him standing in the rain, his jacket over her head as she climbed into the taxi. Him leaning through the window to give her a kiss as the rain ran down the back of his neck. He shook the memory off. It hurt too much.

Saving her number as 'Train Girl', just in case, he put his phone down and poured himself another drink, looking towards his shed as he did. A wave of guilt at his betrayal washed over him. He had slept with a woman who wasn't his wife. He went upstairs and changed his bed sheets. He hoped she wasn't stupid enough to come back to his house. He hoped she would get the message he wasn't interested when he didn't call. He hoped she wouldn't try to learn any more about him and the contents of his shed. For her sake.

Chapter 26

It took me a while to find my keys and unlock the front door and, as I finally wrestled them out of my bag, Natalie had already opened it. She looked at me in the way she did when she disapproved, arms crossed and eyes narrow. She took a step back, allowing me in, and shut the door.

I wanted nothing else than to get a cup of tea, maybe a piece of toast and go to bed. A full day of managing accounts after a night with barely any sleep had made me feel unwell but I knew she wasn't going to let me off the hook. I walked into the kitchen and flicked on the kettle.

'So, are you going to tell me where you were last night?'

I should have told her I had been back to see Chris, to give him the stone. But I didn't.

'I told you, I went out with work friends.'

'Sarah!'

'I got drunk, crashed on a friend's couch. I'm sorry, I should have texted.'

'What friend?'

'Just a friend.'

'You were with John, weren't you?'

I hesitated before answering. She had given me a get-out clause. And I was more than prepared to take it.

'Fine. Yes.'

'Sarah!'

'I know, I know. I was out and he saw me and he sounded like he had changed.'

It frightened me how easy it was to lie to my sister.

'I didn't intend to stay. But we talked and talked, and before I knew it, it was early hours. So I stayed.'

'Did you even make it to work today?'

'What is that supposed to mean?'

'It means when you're with him you ... '

'Natalie. Let it go.'

'No, I don't like who you are when you're with him. So, did you go to work?'

'Of course I did. I'm not stupid.'

'Again – not stupid again.'

'When will you ever let that go? So I lost my job once. Big deal, Nat, we all do at some point.'

'I haven't, and not everyone turns up to work pissed from the night before, Sarah.'

'Please, Natalie.'

'That job was the best job you ever had, and you ruined it for yourself.'

'Nat.'

'You decided to go out the day before the owners were visiting. You decided, with John, to get wrecked when you should have been at home. You made those choices, Sarah. And then you turned up to work, pissed.'

'Nat, please.'

'So I think I'm entitled to ask if you went to work; George and I can't afford to carry you again if you cock it up for yourself.'

'Nat, please, I get it.'

My plea worked and I watched my sister take a deep breath, calming herself.

'Good. You need to know, I don't approve.'

'I know.'

'He's bad for you.'

'Please.'

'Look, I just don't want to see you get hurt again.'

'I know, thank you.'

'Do you really think he's changed?'

'I don't know, but it's okay. I've changed; I'm tougher.'

'If you're tougher why go back?'

'Because I still love him.'

Saying it out loud felt strange. When a man holds your soul for so long it's tough to shake it free. I didn't want to talk about John any more, just saying his name made me feel uneasy. I offered her a tea as a way to change the subject. Natalie knew what I was doing but allowed it. For now, she was satisfied.

It felt awful to keep secrets from my sister. I didn't know how she would react if I said I had been with Chris. I'm sure it wouldn't have been as easy.

It was shit of me to lie, but I now had an alibi if Chris ever messaged or called. I could go to his and say I was seeing John, knowing Natalie wouldn't suspect anything. She'd just be disappointed in me for being weak. But I knew I wasn't weak, I was strong. I knew being around him might be tough, and sometimes heartbreaking, but I was going to find out what his secret was and show him a way to be happy again. Then I would tell Natalie. She would be angry with me for lying, but then, she would see my courage to do what I needed to. She would see, as I see, that Chris is a good man.

We had our tea and talked about our days, then George came home and they had dinner together. Giving me the excuse to go to my room. As I said goodnight, Natalie gave me a look as if to say: *I hope you know what you are doing*. It meant she wasn't going to tell George, which was good. He didn't like John very much and would no doubt try to talk me out of seeing him. She was giving me the benefit of the doubt. A free ticket, for now. It made me feel even guiltier. I tried to reassure her with a kiss on the head before going up.

Once in my room, I walked towards my curtains to close them. Looking outside, I saw someone on the street: a man. Looking my way. I couldn't see his face as the evening sun was behind him, making him a silhouette, but no sooner had I noticed him than he turned and walked away quickly. I closed my curtains and climbed into bed, spending the rest of the night trying to sleep, hoping for a message from Chris.

Chapter 27

Julia's diary – November 2013

I have never felt so lost as I have in the last month. It's like a giant shadow has been cast wherever I stand that leaves me cold and alone. I don't even feel like I should write anything down but he suggested it might do me some good to talk about how I'm feeling, despite being unable to talk about it with him. He's even given me some space and is waiting in the car for me. He told me I'd not written in my diary for months and today would be a good day to restart.

Perhaps it's being here at Mum's that has finally allowed me to let myself feel something. So, here I am, listening to the rain beat down on my mum's kitchen window, feeling guilty because I'm relieved that she is gone. Over the past year she deteriorated fast and all but lost who she was. In the times she was with us I could see she wanted to die. Seeing that look in someone you love is so painful. I can't put it into words other than to say it's like my blood cried.

I want to tell Chris about how I am feeling but I don't think he'll understand, despite me knowing he would try to. I feel like it would make my guilt worse.

We came here so I could grab the last few things before going to the estate agent and putting Mum's house on the market. It is far too big for me and, besides, it was her house, not mine. But I can't sell it. I knew as soon as we got here it would break my heart. I worry that when I leave I'll lose her too. Which, even as I write it, I know is silly. A person isn't tied to a house. It's just a house. Just bricks and mortar. It's not like I even grew up here. She bought it when I was twenty and moving in with a friend. Yet, I can't bear to say goodbye to it.

I spoke to Chris about all of this and he said that I need not rush, that the house wasn't going anywhere and wouldn't cost much if it sat empty for a while. I told him that if we sold it quickly we could use that money to go towards our wedding and honeymoon. He said money wasn't everything. He said that some things are much more valuable. He said that one day it might feel right, and until that day, I shouldn't force it. I don't know how, but he always finds a way to settle me. So, it's not a goodbye, not yet.

Mum's funeral was last week. A small but nice service, if you can call burying someone you love nice. She had a few friends there. Rita, who I called Aunty, even though we weren't related. I'd not seen her in years. Maureen from her old job and June who Mum met at church. They knew it was going to be a quiet service so they brought along their husbands who were polite and kind but not emotionally connected.

A few people from work – Susan, Helen and James – said they would be there if I needed them but I told them it wasn't necessary. It was nice of them to offer though. I am lucky that I've got such sympathetic colleagues. Especially James, my boss. He's been really understanding with my workload, ensuring I'm supported and not taking on too much. Throughout this time, he's become a friend when I've needed one. An ear to bend. He even picks me up and drops me off so I don't have to get the bus. With everything that has been going on recently and how busy life is, sometimes he feels like the only friend I have, besides Chris, of course.

Chris came with me and I held his hand tight when the pallbearers – six professionals who were not family – carried my mum into the crematorium. She had always said she didn't want to be buried, just in case. I cried into Chris's shoulder when they played her last musical request: Canon in D.

As people left I was so sad she was gone and even sadder that she only had a handful of people come and say goodbye. The only thing I could take solace in was the fact that at least she knew I was going to be married.

We told her when she was in hospital. She had been there for a week and she was bad. Morphine given throughout the day to help manage her pain as her body began shutting down. It meant most of the time when we visited she wasn't really with us but off in a pain-free dementia dream. But the day we told her we were going to get married I could see in her eyes she was there. And she was happy. I know remembering that will help me walk down the aisle on the day. My mum, smiling because I was going to be a bride.

On the night she died I told her how Chris proposed to me on the River Nene. We go there often. It's close to home but far enough away that you feel like you're somewhere else. We walked along the river, over the small stone bridges that line it, watching the birds fly. There is this one bridge – it's about a mile away from the city centre so the parkway traffic is barely a hum. It had been raining, but the clouds were still thick and laden, like it might start again at any moment.

I love the rain. Mum and I used to sit in the back doorway during storms in the summer. She told me her and Dad used to do it all the time when they were young. I like to think Chris waited for a wet day. I like to think he knows it meant a lot to me.

Anyway, we were on the bridge watching fat droplets run from the branches of trees and drip into the river when I pointed out a grey heron tiptoeing from the banks. He told me there was a nest there every spring. He then told me about their feeding and mating and migration habits. A keen ornithologist. Even after two years he still manages to surprise me.

I watched him as he observed the giant grey bird, seeing the same expression I saw with the seagull on the beach from when we were first dating, and he turned to me and told me that recently he had reconsidered time, and how it's something to not take for granted. And then he got on one knee and asked me to be his wife.

I like to think that knowing I was going to be a bride helped Mum feel at peace and ended her own suffering.

I miss her. I miss her so much and I'm so glad I don't have to face this alone. I'm so glad he is with me, waiting in the car. I'm not sure how I would cope without him …

Chapter 28

10.33 a.m. – St Luke's Street, Cambridge

I really thought after our night together he would message. And, stupidly, when he didn't, I messaged him. Just to say thank you for a nice night. He hadn't replied and that usually meant they weren't interested. But I didn't get that feeling with him. I felt like he wanted me there. Even needed me there with him. And he had said I could return the cup next time we saw each other.

I was starting to worry something had happened and looked at the obituaries in the back of the local paper, just once. I stopped. Telling myself I was being silly. Jane, who sits opposite me and eats too loudly, caught me reading the pages and I could see she thought someone I cared for had passed. She smiled meekly and gave me a wide berth afterwards. People don't know how to be around others who are going through grief. It's treated like a disease that should be avoided.

I had thought of paying Chris another visit but it felt too invasive. Still, I needed to know if he was okay. So, sitting at my desk with a mountain of work and no motivation, I googled his name. Nothing came up.

Making sure I wasn't being watched by one of the bosses I might someday be, I logged on to Facebook and typed in Chris Hayes. There were several hits and, as I scrolled down, I recognized his picture. It was the same one I saw in his living room. It made me feel sad for him. His profile was secret so I couldn't look at any pictures or wall posts. But, as I hovered my cursor over the picture, it showed that the other man was tagged. Steve Patterson.

I clicked on his page and it wasn't hidden. I could see his photos. I could read his posts. I didn't delve too deep into this stranger's online world, but from what I could see he and Chris were close. There were also two women: first the blonde. She only popped up in a few of his pictures, always with Chris and Steve together. Then a beautiful Mediterranean lady who made me feel a twinge of jealousy. Her smile perfect in every picture. Her gaze one of someone who didn't have a care in the world. She and Steve were married. The wedding picture he had used as his profile was stunning.

I clicked on the wedding photo album. I could see Chris wearing a top hat and tails. Looking healthy. Looking strong. Attractive. I zoomed in on one of them and looked at his smile. The blonde was also in a few of them. They were dancing together, drunk and happy. I couldn't look any more.

I knew I had to message Steve. Not because of the night I had with Chris, but because I was worried for him. I had got close to him, but, he still hadn't reached out, he still hadn't shared his pain, and I felt the need to do something to help that happen. Messaging Steve would make me look like a crazy lady who after a one-night stand had fallen for Chris. But, knowing what I knew about him, I needed to, however it would appear. I rationalized that messaging his friend through Facebook was less stalker-ish than turning up at his house uninvited. I knew I'd done it three times already. But now we'd had sex, it felt different.

So I drafted a message. Telling him I was a new friend of Chris's and I couldn't get hold of him. Asking if he knew whether Chris was okay. I hovered the cursor over the send button, wondering if sending it was a stupid, childish thing to do. But I had to know. So I closed my eyes and clicked the mouse. Then I tried to get on with my work. Less than an hour later, a reply popped into my inbox.

Chapter 29

1.11 p.m. – Somewhere along the A605

As he made the eighteen-mile drive from his house towards March train station, Chris tried to manage the growing anxiety he felt in his stomach, and he was failing. Each mile passed, the knot inside doubled in size, until he could feel its twine pressing on his diaphragm. It was the same drive he had made in the pouring rain eleven months before. He knew he wasn't going to stop. He was just going to slow a little as he passed, get to the next roundabout, turn, and drive past again on his way home. Drawing no attention to himself. That night it was raining hard but now the sun was out making the road look entirely different. With the road being one that cut through the Fens, he could see for a few miles ahead, and that meant he didn't need to concentrate as hard as he would driving through a city. He noticed a small chip in his windshield but didn't know how it came to be. He didn't see the point in replacing it, soon it wouldn't matter if it became a crack. Besides, he didn't want to replace a window in his car for the second time in a year. Of course, the first time wasn't due to a chip. The first time the window had been broken by the man who attacked Julia, moments before she died. Chris remembered how he had to clear her blood from the car so no questions would be asked when he took it to the garage. His heart pounding, waiting for them to notice something odd. Of course, they didn't.

Up ahead, Chris saw the tree he came to see and forgot about that day in the garage. He was moving towards it on the other side of the road. It was magnificent and tall, leaves in full display, casting shadows over the road. As he drew level with it he looked behind. There were no cars following so he slowed to a crawl. The grass was long, untouched. The wild flowers showing beautiful soft colours. It seemed the flowers near to the tree were brighter than others that lined the road. For a second he wondered if any of their colour was because of her and that memory of them underneath it. Him holding her head in his hands, stroking her hair. Neither speaking. Neither needing to.

Passing the tree, he drove a mile to the next roundabout and turned back on himself to see the tree again before heading home. His mind once again drifted to the memory of that moment and as it was about to take hold he shook it off. He wasn't strong enough for that one. Not yet. He did it just in time to swerve and miss an oncoming lorry, its horn blaring and the driver shouting obscenities.

He tried to mouth a sorry but it had already passed. Looking in his rear-view mirror he watched it drive away. Then he caught himself in the mirror, just his left eye. Easing off the accelerator, he leant forward to see himself fully. His hair was cleaner this time but messy. His beard longer. He looked cornered, defensive. Focusing back on the road with his heart racing, he continued on his drive home. His only thoughts on the tarmac in front of him, mile after mile, until it was interrupted by his phone buzzing in his pocket. He pulled it out and looked at the screen. He was shocked to see it was a message from Steve.

'I don't want to call, because quite frankly I don't know how to talk to you at the moment. But your lady friend Sarah messaged me. I don't think you shagging another woman is a good idea.'

Chris messaged back five short sharp words.

'What have you talked about?'

The reply was instant.

'Nothing … '

***

That was a lie. Steve had told Sarah about Chris's wife and how she had left nearly a year ago. So she shouldn't be offended if Chris didn't message quickly. Or if he backed away. When she probed a little deeper, he told her his wife's mum had died and she couldn't cope so left one day. The simple note she'd left contained no apology, no warning. She just left.

He'd told her that he was worried about his best friend's mental health and that he was a little worried about others being around him, people like her. Chris was unpredictable, even before their fight. She insisted she had it under control and he asked that if she did see Chris, would she keep him in the loop. Something that she had agreed to.

***

Steve messaged Chris again.

'Are you going to see her again?'

Chris's initial reaction was no, she was just a one-night stand; but she had found an unlocked back door into his world and it limited his options. He could cut Steve out of his life – he had managed successfully so far – but she was more difficult to shake. If he ignored her, she would continue talking with Steve and questions would be asked. He could tell her to leave him alone, but somehow he knew she wouldn't, and questions would still be asked. He could get Steve to tell her to go, but then, again, questions would follow.

Questions meant having to give answers, which could expose the gaps in his progressively delicate plans. He couldn't let that slip now. There was only one thing he could do to make sure he was in charge.

He had to keep her close to keep both her and Steve quiet.

'Yes.'

Chris felt as if he was about to pass out so stopped the car. He needed air badly and, getting out, he took deep, measured breaths, trying to calm his heart rate, to get it back down to a normal level. It took him ten minutes to feel like he could drive again. As he sat behind the wheel once more and put the car in gear he tried to figure out what he was going to do.

Once home, he stepped into his quiet house, grabbed a beer, opened the back door and sat by it. He thought about going to the toolbox. He hesitated. Now was not the time to be lost in his past. He needed to focus on the immediate future. It saddened him to know that for the final few days he might not have a chance to hear his wife's voice.

Taking a sip of his beer, Chris closed his eyes. He tilted his head back and felt the summer sun warm on his skin. He tried to calm his chaotic mind. Knowing that after he sent the text he had to send, everything would become so much more complicated. 'Okay, Chris, what the fuck are you going to do?'

He thought about the facts. Julia had been killed; Steve didn't know and believed she was in Australia, but Chris knew he was getting suspicious. If he found out Julia had died, he would also know what Chris was planning. And Sarah knew he wanted to kill himself but probably believed she was changing that. If the dots were connected there was every chance his plan would fail and they would end up in danger. The killer was still out there. Steve and the train girl therefore couldn't speak to each other again and he had to find a way to make sure this didn't happen.

He took his phone out and scrolled to her number.

'Hi, sorry it's been a few days. I've been swamped with work. I was wondering if you wanted to do something tomorrow. I hope you're good.'

After hitting send he cursed himself and took another mouthful of beer, a large one. Half the bottle was already gone. He threw his head back to drink quicker. He saw a spider's web neatly constructed between the outside wall of his house and the back porch light. Tucked up in the dark corner was a small black blob, the spider, quietly waiting for dusk to fall and the outside light to come on. Chris couldn't help but marvel at the little arachnid's ingenuity. Somehow it knew that small insects were attracted to the light created by his porch bulb and it had built its trap exactly where it would work.

It made him think about how these tiny creatures were losing their natural habitat as their worlds were being replaced with concrete, but still they managed to overcome and even thrive. Before finishing his beer, he couldn't help but raise his bottle to the black blob, in awe of its strength.

Chapter 30

3.03 p.m. – St Luke's Street, Cambridge

I was sitting at my desk when my phone pinged, telling me I had a message. I hoped it was from him but assumed it was probably Nat. So when I opened it and it was from an unknown number my heart skipped a beat.

It didn't say much, or who it was from, but I knew it was him. I wanted to tell him I could come and see him in a few hours, after work, but I needed to play it cool. Jane, who had been keeping an eagle eye on me recently, saw me smile.

'It's nice to see you happy,' she said, meaning well.

But it highlighted that perhaps for the past few weeks, perhaps even years, I'd not been. I thanked her and returned to my computer screen. Not being able to focus on anything other than how to respond, I felt like I was in secondary school again, all nervous about how to respond to a boy. I wasn't good at this whole playing it cool thing. My heart was always on my sleeve. Every now and then I picked up my phone, rereading the message to see if there was anything in it that suggested he had feelings for me.

I wrote a text message back. *'I'd love to see you. Are you free later?'* But before pressing send I deleted it.

You can't say love in a text. It was too easy to read into. Keep it neutral, clean. I had no idea what to write. So wrapped up in how to construct one sentence, I hadn't noticed Jane, who had been watching me the whole time.

'Sarah, you want my advice?'

'Advice?'

'About your man issues.'

I laughed. She was good.

'Make him sweat a little.'

'Really?'

'Yes. What has he said?'

'He's asked when I'm free.'

'When are you free?'

'Now, today, this evening.'

'Oh God no, that will make you appear desperate.'

'Will it?'

'Yes, Sarah – didn't anyone teach you these things?'

'No.'

'Do you like him?'

'Yes.'

'Then make him wait. Make him the desperate one. Say you're busy tomorrow, but maybe the day after.'

'But what if he doesn't become desperate?'

'Oh, sweet, they all do. Men like to sweat a little, feel unsure. Like you're a game he must win.'

'Really?'

'Of course. It's that whole hunter-gatherer thing they all have. So give it a few days, make him feel like he's honoured to have time with you.'

'Are you sure?'

'It's always worked with me. How do you think I bagged a husband like mine?'

I laughed out loud, causing a few in the office to turn and look at me.

'Okay, I'm busy tomorrow but maybe the day after.'

'Yep.'

I drafted it, word for word what Jane said, and hovered over the send button. 'Do I put a kiss?'

'If you must, but only one.'

'Okay, one kiss – thanks, Jane.'

I hit send; it was gone. A few minutes later, he replied, the phone's ping making me jump.

'He's messaged back already.'

'Of course he has. He's now in hunter mode. What's he said?'

'Just one word: great.'

And it was. I couldn't wait to see him again.

Chapter 31

Chris grabbed a fresh beer and returned to his lonely chair by his back door. As he sat down, his phone lit up, saying Sarah had replied. Putting his bare feet on the wall, he thought of how he would play the next few days. He knew he needed to use her affections towards him against her. Keep her blinded. Keep control. It was the only way to keep her safe. He had to make sure nothing got in his way when he stepped onto the station platform in five days' time. Just five short days, and yet, it felt like a lifetime away.

He opened the message. She was playing it cool. Making him wait was a good thing. It meant she would start to be consumed by him. Think of little else. He replied. One word. But enough to keep the hooks in.

Putting his phone down, he looked at the spider again. It seemed so patient and calm. Waiting for the moment when there was a vibration on its web before it pounced with a viciousness humans couldn't compete with. It was perfect. In control. He knew he needed to become more like the spider. He had spun his web, and was about to entrap. He would wrap her in him, binding her from interfering until the day he could climb off the delicate silk thread and under a cargo train. Admittedly, it would damage her more this way than if he had just killed himself on the fifth, but that didn't matter any more. It would keep her from a worse fate.

Standing, he flicked the edge of the web and the spider reacted, becoming poised and alert, but then it didn't move. It knew it was being teased. Clever little thing. He grabbed it and pulled it off. Holding it in his hands, and keeping still, it remained passive. Assessing him and its situation. Processing its next move. Chris flicked it and it threw two of its legs in the air, warning him off. It was a brave little thing.

After a few moments it lowered its legs but Chris could see it was still very alert to him and what he would do next. It remained still until Chris grabbed one of its legs. It began fighting for freedom and, as it did, Chris pulled. Tearing it away from the arachnid's body. It tried to escape but Chris didn't let it; he watched it squirm. Watched it fight as he pulled another leg, then another, until all eight sat in his hand like fine dark hairs. Its black body no longer fighting.

Chapter 32

4 days left

10.15 a.m. – London Road, Peterborough

Steve kept his car in third gear to keep the revs low and the engine quiet as he slowed down past Chris's house, he and Kristy trying to get a look inside. They couldn't see anything; the curtains were closed. Whatever he was doing, he was doing it in the dark.

'Steve, why are we kerb-crawling past his house?'

'I just want to see if he's okay. His curtains are still shut.'

'Why don't you just go and knock on his door?'

'Because I don't just turn up at his house; he knows that. Besides, if I do he'll know I'm on to him and that will make it even harder.'

'On to him?'

'He's acting really strange, Kristy.'

'His wife left him. You said he's depressed; that's understandable.'

'It's not that.'

'Of course it is. Julia up and left him and he's not had closure from it.'

'It's not that.'

'Well what is it then?'

Checking his rear-view mirror to make sure he was far enough down the road to not be seen, Steve parked his car and turned off the engine. As he spoke with Kristy, he kept his eyes on the mirror and behind. From where they were he could just about see the bay window of Chris's lounge.

'A few nights ago I came and parked behind his house.'

'Oh God, Steve, why?'

'To watch him. I'm telling you something's going on.'

'Steve, you're reading too much into this.'

'He was acting like he was hiding something.'

'What could he be possibly hiding?'

'I don't know.'

'Have you tried talking to him?'

'Of course I have. And the work thing? Him lying about it?'

'He just doesn't want to worry anyone and maybe he's embarrassed by it.'

Steve looked away from the mirror and into his wife's eyes. He could tell she was humouring his little secret spy moment.

'I don't know. It's weird. He's not been there since Julia left. Have you really thought about it? Julia, Chris's Julia, just leaving with no indication if she would come back? Not even saying goodbye to

241

anyone before she went? She never struck me as the sort to be so cold.'

'Her mum's death hit her pretty hard.'

'I know, but still. Don't you think it's a little weird?'

'Of course I do, who wouldn't?'

'Something isn't making sense.'

'Sometimes you just don't really know a person.'

'I guess.'

'As for Chris, give him a little more time. He'll come around and then be mortified he hit you.'

'I'm not so sure. He's reminding me more and more of the twenty-two-year-old version – getting into trouble.'

Kristy reached over and rubbed the back of Steve's head, trying to knead out the tension she could see in his muscles.

'And if he does get himself into trouble, you'll be there to sort him out again, because you're a good friend.'

'Okay, honey, you're right. It's just … I've known him for most of my life. I've always been able to read him. Now I can't. These past few months he's become a different man.'

Steve knew in his gut something was not quite right. Something was amiss. And although he couldn't say anything to his exasperated wife, he couldn't shake off the idea it had something to do with Julia.

He looked once more in his rear-view mirror. He saw the curtains in the living room twitch, and it felt like Chris had been watching. For the first time in their friendship Steve questioned whether or not Chris could be trusted. If he could lie about his work commitments, what else was he lying about?

'Can we go shopping now, Steve?'

'Of course, love, sorry.'

'It's okay. What are you going to do?'

'About Chris? I don't know.'

He did know what he was going to do. He didn't want to tell Kristy as she would be mad. He was going to try to find Julia. After she left Chris he promised not to talk with her, to give her the space she needed and Steve didn't make promises lightly. Chris told Steve how Julia had blocked him from her Facebook account and in turn Steve had done the same. As far as he was concerned, he no longer had a friendship with his best mate's wife and had no intention of talking with her again. However, that was then. Things were far worse than he imagined they would get, and he needed to act. He would start by ringing the number he had for her. If he couldn't reach her there, he was going to ring her work, see if they had a number in Australia for her. Something was telling him he might not have the whole story about what went on between them.

Chapter 33

3 days left

7.09 p.m. – London Road, Peterborough

Using my phone's camera as a mirror I made sure I looked all right one final time before getting out of my car. I looked anxious. I'd been to his front door a few times now but this time was different. I was no longer turning up unannounced. He had invited me to come.

Before leaving, Natalie had said I wasn't looking well, that I was washed out. Great. Just when I needed to feel sexy I was being told I looked like I might collapse. Stupidly, I'd told Natalie I was just nervous and she looked at me questioningly. *Nervous about seeing John?* I could hear her think. I didn't wait for her to say it out loud and went to my room to grab my bag. When I came back downstairs, Natalie was standing, arms crossed, watching me.

'Sarah, what's going on?'

'What do you mean?'

'I mean this: look at you; you're a wreck. Are you and John okay?'

'We're fine.'

'You know I'm not happy about this, right?'

'I know. You've made it quite clear. Don't worry.'

'Just ... be careful.'

She gave me a kiss on the cheek and disappeared into the lounge to join George. As I left, he shouted for me to have a good time. She still hadn't said anything to him.

After getting out of my car, I adjusted my jeans, smoothed down my top and, faking confidence, I walked to his front door. Hesitating before knocking. *This is it,* I thought. Although I still wasn't sure what 'it' was.

***

He heard three gentle taps on his front door. The first being quieter than the other two, it told him she was nervous. Perfect. A nervous woman was a woman who couldn't think clearly – exactly what he needed her to be. He waited. Wondering how long she would wait before she knocked again. Counting in his head, he made it to thirty-eight before she did, more hesitantly.

He heard her call his name and for a second he felt sorry for her. She wasn't supposed to end up in his mess. But she had forced herself into his world. He had no choice but to use her, knowing it would hurt her once everything was done.

She called his name again, quieter this time, more unsure. Chris unlocked the door, smiling warmly at her.

'Sorry, I didn't hear the door.'

'It's okay.'

'You look lovely.' He saw her cheeks redden slightly as the blood rushed around her face.

'Thanks.'

'Come in.'

As Sarah stepped past Chris, she touched him on his shoulder, too close to his scar for Chris's liking. It made him flinch, but not enough for her to notice. Checking the street to make sure they weren't being watched, he closed and locked the door behind them.

***

He told me to make myself at home as he disappeared into the kitchen. So I sat on the edge of the sofa and looked around. My eye was drawn to the photo beside me. It was clear now who the girl in the picture was. It was the wife who had left him. She was the one who had made him feel so low. Part of me understood. But part of me thought it was also a cry for help. Maybe he had been to the station several times hoping someone would turn up and I eventually did. Maybe he wanted to meet someone like me. Maybe we were fated to know one another.

He came into the lounge with a bottle of red wine and two glasses and poured. He then raised his and I joined him. He didn't speak. It made me wonder what he was raising the glass to. Could it be us? I hoped so but it didn't matter really; his silence excited me.

We sat and drank quietly and it wasn't awkward to sit with him in silence. Not like with John, where our silence usually meant he was thinking of another woman. This was safe. Nice. It felt good to be able to not force conversation. As we were close to finishing our first glass, he said it was a nice evening and would I like to go for a walk.

'Yes, of course, a walk would be lovely.'

I thought he was going to go straight for sex. I was expecting it. That was how it usually worked. I didn't mind that either. I'd been picturing it all day. But, a walk was romantic and wonderfully unexpected.

As we left his house, his hands were in his pockets. I wanted to link arms with him but hesitated. I noticed how this one small act seemed a bigger deal than when we had sex. After a few minutes, we came to a bridge with a small walkway leading down to the river and we left the city behind. The concrete and noise of passing cars was replaced with a calmer, more natural setting. A place where lovers would walk.

The path was lined with blue LED lighting that gave it a soft, safe feel. A couple passed us in the opposite direction and because the path was narrow I had to step closer to Chris, using it as an opportunity to link my arm in his. He didn't acknowledge it, but for a second I thought I saw him smiling out of the corner of my eye.

'I hope you don't mind us walking. It seemed like a waste of a nice evening if we didn't.'

'No, no of course not.'

We walked for about twenty minutes before crossing a small bridge over the river and heading back, pausing on it for a second as he pointed out a grey heron nest on the bank.

'They nest here every spring.'

'Do you know a lot about that sort of thing?'

'Not really.'

I felt silly for asking, but then I realized, besides knowing that he had tried to kill himself, I knew little else about him. I watched him looking out over the river, lost in his own thoughts, and wondered what was going on inside his head.

I wanted to ask him about his childhood, his family. I wanted to know about his first kiss and what he wanted to be growing up. I wanted to know what he did with his days now. I didn't even know what he did for a living. And, equally, he knew just as little about me. But asking felt unnatural and the evening carried an air of magic that coexisted with his air of mystery. I wanted to know, but it was exciting not knowing also. So we walked back in silence. Our strides in unison, my arm now comfortable in the space between his and his torso.

Halfway along the path, I spotted what looked like a homeless man on the other side, the side we had just walked on. I was so wrapped up in Chris that I hadn't seen him until now. He was watching us, intently. At first I felt uncomfortable but then thought to myself, he was alone, probably sad.

Seeing a young couple arm in arm would be what I would want to see if I were him.

I gave him a smile and he turned away from me, camouflaging himself in the reeds and trees that lined the river before getting up and walking away quickly. I stopped. Everything about what that man had just done reminded me of the man the other night outside my house.

'Did you see that man?' I asked.

'What man?'

'On the other side of the river, watching us. It's funny, I think I saw him near my house the other night.'

Chris unlinked from my arm and walked closer to the river edge, looking intently, almost in a panic, at the other side.

'Where was he?'

I pointed to where he had been sitting, but he was gone. I walked to Chris and took him by the arm. I could feel his muscles, tensed to the point he shook a little.

'It's okay, Chris, it's just a coincidence. I'm just being silly.'

'Are you sure it was the same man?'

'No, of course it wasn't. It's just been a long week and I'm being over-imaginative.'

I relinked arms with him and we continued to walk, quicker than we had previously. The rest of the journey back I could feel his heightened tension on my arm, his senses engaged. I would almost go as far to say he was jumpy.

Once back in his house, Chris told me to make myself at home as he dashed upstairs. I walked into his kitchen and poured us both another glass of wine. Above me, I could hear him opening and closing windows. It was obvious he was making sure the place was secure. Although I didn't know why. I also didn't know why he was so jumpy. When he came back down, I handed him the glass of wine and we both had a sip. He was calmer, although not entirely.

'Is everything all right?'

'Yes, sorry, I'm fine. I suffer from anxiety from time to time.'

'Me too.'

'Sorry.'

'Hey, don't be.' I put down my glass and wrapped my arms around him. 'You feel so tense.'

'I'm sorry. I'm embarrassed now.'

'Don't be embarrassed. Come with me.' I led him into the living room and sat him on the sofa. I climbed over the arm and sat on the backrest, so his head was between my legs. Pressing firmly, I massaged his shoulders.

'That feels nice.'

'Good, I'm glad.'

I could feel a fresh wave of anticipation begin to build, knowing once I had calmed him I would kiss him and he would kiss me and we would go upstairs to have sex. Then, afterwards, we would wrap ourselves in each other's arms and make each other feel safe.

Chapter 34

11.43 p.m. – London Road, Peterborough

Standing over his bed, Chris watched the shape under his covers twitch and then roll over. Her breathing deep and slow. In, out, in, out. He tried to mirror her calm rhythm. To ease his pounding heart from his dream that had startled him awake. This time he was the one sinking into the wet soil, his eyes forced open, a sharp pain as mud and water blurred his vision. The only thing he could see was the man, hunched and panting hard, like he was that night.

In, out, in, out.

It worked. His heart rate dropped to a level at which his hands didn't shake any more. Still, he watched her for a few more seconds. She slept in the same way Julia used to. It made him feel a longing for the past and hate for the woman next to him.

She mumbled something in her sleep, obviously dreaming. In the low light, her dark hair that invaded his pillow reminded him of the spider's legs that had lain snapped off and fragile in his hands. She turned again, this time facing towards him, her jaw flexing a little. Her neck exposed once more. He didn't know why he had taken her for a walk to his place with Julia. That place wasn't for her; that place was for him and his wife.

He focused on her neck, on the vein that pumped blood away from her brain and again pictured pressing on it. Pressing until she woke and fought and in doing so invited him to press on her entire throat until the whites of her eyes were dyed red with burst blood vessels. He forced the image out. One that was there because of a year of remembering how his wife died.

Reaching forward, he touched her and felt her pulse thump through the vein, before quietly walking backwards out of his room and heading for the shed. Outside, he noticed something was different. Lowering himself, he waited patiently for his eyes to fully adjust. Once they had grown accustomed to the darkness, he could see the grass was flattened in an area he didn't walk. He scanned the garden and could see a new pathway leading from the back fence towards his shed. Straightening up, he looked around. There was no one there, but someone definitely had been.

He tried to remember exactly when he had last been out. Was it two days ago? Three maybe? The shed was still locked, and there was no sign of forced entry. Maybe it was just an opportunist burglar trying to get a bike or lawn mower. But he doubted it. Someone had been there, trying to check up on Chris, probably after that moment at the river.

The toolbox would have to be hidden somewhere else, somewhere in the house. He'd intended to come and read his wife's diary again, to feel that closeness he couldn't feel anywhere else, but it had turned into a precaution mission instead. After unlocking the door, he leant over and picked up the toolbox then carried it back to his house. Locking the door behind him, he looked out into his garden and jumped at his own reflection.

'Take a deep breath, Chris; get yourself under control!'

After setting the toolbox on the dining table, he opened it, counted the items. They were all there. That much hadn't changed. That much was still the same as it was before May. He picked up her diary and fanned the pages; it still smelt of her. He wanted to read it but knew it wasn't safe. Not yet. He took her phone out and tried to turn it on but her battery was flat, so he got her charger from a drawer, plugged it in and waited.

He had turned that phone on once a month on average, just to make sure, and every time the only messages that came through were texts from PPI companies or accident claim specialists. Each one would send a wave of anxiety pulsing through him until he read who the sender was. There were never any voicemails, and yet, when the screen lit up his heartbeat doubled as it notified him there was one sat waiting to be heard.

'Hi, Jules. It's Steve, Chris's friend. Look. I know I shouldn't be bothering you; you had your reasons for leaving. But I was wondering if you could call me when you get this. I need to talk to you. Just between you and me, Chris has been acting odd lately. He doesn't know I've called. So, please, give me a ring. He won't know we've talked. It would be nice to hear your voice.'

He listened to the message again, before turning the phone off and putting it back in the toolbox.

'Fuck.'

Chris knew when Julia didn't call back, Steve would go digging. It was only a matter of time before he would find out she was not on sabbatical like he had said and then Chris would be questioned as to why he'd lied.

He buried the phone under some shoes and the hoover in the cupboard under the stairs. It wasn't as discreet as in the shed, but it would have to do. There were only just over three days left. Three difficult days. He knew Steve suspected something. He'd watched him crawl past his house, him and his wife looking in. He also knew Steve wouldn't understand if he tried to explain. He wouldn't see it from his perspective.

Tiptoeing back into his bedroom, Chris wondered how he should respond. He was tempted to ignore it, but that would arouse suspicion. Instead, in his head he composed a short message that would hopefully throw Steve off the scent. He'd send it tomorrow.

'Steve, nice to hear from you. Sorry I've not been in touch. Listen, I don't mean to be rude, but I need you to understand I need more time. Please don't contact me again.'

***

As he climbed into bed, Sarah stirred but didn't wake. Or so he thought. He didn't know she had been awake since he cried out in his sleep moments before he got up. He didn't know she faked her mumble and controlled her breathing until he left. He didn't know she watched him carry a heavy box from the shed into the house and she was planning how she was going to find it.

Chapter 35

Julia's diary – January 2015

Mum's been gone now for over a year and it still doesn't feel any easier. I've been a wife for a similar amount of time and, if I'm truly honest with how I'm feeling, it's just as hard. They don't tell you that once you're married things change. It's almost like putting on the ring and the dress means that you don't have to try any more.

I'm not talking about Chris here. I wish I was; it would make this easier to write. He still works on us. He gives surprise gifts and wants to talk all night about silly little things. He is still calm and reassuring about my mum's, despite me knowing that he wants me to sell it. He'll never say, but I can see it in his eyes whenever he is about to leave to do the monthly visit to my mum's house, trips I cannot do with him. He makes sure the old place hasn't fallen down. He's waiting, hoping I'll tell him I'm ready to say goodbye to the place and put it on the market, but I'm just not there yet. And he'll not ask me to do it, he knows it would break my heart. Don't get me wrong, since we've been married

I've seen his flaws. He takes up the whole bed and can't sing (despite always doing it), he is a terrible drinker, and sometimes when he does I can see a rage behind his eyes. It's never directed at me. But it's there.

Once or twice I've had to calm him from hitting someone after a few on a night out. Him usually wanting to because some guy has tried it on with me. It's great that he's protective, and sober he handles it well, but drunk, not so much. I'm not unrealistic. I know we all have flaws. I most certainly do. Chris isn't the issue in our marriage. I am.

Because I'm bored.

I question why. It's only been a year and I thought people didn't get these feelings until the itch in the seventh. The problem is, our relationship started at a time of turmoil. It was a marriage born out of a waiting grief. I wonder if I would be married at all if Mum hadn't died and I think Chris asked me so she would know. And it's wonderful that he did. It says more about him than anything I could ever say.

But, I feel it may have been the wrong thing to do, for me at least. There was still a part of me that needed to explore the world, meet new people and do things a married woman doesn't do. The problem is that I was so caught up in seeing my mum happy, keeping the man I'm married happy too, that I didn't stop to try to ensure that the happiness I felt doing so was enough.

I don't regret falling for Chris; I really don't. But married life is one without adventure, or risk. It's about trying to manage two houses with all of their bills whilst juggling work commitments (although still being part-time, his are far more committing than mine), and spending quality time together. It's about being normal. It's normal to be married. It's now normal to be a woman whose mum has died. And normal isn't what I want. The ring on my finger has kept me safe and I wanted that. I still do, I think. But surely life is about a risk or two along the way?

And I don't want to end up like my mother: alone, sad. A life full of moments past and life missed. She stayed at home to raise a small family as Dad worked, and then he left and her desire for adventure left with him.

I love that I'm Mrs Hayes and I know my husband is a good man, a man who loves me and wants to protect me. I know I am lucky. I just needed to get it out of my head. Then I can accept that life isn't a fairy tale like I read as a child. I can be happier that my adoring husband is breaking himself at work to make sure we have enough. But, even now, despite me saying all of this, I still need some excitement in my life that is beyond what being a wife is. I need an adventure. I need to be a little more like my dad and a little less like my mum.

And it frightens me to know it …

Chapter 36

2 days left

5.42 a.m. – London Road, Peterborough

It was nearly six when he began to stir, stretching, yawning, his back to me. I knew he had only been asleep for a handful of hours because I hadn't slept at all. I spent the night wondering about him. Wondering what was inside that box he carried in from the shed. Wanting to know its contents. I have thought about asking him, but, whatever was inside, it was obviously something he wasn't ready to share, and if I pushed it he would probably close up on me. If I was going to help him, I needed to be patient, or if that failed, I needed to find out things without the need to ask him questions.

I don't know if it was my sleep-deprived mind but things weren't adding up. I couldn't work out why a man who wanted to kill himself only weeks ago now seemed happy with me being beside him. I started to question if I was a rebound fling.

The night before felt a little like rebound sex. It was completely different to the first time. It was a little rough. At times a little *too* rough. My hands ached from where he'd squeezed them. I could feel bruises under the skin on my arms where he had pinned me down. Although I was so caught up in the moment it didn't matter. But it was hard, like sex you had after an argument that hasn't been fully settled.

I guessed it was anger, not at me, but directed at his estranged wife. I felt used. But still, the walk before along the river – surely that meant something too? Natalie would know; she always did. I knew I would need to talk to her but after lying about seeing John it was becoming increasingly difficult to try to tell her the truth and I didn't know how to start such a conversation.

What I did know after a night of pondering was that I wouldn't be able to do a thing to help him if I didn't learn more about the burden he carried. He rolled onto his side to face me, wafting his smell in the duvet as he did. He smiled. I wasn't expecting it. I was expecting that same difficult-to-read expression that turned me on and made me feel repulsed in equal measure. There was no confusing it this time. He was happy. He was happy that I was in his bed. Just as I started to smile back it was gone and he was getting up, speaking as he moved towards the door.

'I'll put some coffee on.'

'Thank you.'

I lay there for a minute not knowing if I should get up, quickly get dressed and join him, or wait for him to return with the coffee. I could hear him downstairs, opening and closing cupboards. Flicking on the kettle. Waiting for it to boil. I wondered what he was thinking.

Knowing I was on my own in his room presented an opportunity to try to discover something that might help. I couldn't fight my urge to snoop and see if I could find out anything about him. It was wrong, but I justified it because of the intensity of the situation. I knew what I really wanted was somewhere downstairs, but I decided to look up here anyway. Starting with his bedside cabinet. I could feel my heart beating in my fingertips as I opened it slowly. I stopped myself, questioning if I should continue down this road. Again I justified it in my head and continued. Sometimes you have to do things that are wrong for the greater good. The top drawer only contained a book and a blue jumper. The bottom had two loose keys in a small jewellery box. A car key and what looked like a front door key. I put them back quietly.

Treading as carefully as I could, I walked to his wardrobe and opened it. There were seven shirts, all white, and several pairs of dark trousers. It screamed office job, although I couldn't picture him doing a nine to five. There was also something green tucked in the corner, the colour catching my eye, intentionally hidden.

I slid his shirts to the left and pulled it out. It was a jade-green dress. Smelling of dust and time. I didn't know what it meant. But it was clearly something very important to him. I pictured the blonde woman from the photograph downstairs wearing it. Knowing she would have looked beautiful. It made me feel a pang of jealousy.

After putting it back, I got on my knees and looked on the floor of the wardrobe. I found some shoeboxes stacked two high. Six in total. I opened the first one. It was full of photos. Pausing to listen I made sure I could still hear him downstairs. I picked up a handful of the photos. Each one containing him and the blonde woman. In one they were arm in arm, beaming with smiles in front of an old church somewhere. No doubt a picture of their wedding venue.

I hastily put the pictures back in the box and quickly looked in the others. They all contained old shoes and phone chargers. Hearing footsteps coming up the stairs I leant forward and pressed my hands on the floor to stand, but something caught my eye under his bed. A card. I reached under to grab it but it was just out of reach so I knelt up and snatched my handbag. I rummaged inside and took out a biro, scattering lipstick and change onto the floor. I cursed myself for panicking so much. Using the pen, I managed to hook the card, pulling it into my hand just before he walked into the room. He looked at me puzzled.

'I dropped my purse,' I said, almost too quickly.

'You need a hand?'

'No, I'm almost done. Clumsy me ...' I laughed, hoping it would hide my panic. It seemed to work as he relaxed and smiled back.

I picked up my things and put them in my bag, along with the card that was pressed into my palm, before joining him back in bed for coffee. He leant over and kissed me on the cheek, thanking me for a wonderful night. It made me feel terrible for looking through his things. I knew that taking the card had clearly crossed the line from wanting to be nosey in order to help to something that probably meant I was the one who needed help. My actions made me feel uneasy, but I was also elated that I was beginning to mean something to him.

We stayed in bed for another hour before I had to get ready to leave. I didn't want to. I wanted to stay in his bed forever but I had to get to work. As I left, he kissed me on the lips. Said he couldn't wait to see me again. I felt like I could have died in that moment.

***

So consumed with playing the part, Chris almost believed his parting words to her. He watched her walk down his path, turn, smile, wave and get into her car. Once her car could no longer be seen, he felt the tension he didn't know he was holding in his shoulders release. He knew he had to deal with Steve and his message to Julia, but he needed to hear her first.

After climbing over loose shoes in the cupboard under the stairs, Chris opened the toolbox and pulled out her diary. He scanned it and stopped at random: March 2015. Two months before she was murdered.

'I don't know how it happened but it has now, and I can't undo it. There is no delicate way to write this so I'll just say it as it is. I'm leaving ...'

He knew what was coming next and closed the diary carefully. He'd only read this entry once, and he vowed he'd never do it again. However, he knew he needed to. Part punishment, part catharsis. But not now. He needed to read it in a place where it would have the greatest impact, test his resolve. Show his commitment. He would wait for the cover of darkness, drive to March train station and read his wife's words after the 10.47 passed.

Chapter 37

After a long and shitty day at work, all I wanted was to crawl into my bed and think of him. I didn't even have enough energy to eat. So when I pulled up outside and could see Nat looking through the window at me I braced myself. She knew something; I could see it in her face. I just didn't know how much she knew. When I opened the front door both her and George were standing there – her hands were on her hips ready for an argument; his arms were crossed, disapproving. I thought Natalie would lead so was shocked when George spoke, his voice deep and wounded.

'Sarah, where were you last night?'

'I told you, with John.'

'John, as in your ex John?'

'Yes.'

'I cannot believe this.' Natalie walked away. It was clear she knew I was lying. I tried to say something but she was gone, the door behind her that led to the kitchen closed. I couldn't help but hang my head in shame. George spoke, making me jump, his tone softer, but no less annoyed.

'So then why did he call today asking to speak to you?'

'He did?'

'Yes. Sarah, what is going on?'

'When?'

'Does that matter? What matters is he called your sister, saying he's been trying to get hold of you and wanted to make sure you were okay. He said you'd not spoken in weeks. It was a good job you weren't home.'

'Was she angry?'

'Was she … Sarah, you need to tell us what has been going on.'

'Shit. Look, I'll tell you everything, I will. But can it wait? I've had a rough day.'

'Bloody hell, Sarah. Do you know how much you've hurt Nat by lying?'

'I can guess.'

'Yeah, well, even guessing you're miles off.' He paused for a moment. I could see him thinking of the most diplomatic way to handle the situation. 'You look like shit.'

'I've not slept much.'

'She'll want answers.'

'I know.'

'Tonight.'

'Okay.'

'Go get in the shower or something and freshen up. I'll do our dinner and then make you a coffee. It's time for no more bullshit.'

'What about Nat?'

'Just go; I'll calm her down.'

'Thanks, George.'

I wanted him to give me a hug in that big brother way he sometimes did, reassuring me everything would be all right. But instead he nodded and headed for the kitchen, no doubt to hug Nat. It was selfish of me to expect anything else. I thought about how much they did for me and how I'd been lying, so I went upstairs and did exactly what was asked of me. Knowing it was time to come clean.

Half an hour later there was a hot cup of coffee waiting on the kitchen table. Natalie couldn't look at me as I sat down and George just looked at me in a way that told me not to fuck it up. Seeing my sister so hurt by my actions was a kick in the stomach. I had been so caught up in my feelings and what I wanted I had neglected hers.

So I told them everything. How I lied to return the stone and ended up in his bed. How I messaged his friend to find him again and how I had spent the night once more. They both said that it was stupid and dangerous as he was suicidal, but I told them I had got through. He was just a damaged man, like I was a damaged woman.

When they asked me about John I told them I didn't care. I could see George liked that but Nat told me I was replacing one fuck-up with another. It wasn't like that. Chris was sore, wounded, but not a fuck-up. I didn't tell them I saw a future with him, but they could see it. They could also see I wasn't going to stop seeing him because they were concerned.

Nat was too angry to see it from my perspective, and I didn't blame her. I was angry with me too. But George had calmed and made me promise, no more lies. If I was going to see him I had to say, so they both knew where I was.

I then had to write his address on the calendar. I felt it was a little unnecessary but I was in the wrong so did as I was asked without question. George got up and left, leaving me with my sister. It was clearly something Nat had asked him to do before our talk had begun. The room shifted from one of open discussion to something sadder. She still couldn't look at me so I sat patiently waiting. Eventually she looked up, her eyes red and puffy.

'I need you to grow up and start taking care of yourself.'

Before I could respond she left. It broke my heart to upset her as much as I did. But I knew what I was doing, and I knew one day she would understand I wasn't as stupid as she thought.

Chapter 38

10.45 p.m. – March train station

Chris felt ill knowing that he was stood once again on the platform where he should have ended his life weeks before. He had no note to place under the bench this time instead he held his wife's diary, knowing that after the train passed, he would read the entry he'd started earlier that day.

Chris came at this time knowing his train would come. He did it to cement his resolve and commitment to his wife after his failings. He knew that when the train passed it would hurt, and that mattered. He hoped she was watching, seeing him suffer, knowing his regret.

It had been twenty-seven days since he failed. It felt like twenty-seven years.

It was as quiet as it should have been that night in May, besides the sound of raindrops hitting the old tin roof. As the pre-recorded voice-over announced that a train was coming, he noted the irony of the fact that right then he could do what he set out to do but at the same time he couldn't. As expected, the realization that with one small step it would all be over for him was a step he couldn't take. He had to wait two more days. The date had to be right.

As the train rushed past, not stopping on its way to wherever it was going, Chris looked up and hoped Julia was watching him and could see what he was doing for her, and he hoped she would forgive his weakness.

Once the noise had passed and the tail lights had disappeared into the distance, he calmed slightly, allowing himself to feel how he truly felt. Beaten, beaten by time, beaten by his weakness with the opposite sex, beaten by the grief of his wife's death. He wanted nothing more than to give in to the fight, to throw in the towel. He knew that coming back early would test his resolve, but he could do it when the time was right, he was sure of that. Part of him, a quiet part, suddenly thought about a different future, one that contradicted his plan.

He couldn't believe he'd thought it.

He wanted to say something to her, something new, but there was nothing new to say, not until she could respond in a way that wasn't through memory. So, instead he quietly sat, noticing how much he shook in doing so. He opened the diary and began to read.

'May 2015

'I don't know how it happened but it has now, and I cannot undo it. There is no delicate way to write this so

270

I'll just say it as it is. I'm leaving nothing unsaid in these pages.

'*I've got close to James from work. I have been since before Mum died and last night I lied to Chris, telling him I had to work late, so I could see James. Now, despite everything I believe in, everything I have been taught, I'm a woman having an affair …*'

He rubbed the ball of his free hand against his eyebrow, despite it not being the first time he had read it, her words hitting him hard. She hadn't disguised it, or tried to soften it. Just laid it out, bare and painful. He wanted to throw the book on the track, wait until the next train passed and watch it be obliterated, her deeds and words dying for good. But he took a deep breath. He wasn't being rational. He knew he had to carry on.

'*… I never intended for it to happen. It just did and I'm not sure how much longer I can live with the lies I have to tell to my husband. I feel so ashamed. Despite his flaws he is a good man, a loyal man who doesn't deserve this. But I cannot help how I feel.*

'*It's different with James. It's like how Chris and I were in the beginning but amplified. He's kind-hearted and patient and I know I shouldn't make excuses as I'm completely in the wrong, but with Chris the urgency is gone. He works so hard for us, but I'm bored …* '

Looking up at the smoke-stained bridge that crossed over the track, Chris took a deep breath. He knew what was coming next. He knew how much it was going to hurt.

' ... I love my husband. I truly do, and despite the fact that I know I will one day end what James and I have, our marriage will also come to an end. I need to tell him. He deserves the truth, but I am worried about what will happen when he finds out. I'm worried it will break his heart ... '

Dropping the diary on the floor as if it was burning his hands, Chris stood and stepped away from the bench towards the platform's edge.

The rain became deafeningly loud and Chris needed to feel it on his skin, so he walked the length of the platform until he was no longer standing under its shelter. His white shirt became translucent in the deluge. His hair stuck to his face and rainwater ran through his matted beard, dripping onto his shoes.

In the distance he could hear the rumblings of a thunderstorm. He hoped it would come overhead. Taking a deep breath, he smelt the world becoming wet, the smell of dry soil turning to mud. The same smell from that night nearly a year before when he and Julia sat under that tree on the A605.

Chris snapped himself out of his memory, unable to let himself remember what came next. He wasn't strong enough. Looking up, he was surprised to see the London train was sitting on the platform. It was either early or he had lost track of time. Glancing at the station clock, he realized thirty minutes had gone missing. In the nearest carriage to where he was standing sat an old man on his own. Chris blinked rainwater from his eyes and, as he focused, he saw the old man was looking at him.

He watched Chris quizzically, probably wondering why he wasn't standing under the shelter, wondering what was running through the young man's mind. Chris wanted to look away but couldn't. There was something in the stranger that mirrored him. The man nodded at Chris but he couldn't nod back.

As the train pulled out, neither blinked until they could no longer see one another. A sadness dripped down him with the rain. A loneliness came over him. Sitting on the bench, he picked up the diary and wiped off damp leaves. He took his phone out and scrolled down to the train girl's number. He hoped she wouldn't be asleep.

For the first time in just under a year he didn't want to be alone. He needed a distraction more than ever. He needed to forget about time, and the train girl somehow managed to do that for him.

Chapter 39

11.57 p.m. – London Road, Peterborough

Steve rubbed his eyes, fighting off sleep that his body screamed for. Refocusing, he – for what felt like the thousandth time that night – looked to Chris's house for any sign of movement. Still nothing. He wondered if he was ever coming back. He hadn't intended it to be a stake-out.

What he wanted was for Chris to answer the door when he knocked and for the pair of them to talk. He wanted Chris to know he knew he'd been lying about work and hoped he would offer an explanation. He wanted to talk about Julia, about what really happened between them and why she'd left. He wanted to raise the point that he had tried to reach Julia and couldn't. He wanted to say he had rung her work and they told him she was gone. That she'd handed in a typed and unsigned letter of resignation, posted eleven months before, and that everyone knew why she had resigned. The affair was public knowledge in the office, and no one had heard from her since.

That was the first time he had heard of Julia's affair. Yet another lie. Her affair was awful, and a shock, but what was more troubling was Chris saying for nearly a year that Julia was on a sabbatical to see her father when she had quit.

For a while he couldn't work out why Chris would lie like that. But then he put himself in his shoes. Chris would feel like he failed her despite her having the affair. He would be too ashamed to talk of it. Steve knew Chris truly loved Julia, perhaps he didn't want to say it out loud in case she came back. Perhaps he lied because of a loyalty to his cheating wife. Regardless, yet more unanswered questions. He wanted to ask them eye to eye to gauge Chris's response. See what his friend's body language told him. But then when Chris didn't answer and appeared not to be in, Steve had decided to wait, to watch, and see what happened next.

Whilst waiting he tried to call Julia again and again it went to voicemail. This time he didn't leave a message. Instead he logged on to his Facebook and typed her name in the search box. It wasn't the first time he had done so. In the months after Julia left he checked her page periodically to see how she was and if there was anything that might indicate when she was coming home. Each time there were no updates to her page.

Her profile picture remained one of her and Chris. She hadn't posted anything new on her wall.

Her last being a comment reading: 'I love my work friends. Thanks for a great night.' He had read it before, several times, but this was the first time he checked the date. It read '27 May 2015'.

It seemed innocent if you didn't know. Julia had never been massively into Facebook, and people gave it up all the time. But in his gut he knew something was wrong. She had stopped posting days before she left to go see a father who had been absent for so many years. Or so Chris told him, and there seemed to be no trace of her since. Steve also noticed that she hadn't been tagged in anything either, no photos, no friends posting about trips away or nights out, and there was no mention of Australia anywhere. It seemed as if Julia had completely disappeared off the face of the earth.

It was believable to some extent: she may have had a breakdown and that was her reasoning for leaving, but all the information about her doing so had come from Chris, who Steve now knew had lied about what he was doing with his days. He didn't want to, but Steve couldn't help but wonder, if Chris could mislead so easily about one thing, what else was he lying about?

Steve's eyes were beginning to sting and he was about to leave when a Toyota Aygo pulled up outside the house. He didn't know the car but he could see two people inside. Chris was the first to get out, soaking wet and shivering. He walked towards the front door and, as he opened it, he removed a book

276

from under his shirt and put it somewhere behind the door before gesturing for the other person to join him. As the other person got out Steve recognized her from her profile pic. It was Sarah.

Watching them both disappear into the dark house, Steve knew he had to say something. But he didn't want Chris knowing, not until he understood a little more. Going into his messages on Facebook, he brought up the conversation he'd had with Sarah and typed.

'Don't tell Chris I've messaged you. Not all is as it seems. Chris isn't the man you think he is. He is hiding something about his wife. Be careful.'

Chapter 40

1 day left

2.18 a.m. – London Road, Peterborough

I was just beginning to fall asleep, the deep, dreamless, content kind after sex – not the rough sex like last time but like our first time – when I felt a movement beside me. At first I thought he was turning over, but then I heard the soft thud of his feet hitting the wooden floor. He was leaving again. One of his nightly walks to the shed. I heard him go downstairs, thirteen in total, before the world fell silent again. I got up and sneaked to the window, waiting to see him outside. Then I remembered his box wasn't in the shed any more. My attention turned from the window to the door.

Quietly, I moved to the doorway and looked downstairs through the stair railings. There was light coming from the kitchen. Not a lot, but enough. I could hear pages being turned. He was reading, no doubt it was the book I saw in his arms when I picked him up from the station.

I wanted to confront him, tell him I had watched him sneak off each time he had, but if I did he was likely to ask me to leave. It was his secret. I couldn't barge my way into it, and I had to be patient, play the long game, so I climbed back into his bed. Unable to switch off and knowing if I strained to listen, it would end up with me losing my patience, despite needing it, I picked up my phone. Logging onto my Facebook I saw I had a message. Steve's stark warning about being careful made me feel sick. I decided to message him back.

'*What do you mean be careful?*'

I wasn't expecting a reply, but within a minute another message popped into my inbox. '*Something's not right.*'

'*Like what?*'

'*I don't know, but recently, I've tried to find his wife. She's completely disappeared.*'

'*Disappeared?*'

'*Like she doesn't exist any more. It's weird. People don't just vanish.*'

He was right; people don't just vanish. Not in the modern world of technology and social media. Everyone's traceable. In that moment I knew there was more to his suicide attempt. It was something other than depression, something more like grief. I also suspected Steve didn't have that information; if he did, Chris's troubles would be public, he would have all of his friends and family acting in the way I was having to, wanting to. I didn't know Steve, but, if he was a close friend like his Facebook suggested, he needed to know about that night at the station.

'*Do you know he tried to kill himself?*'

'*What? No, when?*'

'*Nearly a month ago, at a train station. It's how we met; I accidentally stopped him.*'

'*Sarah. We need to meet.*'

'*When?*'

'*Later today.*'

'*I've got work.*'

'*After. I'll come to you.*'

I paused for a moment and listened. In the silence I could hear him mumbling to himself downstairs, reading out loud. Steve's apparent anxiety began to rub off on me. My heart started racing.

'*Can you meet me at Cambridge station: 8 p.m.?*'

'*Yes. I'll meet you outside. Sarah, I mean what I said: be careful. Something isn't right.*'

I locked my iPhone and put it back in my jeans pocket on the floor beside me. Lying back, I looked at the ceiling, trying to process what I understood about what Steve had just said. His wife had disappeared. It wasn't unheard of, but I knew in my gut that whatever was going on was inside that book and I needed to read it. Then I remembered the key he kept in his drawer, so I quietly opened it, took it out and put it in my jeans pocket just before I heard his footsteps coming back up. Taking the key went against everything I thought I knew to be right. It was just as bad as taking someone's wallet, something

I couldn't do only a few weeks before. Because then, on that night at the station, the line between right and wrong was clear. It was a boundary that shouldn't be crossed. Now, everything had changed. I knew that life wasn't like, and would never be like, a black-and-white movie where there were only two sides, doing good or doing harm. The real world, with all of its complexities, had many shades of grey in between. In those shades, good actions could disguise something terrible, and bad actions, like stealing, could be for the greater good.

After getting back under the covers, I closed my eyes and tried to slow my rapid breathing to a sleeping person's rate. He climbed back in next to me, close, his head over mine. I could feel him looking at me. His face so close to mine I could feel his breath on my eyelashes. I felt like I was suffocating, but after a few seconds he moved and lay on his side, facing away from me.

I stayed motionless and listened to his breathing become deeper and deeper until he was asleep. It felt strange knowing that the man I was falling for was hiding something. Something that meant his friend felt the need to warn me. It felt even stranger that I wanted to ignore the warnings. Perhaps it was the risk taker in me, or perhaps I was so hell-bent on trying to do something to save him I didn't care. But, I didn't feel like I was in danger with him. He was troubled, he needed help, but I could see in his eyes there was a really good man. He needed someone to take action, and because of a night at a train station that person was me. I knew Chris would never volunteer answers that might help him so I would have to find them in other ways. When I had the chance I knew I was going to break into his house. It was wrong, and could potentially get me into a lot of trouble, but I was in a shade of grey and my wrong deed was for the greater good. My only issue was I needed to make sure the key that was in my pocket fitted the lock in his front door.

***

He knew she wasn't asleep; her breathing was off. There was something jagged about it that suggested she was apprehensive, awake, alert. She was easy to read. She must have seen him with the diary. He cursed himself for his vigilance slipping. It seemed every day presented new obstacles. Wanting nothing more than the quiet life he'd managed to create, he rolled onto his side and fought fire with fire by also pretending to sleep until the jagged edge to her breathing had gone, replaced with the deep rhythmic breathing he had come to know. In, out, in, out.

Now, with her sound asleep beside him, he rolled out of bed again, looking back to see if it disturbed her. She didn't stir. He went round the bed and rifled through her jeans until he came across her mobile. He saw a message from someone called Nat. It was locked. But she was predictable. She was someone to whom dates were important. Like him. He punched in 0505. The date he met her, his wedding anniversary. He opened it and read.

'I've seen your note. Not impressed by you sneaking out in the middle of the night. Let me know when you've got this.'

It was obvious the note was about him. The fact she wasn't impressed told him Sarah had talked about him and how they met.

Another potential obstacle.

Looking at the train girl, who hadn't moved, he opened her Facebook and went into her messages. He knew she and Steve had spoken. He wanted to read what was said. But Chris wasn't ready for what he saw. He knew Steve was suspicious, but as he read that he'd been actively looking for Julia, Chris knew he was in trouble.

They were going to meet, Sarah and Steve, to talk about him. With so little time left, he couldn't ignore it. He wouldn't say anything to her. He would wait, and watch and act if he needed to, to make sure the truth didn't spill.

Chapter 41

7.58 p.m. – Cambridge train station

I sat on a bench outside the station entrance, apologizing to an old lady as I did, although I didn't know what I was saying sorry for. She smiled politely. I tried to smile back but was aware it must have looked like a grimace. The lack of sleep was starting to make me feel uneasy on my feet. I looked away, focusing on people who were so wrapped up in their own worlds they didn't see each other, bumping shoulder to shoulder sometimes, chest to chest, without blinking. Their faces became an undefined blur as my eyes lost focus.

When I thought about it, I realized that I'd not slept a full, uninterrupted, blissful night since meeting Chris. I knew it wasn't healthy, but when are the start of relationships healthy? Weren't they always filled with anxiety and fear? If you could call what Chris and I had a relationship. I was starting to feel similar to how I had in the past, with John, a quiet distrust that rattled inside my chest. One I refused to acknowledge properly. If I did it would have surely sent me over the edge.

'Sarah?'

I looked to my left and there he was, standing five feet away from me, a quizzical look on his face. He was definitely the man from the Facebook picture, but as I stood I realized he was much bigger than I thought. His right eye was surrounded by a horrible bruise, deep in colour and clearly new. Not knowing how to greet him I offered my hand and he took it, his large palm encompassing mine, a doll's by comparison.

'Thank you for meeting me.'

His voice was deep, in control. Making me feel more anxious. As I spoke my mouth felt dry.

'It's okay.'

'Can we go for a coffee?'

I hesitated. There was something that made me feel I needed to stay in the open. But, as I looked at him, I could see kindness in his eyes and I knew I was being irrational. I had no reason to think he would harm me. But his physical presence intimidated me regardless. I thought of our conversation online, how he seemed caring. I remembered his pictures, happy on his wedding day. It settled me a little.

***

Sitting in his idling car forty feet from the train station entrance, Chris opened a small bottle of

285

bourbon, took a long swig, and watched the train girl stand to talk to someone who he couldn't see from his position. But he knew who it was, and within a minute she turned and walked into the station, Steve by her side.

They went into the coffee shop and she took a window seat as Steve ordered. Chris could see her shifting nervously. For a second he thought she looked up and saw him, and despite his car having dark windows his heart stopped. Surely she hadn't recognized his number plate? She looked away as Steve returned and sat opposite her with two hot drinks. He paused his thoughts for a moment to consider the possibility that Steve was far more likely to recognise his car and he wondered why he hadn't thought about that before leaving. It would have been safer to get a taxi. Yet another slip.

He put his car in reverse and backed it up, obscuring it partially behind a tree and watched, seething, as Steve talked, no doubt telling her about Julia. Telling her the things he had no right to tell. Their exchange was short, no more than fifteen minutes. And in that time he watched the train girl engage, then look away, perhaps learning about his recent violent outbursts.

He watched her nod and shake her head, hearing Steve's suspicions. He watched her cover her mouth with her hands. He wasn't sure what was said. Just as she looked like she was going to stand and leave, she hesitated and reached into her bag. Then a young woman with a buggy stopped outside the coffee shop to tend to her baby, blocking his view of what the train girl had stayed for. He knew whatever the reason, it wasn't good.

***

Some of what Steve had told me I already knew: he had a wife; she had broken his heart. But hearing it out loud made me feel even more concerned for his mental health. I also learnt that she had not only broken his heart, but she betrayed his trust by having an affair. Maybe subconsciously I had known that all along. Maybe it was the reason I was drawn to him so fiercely. She had made that wonderful man want to hurt himself and I felt even more compelled to find a way to get through the wall he was hiding it all behind. Shine a light into his soul and help him come towards it. I had to fight the urge to leave there and then and rush to his side to tell him I knew his pain, I felt the anguish he felt and it can get better. However, I didn't – the fact she had seemingly just vanished without a trace was troubling. Maybe Steve was right to be alarmed. Maybe he was right to warn me about Chris. Maybe it was right that I still didn't want to believe it. And I knew Steve could see my scepticism. I mean, Chris was mixed-up and sad, and yes, he did try to kill himself, but being involved in his wife disappearing? I couldn't quite get there.

He asked me to 'report in' when I was with Chris and, feeling disgusted by the idea of spying for Steve, I stood to leave. Then something stopped me. Steve was just trying to help his friend, he and I were on the same team, and besides all he wanted me to do was talk about it with him, hardly a crime. Unlike stealing a card from under the bed and a door key from his top drawer. I felt hypocritical for even thinking of saying no. It made sense to keep an open line of conversation. I reached into my bag I pulled out the driving licence I had found in his bedroom. Maybe it would help us help him if I shared it with Steve.

'What's that?'

'It's Julia's, with a different last name: Walker. I think it was from before they were married.'

'Can I see it?'

I handed it to Steve who examined it for a second. 'The address is different.'

'I think it was her old house perhaps.'

'She lived on and off with her mother before she moved in with Chris.'

'Have you tried contacting her?'

'She died.'

'Father?'

'Nope, we never knew anything about him, other than that he lived in Australia. It was a bit of a shock when Chris said she'd gone to him. We never thought they were close.'

'Do you think she's out there?'

'Honestly, no. I don't think she is. I think, I hope, she's still in the country and we can get some answers.'

'But she could be anywhere.'

'Maybe.'

I watched as Steve looked away, lost in his own thoughts. I didn't think to consider our conversation about the poor state Chris was in would have an effect. I could see the hurt etched into his face. Then his eyes widened and he sat upright again.

'They never sold the house!'

'Sorry?'

'Chris and Julia, they never sold her mum's house.'

'Even after she died?'

'Chris said she couldn't say goodbye to it, she couldn't let it go.'

'And you've not thought of looking for her there already?'

'I've never known where her mother lived. Sarah, would you mind if I take this? I'm going to pay the house a visit. Maybe there's something about Julia there.'

'Of course; do you think she might be there?'

'I don't know, I hope so. It makes sense, where else would she go?'

'Surely if people thought there was something suspicious about her disappearance it would be on the news or something. Surely someone somewhere would ask questions?'

'I thought the same at first, but then I really thought about it. Besides Chris, she didn't really have anyone. I've never met any of her friends, not since that first night when Chris and I met her and because of the office affair I bet none of her work colleagues thought to look for her.'

'Was it someone from work?'

'Her boss.'

'Where is he? Maybe he knows where she is?'

'He left too, I don't know where he is either. From what I could gather from Julia's work their affair was a scandal, she resigned and he also handed in his notice, although, when I pressed, I got the impression he had to choose between the affair or his job.'

'So, you're telling me he is missing too?'

'I don't know about missing, he's still active on his Facebook.'

'How do you know?'

'I checked straight after I found out about it. It seems he's now in Luton with a new job.'

'But she isn't there with him?'

'She isn't there with him.'

'So, he loses his job and she gives him the cold shoulder.'

'Maybe, yes. I mean, I hadn't thought of it, yes, it definitely looks that way.'

'Don't you think he might be connected to her being missing?'

'Honestly, I hadn't considered it.'

I pictured it in my mind. Julia and he being caught and then her backing off to clear her head. It looked like her boss cared for her more than she did of him. He was willing to give up his job for her. It seemed like she potentially broke the heart of two men. And there is nothing worse than a lover scorned. I thought about the man outside my house in the middle of the night, and then the one that I thought was the same on the opposite side of the river. Could it be that it was the same man both times. Could it be Julia's lover who lost his job keeping an eye on things. Could he have done something terrible as a scorned lover? In that moment I felt in my gut something terrible had happened.

'What happens if she isn't there at her mother's house?'

'I don't know, Sarah. Let's just hope she's there. Regardless, after trying to find Julia I'm going to call him, tell him we need to meet tonight. Somewhere public. I'll put on a little bit of pressure. He'll either tell me what the bloody hell is going on, or start making mistakes if he is covering something up.'

Steve's apparent certainty that Chris was somehow involved in Julia's disappearance unnerved me. Especially after we had talked about the lover. I forced myself to not believe it. Everything went back to the toolbox and that book he'd tried to hide. I needed to read it. As we said our sombre goodbyes, Steve reiterated that I needed to be careful.

I left knowing what I was going to do next. I had a spare key and I knew it worked. When leaving his earlier, I intentionally forgot my coat so I could walk back up to his doorstep, slip the key in and test it by quietly turning the lock. I didn't let myself in; once satisfied it worked I pocketed it again and knocked. Then I put on my best 'silly me' expression to get my coat back. It was calculated and dishonest. I was under no illusion it was wrong. But the greater good had to prevail, even more so after discovering some of the reasons for Chris's grief. I would wait until Steve called to meet and would break in, if you could call it that. I didn't care if he caught me. I needed to know everything. I knew he would never tell me. I still held on to the idea that Steve was entirely wrong about what was going on. Chris wouldn't hurt anyone. I could see it wasn't in his nature. If he did catch me with the diary, I would explain. He would understand. Walking quickly, I headed for home and my car. If I didn't do it then, I knew I would lose my courage.

***

The woman with the baby finally moved but Steve had already seen whatever the train girl was taking from her bag. Moments later, she got her things and left. Chris watched her walk away from the station quickly, deep in thought. He contemplated following her, but he knew he needed to stay with Steve, watch his movements, and see what he did next.

Chris hadn't realized how delicate his existence had become since May. Before then, everything had been fine-tuned. Decided. Now it felt similar to the weeks after Julia died. But somehow worse. One false step. One minor issue and the tapestry of his design would unravel and the monster who killed his wife would win.

The stress was becoming unbearable, but the bourbon, half of it now warming his belly, helped. It clouded his thoughts, however, making him feel as if he was seeing the world from underwater. Unable to breathe. As Steve got into his car and pulled away from the station, Chris followed three cars behind until they left the busy city and went westwards. The opposite direction to where Steve lived.

Alarm bells began to ring in Chris's head. He knew, whatever the train girl had shown to Steve, he was following up. Opening his car window to cool the sweat that stuck to his forehead, Chris followed far enough behind to not be noticed but close enough to not lose him as the city faded and the open countryside rolled in.

The sun was beginning to sit heavy and washed out in the sky. Within an hour or so it would be completely dark. That was a good thing. Darkness was better at hiding secrets. Taking deep breaths, he tried to remain calm. He tried to convince himself it could be nothing. That it was his paranoia. But still, he wasn't going to take any risks. Not when he was so close. Steve would either remain in the dark, or, if not, Chris had to convince him to remain quiet.

Chapter 42

8.49 p.m. – Columbine Road, Ely

Chris watched as Steve's car turned left into Mallow Close and stopped fifty feet from the junction. After putting his car into neutral, he turned off his lights and engine. He didn't need to follow Steve any more. He had questioned, then suspected, then known where Steve was heading. What he didn't know was how the train girl had found out the address to give to him.

She was proving to be smarter than he gave her credit for. Getting out of his car, he stuffed his hands into his pockets and let his eyes adjust to the twilight that had now set in before walking towards the corner at which Columbine Road and Mallow Close met.

If Steve was still in his car or by the front door Chris would continue to walk by, like he was just a guy casually going home after a few beers in the pub. He certainly looked the part, staggering a little as he walked. Trying hard to keep both his balance and focus. But he doubted Steve would still be sitting in his car. He knew Steve and suspected that after a quick look through the front door he would more than likely be at the back of the house. Trying to see inside without alerting any neighbours. If that was the case, he would follow.

Crossing the road, he dared to look at the back of Steve's Audi to check he wasn't inside it or at the front door. He loved how predictable his friend was. He took his phone from his pocket and pretended to text. As he turned right, he walked quickly towards Julia's mother's house. Texting meant two things. The first was his head would naturally be cast towards the ground. Just in case anyone recognized him. The second was that a man who was texting casually wasn't the type of person who was about to have a confrontation. He would look above suspicion – well, he hoped so.

As he approached the front garden gate he saw the small patch of lawn was now overtaken with weeds that were knee-high. It looked obvious the place was unoccupied. Steve would know that now. Opening the rusting gate, he cursed to himself as it squeaked angrily. It caused him to involuntarily pause, listening for the sound of Steve's footsteps. None were forthcoming. Opting to leave the gate ajar, he walked towards the taller, wooden gate that shut off the side of the house. It wouldn't be locked. It never was.

As he passed the large bay window of the empty front room he thought he saw a shadow inside.

He looked again: nothing. Chris forced himself to calm his mind. He knew that soon the pressure and stress would make him lose it entirely so as he stepped towards the gate he repeated to himself: 'Just over twenty-four hours, Chris. All you have to do is keep them safe for just twenty-four more hours.'

After stepping through the gate, he closed it behind him and pressed his back to the wall of the house. With the fence being over six feet tall and only a few feet from the house, he was now perfectly hidden in the passageway that led to the open-plan garden. Looking up, he could see a gap in the clouds. He started to look for his father's star but stopped himself.

A sound came from the back garden. A muffled smash of glass. It snapped him away from thoughts of his father. Steve was not as predictable as he thought. He hadn't envisaged him breaking in.

He waited and listened as Steve made noises that suggested a struggle before a lock snapped and a door quietly opened and then closed. After counting to ten in his head, Chris walked around the corner and looked inside to see Steve's back as he walked through the kitchen towards the lounge. Quietly calling for Julia as he did.

Once he was out of sight, Chris opened the door and stepped inside. A fusty smell coming from the carpets filled his nostrils. It had been empty for just over two and a half years. Though it felt longer. As he stepped through the kitchen, he saw his reflection in the glass of the bay window in the lounge. He looked as tense as he felt.

As he walked into the living room, he realized the furniture had remained untouched since the day he came alone to cover it with dust sheets a few weeks after Julia's mother died. Julia had never been there with him; although after reading her diary he knew she had been back a few times, with James.

Chris heard footsteps above him, two soft, followed by two heavy. Steve was going from room to room, his shifting weight almost seeming like he was in two places at once, no doubt with each step his conviction of Julia not being in Australia was cemented.

Chris thought about going upstairs, but as he began to move he heard Steve descending. He backed up against the fireplace, bumping into an iron stand that held a small shovel for the fire. He waited. The stairs creaked. Steve was on the third from the bottom. He knew that because of the times he and Julia stayed over, near the start of their relationship. Chris having to sleep on the sofa, in keeping with her mother's requests. His mind flashed to the first night he sneaked upstairs to be with her. Julia's quiet giggles from the upstairs banister as he tiptoed towards her, the third step almost giving him away.

Shaking his head, the memory vanished, Julia's giggles replaced with the deep voice of Steve talking on the other side of the living-room door.

'It's Steve. Yes, I'm here now. No, it looks like she's never been here.'

There was a pause.

'Okay. Okay. I won't, not yet. Where are you? Where? At his house? How? Jesus, Sarah. I've told you; it's not safe. Is there any sign of him? Good, don't go in. Do you hear me? Yes, I'm going to call him now. Be careful okay?'

Chris was shocked that Sarah was at his house. Something he would have to tackle after dealing with Steve.

Steve walked into the living room, closing the door behind him. He didn't see Chris standing with his back against the wall, watching. With his phone still in his hand, he pressed the screen a few times and a few seconds later a quiet buzzing could be heard. At first Chris didn't realize it was from his phone. Steve looked towards the source of the sound, shocked to see Chris in the shadows.

'Shit, Chris, you scared me.'

'Steve.'

'What are you doing here?' he asked, trying to sound light and interested. His high tones suggesting it was more fear than anything else.

'I should ask the same of you.'

Chris knew he had worked it out. What he didn't know was how and, as he kept his eye on him, Steve looked towards the back door in the kitchen, no doubt planning on bolting for it. Casually, Chris stepped from the shadows and blocked the doorway.

'So, Steve, why are you in mine and my wife's house?'

Steve hesitated for a moment, unsure what he should do next.

'This is Julia's mother's … '

'Left to us after she died. Don't deviate from the question.'

'I came to see if I could find Julia.'

Chris didn't speak. He didn't blink. He just kept his eyes on his friend, on the man in front of him.

'Chris. Please, mate, you need to tell me. What's happened to Julia?'

Slowly moving from the doorway back towards the fireplace, Chris spoke calmly. 'She's gone.'

'Gone, gone where?'

'You know this, Steve. She left me.'

Steve took a step forward, closing the gap between them to two arm's lengths. 'Where, Chris, left you for where?'

Chris backed away and, turning, he looked out of the living-room bay window into the street that was now dark. 'Australia, I've told you.'

Steve took another small step. His hands raised ready to defend or restrain if he needed to. 'Where is she, Chris?'

'Steve, please. Don't.'

'If you don't speak to me, I'll have no choice but to call the police.'

'No. Please don't, Steve, it's too dangerous.'

'Dangerous? What do you mean dangerous?'

Chris turned back to Steve and almost spoke but caught his words, prompting Steve to press further.

'I've tried to find her, Chris. Her phone isn't on, and her Facebook is dormant. She's not been at work since last June, resigning, because of her *affair*, which you've never mentioned. An AFFAIR, Chris – why the hell didn't you tell me about this! She's not on sabbatical like you've told everyone. She's completely disappeared and then I find out that you were trying to kill yourself a month ago. That's how you met Sarah. You know more than you're telling me. So I'm going to ask you again. Where is your wife?'

'Steve, please, just give me one more day; that's all I ask.'

'One more day for what? Chris, what the fuck is going on?'

Steve was shouting. It prompted Chris to raise his hands and try to quieten his friend before the neighbours heard.

'Steve, you need to calm down. Someone will hear.'

For a second Chris swore he heard creaking from the stairs once more and shot a look towards them.

'No, I'll not be quiet. That's it, I'm calling the police!'

Steve turned and began walking towards the door. Chris knew he had no choice. He had to come clean, so he ran and grabbed his friend and spun him round. They were eye to eye.

'Okay, Steve, just calm down, okay. I'll tell you. Just calm down.'

'Chris, where is she?'

Chris stepped back from his friend, just a few steps until he walked into the covered sofa, stumbled and ended up sitting on its arm.

'She's dead.'

'What? What the fuck have you done?'

'I haven't done anything. She was killed. I was forced to watch.'

'Killed? Killed by who?'

'I don't know his name. He was from that night years ago, remember? The one where you had to come and get me out of jail.'

'What?'

'He killed her, Steve. He killed her and he made me watch. He strangled her right in front of me and there was nothing I could do to stop him.'

'Shit.'

Slumping to the floor, Chris let the tears fall. Steve stood, unmoving.

'He made me watch her die.'

Steve lowered himself to be nearer to his friend. His voice calmer, quieter. 'Why haven't you gone to the police?'

'Because he promised to kill you, or anyone else I got close to, if I said a word. And now you know.'

'I don't get it. If it's who you say it is, why would he come back after all this time? Why would he kill her?'

'To punish me.'

'Jesus, Chris, you can't keep this to yourself. You have to call the police.'

301

'Didn't you hear? I can't do that, Steve.'

'Chris, we have to do something.'

'Just give me twenty-four hours and it will all be taken care of.'

'Why, what's happening in twenty-four hours?'

'I can't tell you. You just have to trust me, okay?'

'Trust you? You've lied to me for nearly a year, Chris, and then tell me my life is in danger. No, I'm calling the police now.'

Steve stood and walked towards the back door, dialling 999. As he did, Chris saw a movement out of the corner of his eye. He spun around, coming face to face with the large bay window, and there he was. The man who murdered his wife.

Suddenly Chris felt a shift, his breathing turned heavy and hard like a caged zoo animal wanting to fight its spectator. Somehow this monster had gotten in whilst Chris was focused on Steve, on fixing the problem. In his hand was the fire shovel. Chris could feel his heart beating wildly, so hard his hands began to tingle.

Chris tried to speak, to warn Steve, but found no words. His legs began to buckle as the man pushed past his last resolve. Raising the shovel above his head, he charged at Steve, bringing it down upon the back of his skull. He watched his best friend's body fall limp on the floor. His right leg twitching.

Chris dropped the shovel to the ground, looking down at his friend lying face down in a pool of blood that was slowly growing. As he spoke his voice was different, gravelly. 'He tried to warn you, Steve.' Stepping over his body, Chris made his way towards the back door. His mind already on fixing the other problem. It would be just as easy to fix, for outside his house was the train girl, and it was time they had a little chat.

Chapter 43

9.24 p.m. – London Road, Peterborough

I had been sitting outside Chris's for about an hour, waiting to see a light go on inside as it got dark, or for him to message saying he wanted to see me like he had done the night before. Neither happened. His house remained a shadowed, lifeless mass of bricks and windows.

I looked to my passenger seat, his key catching the orange lights that threw the road into an artificial dead daytime. Grabbing it, I took a deep breath, then opened my car door and stepped into the cool night. There were forty-four steps between where I stood and his front door, each one intensifying as I waited for him to call my name, or a concerned neighbour to raise alarm and stop me. Nothing happened.

When I slipped the key into the lock, I half expected him to be standing on the other side, confused but pleased to see me. Again, nothing. I entered his house without anyone trying to stop me. Almost like it was mine and I belonged.

I let myself fantasize for a moment that it was true. That I belonged here, in this house with him. The neighbours would see us as a young, happy couple and I would often wave to them as I got into my car to leave for work. Their acceptance of me replacing his ex-wife, as if she didn't exist at all and I had been his spouse all along. It was childish to think it, but, regardless, I didn't stop myself.

As I closed the door, I listened, waiting for my eyes to adjust to the darkness. The only noise was the ticking of the clock. Its sound was hard, reminding me of that first moment I stepped over the threshold and into his life. His back to me, his knuckles white.

I walked into his lounge and through to the kitchen. I could almost see him leaning on the draining board. Beside the kettle was a cup and, as I stepped closer, I could see a half-drunk tea. There was also a sandwich on the side near the fridge. For a moment I thought it was fresh, but the tea was cold and the bread hardened and stale.

Doubling back on myself, I went upstairs, first to the bathroom then the bedroom. Secure in the knowledge he wasn't in, I went back down and opened the door to the cupboard under the stairs. The toolbox he had sneaked in from the shed was there and, as I grabbed its handle, a surge of adrenaline shot through me. This was it: the secrets he held dearly I would begin to know.

I was expecting it to be heavy, but it was light and, as I lifted it, things inside shifted and moved. Whatever was inside, it wasn't tools. Once I had wrestled it free, I took it back to the kitchen and put it on the dining table. I listened to the sound of blood rushing to my head before I opened it, hesitating only for moment, and looked inside.

The book I saw him carrying was lying on the top. I opened the first page and saw it was a diary. Reading the first few lines, I learnt it was Julia's. What I didn't know was why he was hiding it in a toolbox.

There were other things in there too, wrapped in a black bin bag. I would look at them as well, but the diary was my first priority. Somewhere within it might be the answer to what had happened. If I could find that out I might be able to save him. But I paused, feeling like I was doing something terrible by looking. The diary felt heavy in my hands and, as I put it on the table, I let myself ask the question that was hiding in the corners of my mind since Steve's message the night before. Had I fallen in love with a man who had done something unimaginable to his wife?

Standing, I leant over to see inside the black bin bag. Its contents something I did and didn't want to see in equal measure. I felt the hairs on my arms stand up and, as adrenaline circulated around my body, butterflies the size of small birds began fluttering inside my stomach, their wings beating as fast as a hummingbird's, making my whole body start to shake. With hands I could barely control, I squeezed the bag as to give a hint to its contents. I could tell there was a shoe, although I could only feel one. I set the bag on the table and carefully pulled away the tape that held the folded top closed, tearing the bag as I did, splitting it completely down one side.

There was no way I was going to be able to put the contents back inside without him knowing it had been tampered with. Although I was starting to feel that once I looked inside there was no going back, no hiding anything. The first item I came across was a carefully folded note. I put it to one side. I couldn't take reading something that mirrored what I had discovered that night under the bench I sat on.

Tearing the bag further, one black evening shoe, size five, from Topshop, fell out. There was nothing remarkable about it. Then I looked at the heel and I could see a dark stain on it. At first I thought it was mud but as I looked closer I saw it was in fact a very dark red, blood red.

I jumped up, quickly moving away from what I assumed was a weapon. Creating some distance before I was sick. I knew I needed to call the police, but I needed to know what else was in the bag before I did. I needed answers. I deserved as much.

Conscious my fingerprints were now all over the possible murder weapon I moved it away from me using just my thumb and forefinger, and then I tipped the rest of the bag's contents carefully onto the table. Four more things fell out. A purse, a car jack, a passport and a mobile phone. I opted for the purse first and, as I opened it, I still hoped it wouldn't be hers. But it was Julia's. Her driving licence in her married name, her bank cards and credit cards. Her Tesco clubcard. Then I looked at the passport. Again it was hers, valid, no sign of an Australian visa, hidden with a bloodstained shoe and her mobile phone. I knew I needed to read the folded note. I picked it up and opened it.

Lat: 52.5862 Long: 0.0140
You will find a tree, under it wrapped within its roots you
will find the remains of Julia Suzette Hayes.
Killed on 2 June 2015
Ensure she is well cared for.

I couldn't hold the piece of paper in my hands any more. My fingers felt numb and I was sure any moment I would faint. I put down the note. I realized Steve had been right all along and I was in the worst place I could be.

I grabbed my jacket and turned to head to the door, but as I did, a yelp escaped from me before I could catch it and hold it in. A man was standing in the doorway to Chris's kitchen. Soaking wet, blood clearly splattered across the right side of his face. His shoulders were hunched; his breathing was hard.

His eyes showed an anger I had never seen before. It wasn't until he took a step forward and into the low kitchen light I realized it was Chris.

I barely recognized him. His face was heavy and distorted. A monster.

He looked from me to the table and back again. The look changed and for a moment neither of us moved. We just looked at each other. It was in that moment that I cursed myself for being so naive for so long. I was so wrapped up in trying to unravel the mystery I didn't stop and question if I should. He even sounded different when he spoke.

'You shouldn't have opened that box, Sarah.'

'What did you do, Chris?'

'Chris did nothing.'

'What?' I looked at him in disbelief, utterly confused by what was going on.

'What did you see?'

I glanced to the table and the contents of the toolbox then back at him.

'Have you worked it out?'

He was smiling at me as he said it, almost proud at making me say what was obvious.

'Sarah, if you had to: take a guess.'

I couldn't look at him any more; he didn't look like the Chris I knew.

'Take a guess. Go on.'

'You killed her,' I said at barely a whisper, hoping if I said it quietly enough it wouldn't be true.

'Bingo.'

I glanced back to the table, to see what was nearest to me, hoping something heavy was the closest but it was the shoe, just to my left, a reach away. It was only a second, if that, but when I looked back to his stare – cold, hard, frightening – I knew he saw the flick of my eye. Without looking away, he closed the kitchen door behind him. His gaze fixed on me.

I could feel fear begin to seep through me, working through my body until it was crawling up my throat, closing it as it travelled. It was what I thought an asthma attack would feel like. I knew I had to get out so grabbing the shoe I threw it at him as hard as I could as a distraction in order to bolt for the back door.

I hadn't anticipated him being so quick, and before I could touch the handle he was on me, one arm wrapped around my waist, forcing the air out of my lungs, the other over my mouth to catch my scream. I tried to fight but he was too strong and he pushed me to the floor, my face hitting the tiling hard. His full weight pressing down on me, his knees in my back. His hand was still over my mouth, covering most of my nose, making it difficult to breathe, his other hand pressing my skull. I tried to fight, but could only use my legs below my knees and as much as I flailed to kick him I could only move air.

'If you fight, Sarah, it will be worse for you. Do you understand?'

I nodded as best I could with my head still pressed hard into the cold floor, a pressure building in my eye as the swelling started to come out. But his grip didn't lessen; instead, lifting me by the waist and wrapping his arm around my neck so tightly I could barely breathe, he dragged me towards the stairs. For some reason, I knew if I went upstairs I might never come back down so I struggled as much as I could, but his strength was too much for me and he quickly subdued me once more, dragging me into his bedroom. Once inside, he closed the door and threw me onto the floor. Standing over me, he leant in close.

'If you scream or shout, Sarah, I'll have to silence you. Do you understand?' His face was only inches from my own. His eyes bloodshot and glazed, his breath reeking of alcohol.

I nodded, and I saw his guard lower slightly, so I made for the door, half crawling, half falling, screaming as I did. He grabbed me from behind and placed his wide hands over my mouth and nose, instantly suppressing my screams.

I tried to fight. I kicked and dug my nails into his hands so hard they bled, but he pressed harder and harder on my mouth, making it impossible to breathe. He leant in close to my ear and whispered, his voice sounding different, like he was another man.

'He warned you not to come back. He told you to leave him alone, but you insisted on pushing your way into his world, and now I'm taking charge. What happens next is entirely your own doing.'

Chapter 44

2 June 2016
The second final day

10.39 p.m. – March train station

Eight minutes.

Chris looked up at the train station clock. It read ten thirty-nine. Eight minutes. That was all he had to wait. In just eight small minutes he would be dead and everything would finally be over. Attempting to calm his inner storm, he looked around. It seemed nothing had improved in the dilapidated station, and although it was warmer than in May there was still a dampness in the air, coming from the dark corners of the old station. It sent a shiver up his spine.

Just a few nights ago he'd been in the same place, distracted with the thoughts and words of Julia's diary. Her betrayal, leading to his. It, along with the other items, were back in the toolbox – their catacomb. Along with his new note, showing where to find everything that would enable her to get a proper burial.

Chris took his shoes off and threw them onto the tracks. He looked at them, lonely and out of place on the grey stones between the iron lines. He wondered why he didn't do that last time. Throwing them down was a statement of intent. It said he would not put them back on. It said, this time he would not fail.

He put his hand in his left trouser pocket and pulled out its contents. Three things: the picture of her, his suicide note and the small black stone. He looked at his wife. It was the same picture he carried on his last attempt. Her crooked smile seeming bigger. Excited. He pressed her into his right palm, which also contained the stone, before putting them under the bench, in the same spot as he had before. The note, although similar to last time, also had new information. Or rather, an apology, both to the train girl and Steve.

He tried to explain that the man who hurt them wasn't him but someone else, a voice that he had long silenced as a young man, who had slowly forced his way back into his life. That man was now dormant but never gone.

He stretched his back and stepped towards the edge of the platform, curling his toes over the end. He looked back to the clock.

Seven minutes.

He ran through his mental checklist, ticking off what he needed. He had checked the trains would still run in a similar manner. He had placed the note and lost the shoes. He had even organized his will this time, leaving most of his belongings to Steve.

He had also left some for Sarah, although both lives were still in the balance.

With very little time left, he let himself remember the day Julia had died.

***

He had found her diary whilst searching for something in the bedroom when she was out having lunch with a friend. His curiosity getting the better of him, he opened near the beginning and read a little about their date on the beach and smiled to himself. Sitting on their bed, he read about their experiences through her eyes and remembered fondly the wonderful moments of their marriage. He shed a tear when he recalled Julia's mother dying and his heart ached at reading the things his wife couldn't say to him about her feelings afterwards.

Then, flicking forward to a more recent entry, only three weeks before, he read about James. Her boss. A sickness washing over him, an anger that started in his chest and flooded to every part of his body like white light. Her words: 'I am now a woman who is having an affair', turned his world blurry.

Heartbroken and not knowing what to do, he continued his day as if he didn't know her secret. Hoping she would say or do something when she saw he wasn't himself. His anger bubbling inside growing in heat, needing to find a way to escape. What was even more heartbreaking was that she was still the same Julia he married when she came home. Bright, funny, caring. There was nothing to suggest she had been cheating and Chris didn't know what was worse: her affair or the fact she hid it so well.

After a quiet dinner he told Julia he was tired. He had to go and do the routine monthly check at Julia's mum's house and seeing he was off she asked to come, saying she would wait in the car. His heart broke knowing she could go into the house with another man, but not her husband. They were on the way back along the A605 between March and Peterborough when the pressure pot finally spilled over. Tears blurred his vision, making it even harder to drive in the torrential rain that night.

'Chris? Honey, what's wrong?'

'Julia, when where you planning on telling me about James?'

***

Six minutes.

Chris thought he heard something coming from outside the entrance to the station. A car pulling up perhaps, or a person walking to catch a late train, and he walked tentatively towards the source, trying to stay in the shadows as much as he could. His footsteps quieter than usual. Reaching the sandstone archway, he peered out. There was no one there. He was alone as he should be, but he couldn't relax.

He wondered for a moment if he was having doubts, but quickly dismissed it. His tension was because of what he'd had to endure over the past month. The person he had become, the things he had done. All for her. All for his wonderful wife.

It wasn't doubt, he was just being cautious. There could be no saboteurs to his plan this time round. He had made sure of that, as hard as it had been. He walked back onto the platform and perched himself on the aged and battered bench. He forced himself to remember that night once more.

***

'Julia, when where you planning on telling me about James?'

She shifted in her chair and gripped the armrest. He waited for a response, watching the pounding window wipers to pass the silence. He knew that if he was patient for long enough she would speak. He knew that much about his wife.

She asked if it couldn't wait till they were at home; he said it couldn't. She made him promise to stay calm so they could talk. He did, knowing he might not. Then she said it. She told him about her affair. For a while Chris sat in silence, listening to the whooshing of blade against windscreen and the hammering of rain. He had lost control of his love, and with it his life. The last thing he remembered was a red mist sinking over his eyes.

He slammed on the brakes and turned the steering wheel hard to the left, making the car veer violently, the back end swinging out as the tyres transferred from tarmac to mud before sliding to a halt. During the commotion the hazard lights had been hit and they began blinking: on, off, on, off.

'Jesus Christ, Chris,' Julia shouted, gripping the seat.

'Are you still sleeping with him?' Chris said, his voice low, his eyes piercing through her.

'You could have killed us.'

'Are you still fucking sleeping with him?'

'Please, just calm down.'

'Answer the question.'

'Chris, please.'

She tried to move, turning her body to go for the door handle, but he grabbed her by the shoulders and squeezed hard. His face inches from hers.

'Please, you're hurting me.'

'Answer the fucking question.'

'Yes, okay, yes. I am sleeping with him. But I was going to tell you; I was. I'm going to end it.'

'Shut up.'

'I promise, Chris. I promise. I've made a terrible mistake.'

'You're only saying that because I know now.'

'Please let me go.'

He cried, and squeezed her harder. Barely able to contain his rage. He knew she had been having sex with him, but hearing it from her mouth, a mouth that should have been his alone to kiss, changed something. She pleaded for him to calm down, to let her go, but her words had become a mumble of inaudible sound, underwater, distant.

His mind drifted to images of her climaxing, another man between her legs, her biting her lip in a way that was only for him. She managed to shake him free, opened the door and stepped out into the rain. Slipping in her heels. One falling off in the footwell of the car. The rain blinding her.

He climbed over to the passenger side and fell out onto the soaking ground. Their eyes locked and he could see her fear, she was thinking about running but decided against it. Getting to his feet he slammed the door behind him. His breathing was erratic, his shoulders rolled, his teeth bared.

'Chris, please, stay calm. Let's talk about this.'

Chris grabbed her again, screaming in her face, crying as he did. He pleaded with her to tell him why she had done it. Not listening as she tried to tell him she was scared and in pain.

She slipped again and fell to the ground and he picked her up by her hair before he felt a sharp pain in his shoulder. He looked and saw her remaining black heel was stuck in it. The pain shot through his chest as his arm went numb. He looked at his wife who stood in shock. She tried to say sorry and stepped forward to help but stopped at his expression.

He pulled out the heel, dropped it to the ground and looked at his wife. Her body lit by the blinking hazards. Light, shade, light, shade. She was crying, begging for forgiveness. Chris looked through her at his reflection in the car. It was a different man who stared back at him. One fuelled by anger, with a dangerous glint in his eyes. His arm hung limp by his side, the heel having done more damage than he thought it could.

Looking back at him was a monster, one that had always been there. For Chris, it was like he was in a dream, a nightmare he couldn't wake from as he watched himself lunge out with his left hand, catching her on her right ear, sending her falling against the side of the car. Her face hitting the window but not breaking it. It was unsatisfying. He needed more.

He needed the glass to shatter around her as she had shattered his heart. It needed to be broken like his trust had been. Grabbing her by her hair, he smashed her head into the glass again and again until cracks appeared. The whole time she begged him to stop. The fourth attempt put her face through it and a thousand shards exploded over her eyes, cutting her flesh. Dropping her to the floor, she was no longer begging but mumbling incoherent words.

Her dress was riding high up her leg, exposing her underwear, and he thought of the other man seeing that part of her body, touching, fucking. He knew he should stop, but the image of her with James wouldn't lift.

'I trusted you, Julia.'

'Chris, please stop.'

'Shut up, just shut the fuck up.'

'Chris … '

'I said shut up.'

He dropped to his knees beside her, took her throat in his hands and squeezed. She put her thumb in the hole in his shoulder and, screaming, he let her go. She tried to run, but failed, in too much pain to get anywhere quickly. Chris grabbed her by the ankle and pulled. She fell once more, her face landing in the wet, soft mud, glass from the window cutting her face even more. A pool of blood began to form around her.

Falling on her, he pressed her head into the mixture of mud, blood and glass. He screamed at himself to stop, begged him to stop but he wasn't listening. The more she fought the harder he pressed, crying as he did until she stopped fighting. The only movement being the involuntary twitching of nerves as they fired for the last time.

After rolling off her, Chris stood and looked towards the car, seeing the monster looking back through the rain-beaten glass. Shocked when through the reflection it spoke to him in a voice that both was and wasn't his.

Look what she made us do. She left us no choice, Chris. We did what we had to do.

'What have you done?'

What you wanted me to do.

'I didn't want this.'

You tell yourself that. We both know it's not true. You know what we need to do now?

'Go to the police.'

Don't be so fucking naive. Now we have to bury the bitch. Bury the bitch, Chris.

'Shut up!'

Chris staggered backwards, the pain in his shoulder intensifying with every laboured, wounded breath. Her body only a few feet away, unmoving. Trying to keep his balance, Chris stumbled to the left and fell down a six-foot dyke he hadn't seen. His body slammed into a tree at the bottom, knocking the wind out of him.

After clambering up the steep sodden slope, Chris fell by his wife's side and rolled her over. Her face unrecognizable, mud inside her mouth where she had fought to breathe. He shook her, shouting at himself as he did. 'Look what you have done to us; look at what you have fucking done.'

Although the animal had taken over, he still expected her limp body would come back to life with every violent shake. But she wasn't moving; she wasn't breathing. From somewhere he could hear himself say that he needed to get to work.

***

Standing up, Chris took a breath. This was the furthest he had ever let himself go when remembering that

321

night. Looking at his hand he could see himself visibly shaking. He clenched his fist three times to try to stop it. It didn't work. Placing his fingers on his wrist, he felt his pulse. It thumped through his vein quickly.

He needed to calm himself down, get himself refocused. He needed to see his crime objectively and then, centred and controlled, like he was a month before, throw himself under a train. He didn't know why but part of him didn't feel as ready as he had. He'd had another month to prepare, and now, with the man he had become in that month, he had even more reason to do what he had to do. He had killed his wife. There was Steve and Sarah too, whose fates were still unknown. This was the only way he could make it right. Julia's body needed to be laid to rest, and the others, they needed to know why.

He looked up to the clock to see how long was left.

Five minutes.

Chris began to pace slowly, one foot directly in front of the other, as if walking a tightrope up and down a short stretch of the platform. He compared this moment to the one from twenty-eight days before and couldn't help but see how different it was. Although he knew what would happen as the 10.47 train came through, the wait felt like the polar opposite.

He felt fear of the pain that he might experience before he was dead and wondered how exactly it would happen. Thinking of it made him feel sick. So once again he forced himself to picture that night. He hated himself for what happened. This was good. Chris knew he needed to hate himself for another four and a half minutes.

***

Her body lay on its back, waiting for him to decide what to do with her. Looking at his wife, Chris felt detached, lost. Like he was watching what was happening to him through an old grainy television set. But it was real; there was no drama. No parting words. His wife lay silently dead at his feet, and he had murdered her.

As his breathing calmed, he felt the cold rain falling on him once more. Soothing, cleansing. He looked in the rear passenger-side car window and saw himself, soaking, muddy, bleeding, and each flash of the hazard lights allowed him to come eye to eye with the monster before him. He looked at what his wife had made him become. A panting, hunched beast with arms that swung loosely at his sides. Its teeth bared, its body taut and ready.

What are you waiting for, Chris?

'No, I have to call the police.'

And say what?

'That you killed her.'

But I'm you, Chris. You killed her, not me. They'll lock you up.

323

'I don't care.'

I do.

Chris took his phone from his pocket, tried to dial 999 but an impulse took over and he threw it to the ground and stamped on it.

I can't have you ring the police, Chris.

'I have to.'

You forget, Chris, I'm you. That means I know everything you do. I know your friends, your work colleagues. All of them. I'll kill them all and you know I will. I'll visit them in their sleep and slit their throats. So I suggest you do what I say.

'Please, don't hurt anyone else.'

I won't, if this stays our little secret.

'Please, don't make me do this.'

We both know that this is what you wanted, Chris. You're just too much of a pussy to say it out loud.

'I didn't want her dead.'

It's too late to change that now. Come on, we have work to do.

With no control over his feet, Chris stepped over Julia's corpse and opened his boot to find the car jack, which lay under the flooring inside. Cradling it in his damaged arm, he grabbed her ankle with his good hand and dragged her to the edge of the slope before pushing her over. He watched her body tumble like a rag doll's before slamming into the same tree he had.

With the Jack in his arms he slid down the bank and ended up standing over her. Her eyes fixed on his, glazed over. And he began to dig, scraping the wet mud and piling it beside the base of the tree. He dug so deep that the thick roots of it became exposed. He thought if he placed her close to them she would be less likely to be found. It made him sick to realize there was some logic in it.

He decided to rest her head first. He didn't want to remember his wife's face as the bloodied, broken and lifeless one that he saw now. He gently laid it into the hole facing the tree. He didn't know why, but it felt important. For a moment the monster backed off, allowing him to stroke his wife's hair tenderly.

He wanted to say something, but the monster wouldn't let him. So he sat in silence for a moment, pretending they were back on the beach in southern Spain. Neither speaking, neither needing to. After giving her one final kiss, he stood and looked at the rest of her lifeless body and the monster took control once again.

The rest of her was the woman who had been fucking another man. Dropping to his knees, he tried to fold her right arm through a gap between root and earth. If he could get her arm in, then her shoulder and half of her chest would follow. But it wouldn't fit, not with it bending the way an arm should.

He looked up at the night sky. The moon was full, peering out from behind a cloud, watching. He then took a deep breath, grabbed her lifeless wrist, and placed her elbow against the root. With her arm twisted so her palm faced upwards, he pressed on her wrist with his other hand. With her arm straightened, the only way for it to naturally bend was if he removed it from the root or released his grip. Instead, he pressed down as hard as he could.

Julia was only petite, but breaking her arm was far harder than he would have imagined. He pressed down so hard sweat began to mix with the falling rainwater until he could feel the arm begin to bend, just before he heard it snap.

Her arm had given way, the snap sounding like a table leg being broken and, because of the force Chris had been pushing with, he fell, hitting his eye on the root of the tree before landing next to his Julia, her arm bent backwards. The bones tearing through her skin. Their jagged angles looking more like a cheap horror prop than belonging to a real person. Breaking it had done the trick, and, twisting it slightly, he was able to push half of her body under the root and around the tree.

She looked like a baby holding its teddy whilst it slept. With her face turned to the tree and her broken arm obscured by the roots, she looked just like she did any other time she was asleep. When she was in their bed, warm, safe.

'Fuck. What have I done?'

***

Four minutes.

Chris needed to snap out of his memories. His train was in four minutes and he was on the verge of passing out. Which would let the monster in once again. Seeing the male toilet door was open, he walked towards it and went inside.

He noticed it was a lot cooler inside the bathroom and the terracotta-coloured floor tiles were mostly broken, several missing. Floor-to-ceiling white tiles gave the space a clinical yet dirty feel. There were four metal urinals lining the wall on the left and two cubicles on the right. He checked them first. Both were empty. Beside the urinals, two of which were blocked with tissue, stood one solitary metal sink. Above it was a mirror that was only six inches squared and scratched, almost to the point of being useless.

He pressed the button on the tap and water poured from it. Cupping his hands, he scooped some onto his face. The coldness instantly making him feel more centred. He splashed himself again then looked at himself in the mirror. He saw the look of a tired child who was unable to sleep because of bad dreams. The beast that used to stare back was gone, dead or hiding. Taking deep, measured breaths, he looked at himself for as long as he dared not to be able to see the clock.

'You have to do this. You have to remember exactly what you did, all of it. Every detail. Because of you, she's dead. So get your fucking shit together.'

Unable to stand the sight of himself any more, he looked away and before leaving took the picture of his wife out of his trouser pocket. The memory of his honeymoon wanted to come back to the foreground. He forced it back. Although smiling, her eyes looked angry. Had they always? He kissed her and then folded the picture, wanting to put it in his shirt pocket, close to his heart, where he had before. Only this time he didn't have a pocket. So he put it back in his trousers before stepping out of the toilets and back onto the platform.

Three minutes.

There were only three minutes left now, not long. He looked around. Still alone. Curling his toes back over the platform edge he took a deep breath and closed his eyes.

***

The ground was so wet he slipped twice whilst trying to get up, both times falling on her. The pain in his eye intensifying as his blood ran into it.

Finally, scrambling to his knees and regaining his balance, he began the process of covering the top half of her body that was wrapped among the roots, scooping a handful of mud with his good arm and packing it around her. Pushing it into every gap, covering her arms, chest, hands and neck. He couldn't do her face, not yet; he would leave that till last. Her body was what he had lost to another man, but he still believed her mind was his. He wasn't ready to say goodbye to that part.

So he covered her torso and wiped mud from her ashen face every time it spilt on it. Once he finished, only that and her legs remained uncovered. As for the rest of her, even he couldn't believe how easy it was to make it look like she wasn't there at all. After taking a deep breath, he wiped blood from his face, flexed his right fingers to try to keep his hand working, and began to fold her legs around the tree. And, as with her upper body, he would have to make her bend in ways that weren't natural, but he took a small pleasure in the sound of snapping bone.

***

Chris threw up on his bare feet and the track beneath. It came so violently he thought he was going to fall over the edge. If he did he would probably knock himself out, then the driver would have no choice but to watch as he ran over his body. He forced himself back and, dropping to the floor, he fought to control his breathing. Telling himself to be calm, get control, nothing had changed from a month before, he'd still done what he did, and he still needed to see it again. He still needed to do so to honour his wife and stop the monster from doing any more harm.

Two minutes.

Looking up he tried to see where the moon was in its cycle. It was almost full. Sneaking out from

329

behind a cloud. There were no visible stars. Looking to the clock, he knew his train, his end, was coming soon. He had to stop wasting precious time so he put himself back in that night.

***

With his hands on her right leg, he forced it into a small gap, hoping he wouldn't have to damage her body any more to make her legs rest against the tree. He scooped up more dense mud to pack around her once she was nested. Her legs were bent up on themselves, all broken angles. Him having to stamp on them several times to snap them and fold them in.

Covered neck to toe in mud, so thick it had stemmed the bleeding from both his shoulder and eyebrow, Chris looked at his work. His wife, his cheating, flawed, wonderful wife was now embraced by the tree as she had been embraced in his arms for years. As she had been embraced in the arms of her lover. But the job wasn't finished. The monster in him backed away, allowing him to kneel down beside her face. He kissed the side of her lips, cold and mud-speckled.

And then he saw that final moment, a fist full of mud, her face uncovered. His final goodbye before burying her completely. Removing her from the world. He dropped his head into his hands and screamed.

330

He screamed at himself so loud the sound bounced off the clouds, like the train horn did a month before.

***

It snapped him back into the present. He screamed at himself for the damage he had caused. He screamed at Julia for having her affair. He screamed at Sarah for loving him and Steve for doing the same. He screamed at his mum for dying so young and his dad for trying to teach him how to be a good man. He screamed at the monster that had robbed him of everything that mattered. He screamed at the wait, the long wait that had filled him with doubt, until there was no more air left in his lungs.

Chapter 45

Sixty minutes earlier

9.45 p.m. – Addenbrooke's Hospital, Cambridge

It took Steve a full minute to focus once he opened his eyes. All he could make out were the blurry images of a window and darkness outside it. Then he saw Kristy, her outline soft and blurred around the edges. It was the only one that he knew and could make sense of. When his eyes did adjust to the light and his vision sharpened, he could see she was asleep in her chair wearing one of his old jumpers.

Looking around the room he fixed on a bag of saline solution hanging from a stand. Its tubes running into a vein in his right arm. He knew what it was; what he didn't know was why he was connected to it. He tried to sit up but couldn't. The pain in his head and face like a lightning bolt that grounded him. Then he called out in panic. His wife was by his side before he could run out of air.

'Steve, darling, it's okay. Steve. Calm down. It's me. It's Kristy.'

'Kristy.'

***

She broke down in tears, relief flooding through her body. They had told her when he did eventually wake they still wouldn't know what the extent of the damage would be. He remembered who she was; that was enough.

'What happened?' His voice was barely a whisper. He was already looking like he was going to go to sleep again.

'Shhh, it's okay, you're okay.' She wanted to know exactly the same thing. What happened that meant he was in a house in Ely belonging to a dead woman she had never heard of? What happened that meant he had been attacked? But she didn't ask, not yet, not while he looked so vulnerable and in so much pain. Instead, she reached over and pressed the call button for a nurse before wrapping both of her hands around one of his, careful to avoid the cannula in the back of it pumping antibiotics into his system.

***

Within seconds a nurse, followed closely by a doctor, entered the room. The nurse flashing a wide smile with crooked teeth and dark, soothing eyes. She almost made it feel like he was a child waking to his mother. The doctor was far more serious, far more assessing. Examining her handiwork like a mechanic.

Steve looked through them and could see two others in uniform who were hovering outside the door, interested in what was happening. The doctor examined his pupils, asked him questions. Can you remember your name? Who is this lady? What day is it? Do you feel any pain? That's to be expected. Does it hurt anywhere else? Satisfied with his answers, she then told him he had been very lucky.

Steve watched as the doctor looked towards the waiting police officers and they began to step inside. They spoke in compassionate tones, held a sympathetic gaze but clearly wanted to know what had happened. They told him he had been involved in an incident, that he had been attacked and hit with a small fireplace shovel. He was told that he was found by police who came because a neighbour saw him break into the house and called them. He might have died if he hadn't been seen.

They wanted to know why he had broken into the residence in Ely. But the questions had become overpowering and Steve couldn't focus. They pushed him despite the doctor insisting he needed rest and before they left they asked if he knew who attacked him. For a second he didn't, then the image of his best friend shot into his mind. Before Steve could begin to tell them about Chris he closed his eyes. Unable to stay awake.

***

With Steve asleep, the officers quickly left the room, asking Kristy to give them a call once Steve was ready to talk. Kristy was left to look out of the window of Steve's hospital room and wait. She felt relieved that after nearly twenty-four hours he was awake and knew who she was. It was a good sign. The nurse who was with the doctor filled in his charts and gave her a weak smile.

'Can I get you a cup of tea, Mrs Patterson?'

'Please.'

The nurse smiled again and left. Returning the room to silence. Knowing he was okay allowed her to reflect on the past day. There had been a knock on Steve and Kristy's front door just before 11 p.m. the night before. When she opened it wearing a dressing gown and slippers, two police officers were there. A PC Hull, and another one whose name she couldn't remember.

She knew straight away something was terribly wrong with Steve. For all her husband's faults he wasn't one who didn't come home at night without letting her know first. PC Hull, a huge but softly spoken man, told her that her husband had been found in a house in Ely. He had been injured and was on his way, via an ambulance, to Addenbrooke's. They stepped inside and told her to get some things; they would take her to him.

She had questions running through her mind as she panic-dressed. She wanted to know what sort of accident he had been involved in. How bad was he? What was he doing at a house in Ely?

As she got into the back of their police car, she finally asked one.

'Is my husband going to be all right?' They couldn't answer directly, instead told her he was in the best hands.

When she got there, Kristy wasn't allowed to see him straight away. He was in surgery. X-rays showed a small fracture on his skull, some swelling, but not as much as they first thought given the state of him when he came in. When he was finally moved into recovery in the early hours of the morning, she was allowed to be with her husband. Seeing him made her choke back a sob. A nurse gave her shoulder a reassuring squeeze, but still, nobody could tell her that everything was going to be okay.

It broke her heart to look at him, but she did so anyway. His head, heavily bandaged and with bruising that ran down the right side of his face. His right eye swollen shut. His eyelids dark, his skin ashen. The rhythmic beeping of his heart-rate monitor giving the only indication he was actually

336

alive. She had sat with him all day and in that time the shock had fully subsided and had been replaced with exhaustion.

***

The police had questions, most like Kristy's own. Apparently, no one had any idea what he was doing at a house in Ely. It belonged to a late Catherine Walker, handed down to her daughter, who they hadn't been able to find yet, and it had remained unlived in for the best part of two years. Kristy didn't know anyone with the name Walker.

The police asked more questions about who Steve associated with. Did he have any known enemies? They quizzed her about the connection to the small fenland city. She knew of none. Without any answers it became clear Steve was leading a double life of some kind. She tried to call Chris. If anyone knew what Steve might have been up to, it would be him. He didn't pick up.

After the police had gone and the doctors' visits moved from every thirty minutes to every few hours, all Kristy could do was listen to the continuous beeping and wait. Wondering what Steve had got himself into and whether he would wake up. She tried Chris again, his phone going straight to voicemail. Something fired in the back of her mind, a question about Chris. No doubt implanted by her husband's doubts recently. But she dismissed it. It had been one hell of a twenty-four hours.

***

Lost in her own thoughts about her horrid and confusing day, Kristy didn't notice Steve wake again.

This time his vision came back to him a lot quicker; this time he knew where he was. But, due to the fading anaesthetic, the events that led to his head needing to be patched together were hazy. Turning his head, he saw his wife, her head on her hands, looking out of the hospital window. He didn't speak at first, just looked at her. The way her jawline angled almost ninety degrees from her small ear. Her delicate nose, narrow and sharp. Her large blue eyes, looking out of the window, lost in a daydream. He didn't remember them ever looking so clear, like an ocean. Her lips were slightly parted, her breathing not as calm as it should be.

'Kristy.'

She turned, her eyes wide, her open mouth turning into a smile. Steve tried to sit himself up.

'Hey, no, don't move. I'll use this.'

Kristy picked up the bed's remote and gently raised the backrest till Steve was sitting up. Not fully, but not lying down either.

'How are you feeling?'

His voice was tired, distant, but more like his than half an hour before. 'Sore.'

'I bet, darling. Can I get you anything?'

'Can I have a drink?'

'Of course; let me get a nurse.'

Kristy tiptoed from the room, leaving Steve to listen to his heart-rate monitor beeping. Its pulses around two a second. It was a little quick, but not dangerously so. Leaning forward on his right arm, careful not to catch any tubes that were in it, he reached to the back of his head, slowly towards the place where Chris had hit him. He ran his fingers through the smooth patch of skin where they had had to shave it before he felt the first of the staples that were holding his head together.

He wasn't sure if it actually hurt touching it or if it was psychosomatic, but he winced and pulled his hand away. Looking up, he saw Kristy watching him. A sadness and resolve in her gaze.

'How bad is it?' he asked.

'Pretty bad, Steve. What the hell were you doing in that house?'

'Trying to find Julia.'

'What?'

'Kristy, I don't think she's in Australia.'

As if on cue the nurse arrived with a jug of water and two glasses, followed by the same two officers who he had spoken with half an hour before.

'Mr Patterson, how are you feeling?'

'I'm fine.'

'Good, we are sorry to press, but do you remember anything about what happened? We just want to find out who did this to you.'

Steve began to speak but stopped himself. He'd forgotten about Sarah; she was going to his house.

'You need to get to his house.'

'Whose house?'

'Chris Hayes.'

'Is he the man who attacked you?'

'Yes, and there's a girl in serious danger.'

Chapter 46

10.45 p.m. – March train station

Ninety seconds.

Chris didn't remember falling over. All he knew was that he was now sitting on the ground on the empty platform, and tears rolled from the corners of his eyes and down the bridge of his nose. Somehow, reliving that night felt more painful than it had when it happened. There was no longer a disconnection to it. There was no shock to help protect him.

He couldn't remove the image of Julia's open eye looking back at him lifelessly as he scooped up the final handful of mud to cover her face. He didn't know why he hadn't closed her eye first. But whatever the reason the image stuck with him. She was gone. Buried in a ditch under a few inches of soil.

After climbing back up the bank, he had sat beside his car, allowing the cold rain to wash the dirt off his skin and clothes. Washing the monster away with it.

Allowing him to cry. Sobbing long and hard until he had nothing left. Chris placed his good hand on the ground to stand and felt something under it. He grabbed the object and held it up. A small black stone, much like how he now viewed himself. His heart cold and hard and black. He subconsciously put it in his pocket. Not knowing how important it would become to him.

He couldn't recall the drive home or that he had to stop three times to be sick. He didn't remember stepping into their house and falling into the shower fully clothed, trying to wash the blood off his skin, both hers and his. He didn't remember sitting on his bedroom floor, stitching his shoulder back together and how for the entire night he couldn't get into his bed or that he couldn't look in a mirror in case the monster was still there to mock his weakness in not being able to control his own body.

All he could remember was thinking about that last image of Julia's open eye being covered.

It had stuck with him all this time.

Chris rubbed his eyes; he needed to focus. His death was so close now. His release was so close he could almost hear his wife calling to him.

Sixty seconds.

He knew that in the next twenty-five seconds he would hear the train rumbling in the distance, coming towards him at speed, not stopping. He had counted it before. At this time of night he always heard the train thirty-five seconds before it arrived. Then, fifteen seconds later he would see the headlights of it, two beams cutting through the night, attracting him like a moth to a flame.

At least that's what it should have done. It had a month before. But it wasn't so clear any more. He couldn't visualize in the same way he had. He couldn't remember what carriage he wanted to aim for or why. Again he asked himself: would he even fit between them? He took Julia's picture from his pocket and looked into her green eyes. The amber flecks pleading with him.

'I'm going to do this, Julia.'

Putting her picture back in his pocket, he looked down the line, hoping it was a fraction early. He wanted it done. Finished. He wanted to atone. It wasn't there yet.

Forty-five seconds.

He wondered: what if things had been different? What if Sarah had never turned up? What if he did it a month before? Or what if he hadn't confronted Julia but waited for her to come to him. What if he never read her diary, or did and divorced her, or sought marriage therapy? What if that night when Steve rang years ago to tell him they were going out he said no and he and Julia had never met? What if he didn't steal that first kiss as the rain warmed his neck outside the taxi? What if he just handed himself in after she died? What if he told someone about the monster in him when he was a young man and knew there was a darkness most people didn't have?

'But none of those things happened,' he told himself out loud. 'You buried her in the mud and then you made a promise.'

Yes, a promise – one he would keep. Taking a deep breath, he focused. He would do it. He would make it all right again. He couldn't hear the rumbling of the train on the track, but it was coming. He would end it all in about sixty heartbeats.

Chapter 47

Twenty minutes earlier

10.25 p.m. – London Road, Peterborough

I was startled awake by the sound of a car door slamming outside, and instinctively I tried to cover up my almost naked body and hide. As I pulled the cord binding my wrists, it bit into me and I cried out, a muffled nothingness behind my gag.

There was another bang, much louder, and I heard the front door crash open, slamming into the hallway's wall, glass breaking, and lots of shouting.

'Chris Hayes, this is the police. Identify yourself!'

I couldn't believe it. I wasn't expecting to be found so soon. Looking at the clock, my eyes struggling to see the red LED digits through swelling in both eyes, I saw the time. He hadn't done it yet. His train was 10.47. But I didn't know what it meant. How did the police know what I knew? How did they know he needed arresting?

I could hear boots hitting the wooden floors in his hallway, lots of them, and they moved through the downstairs of the house, shouting 'Clear', as they moved through the rooms not finding him.

'Sarah, Sarah, are you here?'

I didn't know how they knew I was there. But it didn't matter. I began to scream as loud as my gag would let me and banged my head against the radiator, trying to get their attention.

I heard footsteps coming up towards me and, as the bedroom door flew open, I was blinded by a torch beam shining in my face.

'I've found her, in here. She's alive. Get a medical team up here, quick!'

The main light was thrown on and I closed my eyes to adjust. As I did, I felt something land on my body. It made me jump despite me not wanting to. I opened them to the image of a police officer with a thick red beard, who was knelt down beside me. The thing that had landed on my body was his coat, in an attempt to protect my dignity, like it mattered. As he spoke, I could see a tenderness in his eyes. His voice was a lot softer than his image would suggest.

'It's okay, calm down. If you struggle, you'll end up hurting yourself more.'

I could hear his words and I knew he was speaking the truth but my body wouldn't listen. It kicked and tried to pull away my hands, the pain almost unbearable.

'Sarah, it's okay. You're safe now. Look at me.'

I did as he said and as soon as my eyes met his I could feel my body calm, my muscles relax, and although I was still terrified I knew it was going to be okay.

'I'm going to remove this gag and we are going to get a medic to look at you. Try not to move.'

I nodded and he carefully removed the tape holding my gag in but it still pulled, making my bottom lip bleed. I didn't care though. As soon as he had done it, the sock fell from my mouth and I took a deep breath in. One that was jagged and hard. A pain shooting down my left side as I did, forcing a cry out of my mouth.

'Try to keep still. I know it hurts. We are going to get someone to look at you.' The kind red-bearded policeman helped me catch my breath and offered me some water. Holding a fresh bottle to my lips as I greedily drank, spilling water down my chin as I did.

'Slow down, slow down; you'll make yourself sick.' I nodded and he moved the bottle away.

He asked me if I could talk and was I in any pain. Another officer was behind, first freeing me from the radiator, then cutting the cord off my wrists. As they did, blood flooded into them and my hands hurt badly. I brought them in front and tried to move my fingers. They wouldn't do what I wanted them to. I looked at my hands, swollen so much they didn't look like mine any more. The pain throbbed into them with each heartbeat.

The kind policeman, who told me he was called Peter, gently massaged them, trying to bring them back to life. As he did, I looked at the people in the room with me. There were six in all. Everyone looking at me with either sadness or relief. One, who looked a little younger than the others, was ashen. Our eyes met, and he asked if he could leave the room.

As he left, I caught my reflection in the mirror on Chris's wardrobe. My eyes swollen so badly they looked shut, one had a deep cut running through it that had covered my face in blood. My bottom lip was split. I could see bruising on both of my arms. My left had a deep cut that had bled down my side and onto my lap from where he threw me and I had hit the bedside table edge.

The jacket covered my breasts, but I could still see my left side, black through heavy bruising. With how much it hurt to breathe I was sure some of my ribs were broken. My neck had bruising also, shaped like fingers. There was a portable camcorder. Filming for evidence. I knew then I would never want to see it. A medical person stepped in to check me over, shining a torch in my eyes, hooking me up to a blood pressure monitor, examining the cuts and bruises to my face and arm. She was talking to Peter, using words I didn't understand. She checked my hands, wrists and ribcage before conferring for a second and deciding I needed a body board to transport me due to bruising and swelling on my neck as well as my ribs.

I felt myself begin to shake. Peter lowered himself so we were eye to eye and held my hands gently.

'It's okay, Sarah. It's over and you're safe now. We're going to get you to a hospital.'

I wanted to say something but couldn't. Instead, I just nodded as the medic used more words I didn't understand while she spoke into her shoulder radio. I looked at Peter, scared.

'It's all right, Sarah, I promise you. Is there anyone we can call?'

I nodded.

'Family?'

I nodded again.

'Great, don't worry; we'll find them, okay?'

I couldn't catch my breath. It was all over and I was okay, but the man I had fallen for was a killer and I knew that somehow I was very lucky to not have shared the same fate as his wife. My hands shook even more and it flooded through my body until my teeth were chattering despite not feeling cold.

'Sarah, it's okay. You're safe. Take a breath, that's it; take a deep breath.'

Peter started breathing slowly, and I mirrored him. In, out, in out. It hurt like hell but it helped and I started to feel connected with my body again. With it came fresh pain to my wrists and ribs and a new one to my neck they had spoken of.

'Sarah. Did Chris do this to you?'

I couldn't say it out loud; it hurt too much so I nodded my head at Peter.

'Do you know where he might be?'

I nodded again.

'Where, Sarah? Where is the man who did this to you?'

It took me three attempts to form the words. The pain in my neck from where he choked me caught them. Like broken glass, the words scratched their way into my mouth.

'March train station. But I think you'll be too late. He's gone there to kill himself.'

Chapter 48

10.46 p.m. – March train station

Chris waited for the sound of the train approaching. Waited to feel its deep rumbling throughout his body as it came ever closer. He tried not to let himself panic as he looked at the clock. His train was running late. It sometimes did. He just hoped there wouldn't be much of a delay. Regardless, his train was coming, coming to take him to his wife.

The world made sense again. A stillness enveloped him. It was just his breathing, and his pounding heart, and the rumble of steel on steel approaching. Black and white, all as it should be. But then another noise punched through the silence, a shrill noise. It was very distant and like the train it was building. At first he didn't realize what it was. But when he knew, his stomach dropped.

Sirens.

They were coming for him. Opening his eyes, he looked down the track, still nothing.

The sirens built to a crescendo and, looking to the exit, he could see blue lights flashing, as car after car screeched into the train station car park. Engines running, doors opening, boots hitting the tarmac.

And there it was, on the track, somewhere close by. His train. Its rumblings starting just as a whisper slowly built. Within moments it would take form, passing at speed where he stood. A minute or so until the driver watched in horror as police tried and failed to stop a man stepping off the platform. He knew he wouldn't wait for a middle carriage now. He would let it hit him head on. He looked down the line. Its lights bounced off the steel track that veered to the left. He still couldn't see it, but it was there. He just wished it would hurry up.

Chris turned his back to the track and watched as six police officers came into the station. Chris took a step closer to the edge. He glanced to the clock: 10.47 p.m. If it had been on time, he would already be dead.

'Mr Hayes. Mr Hayes.'

He didn't look at them, but focused on the space under the bench where his note sat. The small black stone that was his heart on top.

'Mr Hayes, step away from the track.'

He could hear them talking, but it was like they weren't there. It was like they were a memory hanging on in a space that couldn't be fully accessed. He looked at them, their actions and calming gestures fake. Animated. In slow motion. He almost laughed at how they looked. So false – like characters from a bad television programme. One took a small step towards him, and immediately stopped when Chris leant back, his heels over the edge of the track.

He hoped that when he killed himself the monster in him had nowhere to go and vanish. He hated the idea of taking it with him.

Seeing his reflection in the vending machine as it flickered, he saw the monster looking back. It looked beaten. Chris knew that it had failed and Steve hadn't died like he thought. It allowed him to smile. Steve was alive and had told the police. They would have found Sarah. It was the only way they would know he was here. He felt a small joy knowing there were two people in this world who loved him and they were okay. It felt like, for the first time in over a year, something was going right for him. But still, Julia was waiting.

There was one more thing to do. One more wrong to right.

To his left, he saw the train begin to come around the corner. He knew, from the many times he had been there, it was twenty-two seconds until it passed.

'Mr Hayes, please. Step towards us.'

Twenty seconds.

'Do you know what I've done?'

'Yes, Chris, we know. Let us help you.'

'If you want to help, leave.'

'We can't do that.'

The lead police officer took a step towards him.

'Don't fucking come any closer. Don't.'

'Okay, I'm sorry. I won't.'

'I didn't mean to do it.'

'Come with us, Chris. We can help.'

Fifteen seconds.

'There is nothing you can do that will help. I'm sick.'

'We can get you a doctor.'

'There isn't a cure for my sort of illness. Have they found her yet?'

'Yes, Sarah is safe.'

'I meant my wife.'

'They are looking for her now, if your directions are correct.'

'They're correct; she's there. Make sure she gets the service she deserves.'

The train sounded its horn, the driver seeing the commotion in front of him. Hoping his signal would clear the man away from the edge.

Ten seconds.

Suddenly everything was gone and he was back outside in the rain, flushed and drunk as Julia pulled him in and kissed him hard. His lips tingling as she did before she closed the taxi door and drove away, their eyes not leaving each other's until she disappeared. He thought of their quick romance, and then marrying to ensure her mother knew before she passed. He thought of the honeymoon with his wife and the lazy Spanish sunshine that he knew was his favourite moment of his short life. He thought of his wife's energy, humour and passion. And how he had robbed her of it.

'I didn't mean to kill my wife,' Chris sobbed.

'Why don't you come with us and tell us all about it?'

'I can't do that. I love her.' He had to shout over the fast-approaching train. 'I need to be with her.'

'Chris, I'm coming to get you. We only want to help.'

'Don't, please, I don't want anyone else to get hurt. If you come any closer I'll end up killing you with me.'

'Then take a step towards me. Let's make sure both you and I don't die tonight.'

Chris took a small step forwards, his entire foot back on the platform. The officer saw it.

'Good, that's it, Chris. Come a little closer.'

Chris raised his left foot to take one more step. One step would be okay. They still couldn't quite grab him despite them creeping closer and closer towards the edge. He placed it down and could see the police officers' body language shift, tension lifting as they saw that he wasn't going to do it. The lead one spoke more softly, his eyes on Chris's, a smile showing on his face.

'That's it, Chris, a few more steps.'

'I didn't mean to kill her.'

'Okay, then let's talk about it. Let's find out what happened.'

He looked towards the train, so close he could see the driver shift in his chair, terrified at what would come next. Chris took another small step towards the safety of the police officer's outstretched hand.

Five seconds.

'Will she get a proper burial?'

'Yes, of course.'

'Will I get to say goodbye to her?'

'Yes, Chris, just come a little closer and we can talk about it all.'

Then he heard it. That mechanical voice.

'The next train to arrive at this station does not stop. Please stand back from the platform edge.'

Four seconds.

Chris looked into the eyes of the speaking officer and took one smaller step. The officer leant forwards, wanting to walk towards him but knowing if he did he could still be in harm's way. He would have to wait for Chris to move once more, just once more. They were only two feet apart.

'Make sure everyone knows what a wonderful person she was.'

Chris took a step back towards the edge and once his foot was planted he pushed off from it, throwing himself backwards towards the track. He heard three voices shout and saw the officer launch for him, both of his feet leaving the ground in slow motion, his eyes fixed and solely focused on saving Chris.

The world slowed down, allowing Chris to look around, take in the station one last time. Leaves and discarded Coke cans on the platform exploded off the floor all around as the wind from the train flooded onto the platform.

Two seconds.

Chris looked to his right, the two eyes of the monster coming to take him. His arms outstretched and behind, ensuring he couldn't try to grab the policeman who had landed on the floor, missing his target. The train lights blinded him, forcing his eyes shut. Finally, Chris could not only honour his wife by fulfilling his promise but he could honour her passion for the truth to be discovered and the record to be set straight. She was a journalist, he learnt that about her in their first moments together all those years ago. She would be paid tribute too and she would be remembered for all of her great work.

And then he saw Julia once more, smiling under the covers, hiding her embarrassed face from his. Her look telling him she knew it was love.

Back when it was something pure, back when it all made sense.

Acknowledgements

There are so many people I would like to thank in helping me bring this novel to life but none more so than my editor Hannah Smith and the team at HQ for seeing the potential, having faith and guiding me through the journey in shaping *Our Little Secret*.

A special thank you also needs to go to the wonderful author and mentor Sarah May who I am lucky to know through the Faber Academy. Without her wisdom, passion and support I would not be the writer I am today. I must also thank the entire group of 2015 – 16 Faber Academy: Aysha, Bryony, Carly, Jean, Jen, Oz, Rob, Rosie, Sarah, Simone, Will, Yair and Zaz. Thank you for listening to the many readings of early versions and giving honest feedback. We had a wonderful six months together, guys. I would also like to thank Nicci Cloke and Richard Skinner at the Academy for helping with answers to the many questions I had in developing this novel.

To Richard and Diane Card, thank you for reading early versions and giving feedback and to

Jacqui Howchin and Jonathan Austin, thank you for taking the time to pick apart the opening ready for submissions.

Mum and Dad, for, well, being Mum and Dad. As always you guys rock!

Hayley Chilvers, thank you for being a part of this since the early days of the first few chapters and being an ear for when doubt dances around me. Darren Maddison for being the rock who pops up when it's most needed and John Ormandy, for helping me see that dreams can work with a lot of work.

I would also like to thank Tracy Fenton at The Book Club for supporting the Kindle edition of *Our Little Secret* and sharing a platform with wonderful readers and Wendy Clarke from The Fiction Café.

The long nights at my computer and constant discussions about characters that has taken over my life have been tough, so finally, to Helen, thank you for your understanding and patience.

Coming Soon

Darren's next book, *Close Your Eyes* is out May 2018!

ONE PLACE. MANY STORIES

Bold, innovative and
empowering publishing.

FOLLOW US ON:

@HQStories